HILL OF THE BEAR

James P. Barber

Also by James P. Barber

Recollections of a Museum Collector

The Collector, the Guide and the Bone Digger

The Gifted Way to Manage Your Career

The Hilgendorf-Haag Connection

From New York to Indiana:
A History of the Ira Barber Family Beginning in 1786

HILL OF THE BEAR

James P. Barber

THE OTHER ROAD PUBLISHING

HILL OF THE BEAR
The Other Road Publishing
630 Nancy Street, Warsaw, Indiana 46580
www.jamespbarber.com

Copyright © 2019 James P. Barber

Printed in the United States of America

First Edition, 2019

ISBN: 978-0-578-49383-1

Cover Design by James P. Barber.

Other works by James P. Barber can be found at www.jamespbarber.com.

This book is dedicated to my grandchildren – Jarod, Tyler, Sydney, Macy, Lindsay and Eliana – whose young and growing minds are filled with imagination and wonder at the world around them. I find their joy in living both inspiring and contagious, providing an energy and a blessing beyond anything I could ever have hoped for.

Acknowledgments

My first novel has been an exciting journey indeed. While there were many days spent alone at the keyboard developing ideas and writing the story, the final product relied upon the keen eyes of someone who could take a fresh look at my words. Of course, I read the manuscript over and over and over, eventually seeing whatever seemed to be the correct words, phrases, and punctuation – whether they were actually there or not. I call this author blindness.

It is only a fresh set of critical eyes that can overcome this condition. Sure, my wife read the manuscript. But, she is too close to me: "I thought it was really good; better than your last book." That's okay for the ego, but it didn't do much for my author blindness.

The work of a good editor is crucial to producing the final product. I have prefaced my thanks to the individual who provided this service for me because I want there to be some understanding of just how important this role is to the realization of the final product – the published book.

I owe a great deal of thanks to my sister-in-law, Michele Barber, for agreeing to serve in the capacity of editor for this book. It is the second book she has edited for me, and I could not be more pleased with all of the errors she found! My author blindness was at its peak after my tenth reading of the book.

Michele is meticulous in her review of every thought, sentence, and paragraph. She is most certainly the "Queen of the Comma" and the "Empress of the Apostrophe!" Her tenacity in researching all of my attempts to reshape the rules of the English language are certainly appreciated.

But, there is more to the editing process than just words and punctuation. Michele also kept a close eye on the details and the flow of the story itself. Her corrections and feedback on key elements in the story were of great value.

So, thanks, Michele! I hope you'll be willing to work on the next one!

Contents

1890   1. Rails West   2

         2. The Beginnings   9

         3. Riding the Rails   17

         4. Before the Judge   24

         5. On to Arizona   29

         6. Working the Expedition   35

         7. Consumption   43

1891   8. Recovery   49

1892   9. The Azuela Family   57

         10. Analena   64

1893   11. The Halls Peak Expedition   69

         12. On the Trail   76

         13. Black Jack Ketchum   82

         14. Return to the Trail   90

         15. Halls Peak   97

1894   16. Working the Expedition   105

         17. Cerro del Oso   114

         18. Loss   122

         19. Unburdened   127

         20. Luz de Oro   135

1895	21. The Mogollon Expedition	141
	22. Alma	147
	23. The Old Prospector	156
	24. River Rescue	163
	25. The Question	171
1896	26. College Years	179
1900	27. Solitude in the Mountains	188
	28. Clay's Bear	194
1901	29. The Southwest Taxidermy & Zoological Co.	200
1904	30. Mexican Expedition	207
	31. Pancho Villa	212
1905	32. Guatemala	220
1906	33. Back Home	229
1907	34. Consumption Again	235
	35. Arkansas	242
1908	36. Hot Springs	252
1938	37. Thirty Years Later	257
1954	38. The Storyteller	261
	Fact and Fiction	268

1890

Chapter 1

RAILS WEST

The boy had climbed high in the knurled branches of a large old apple tree on his grandfather's farm. It was one of those beautiful, warm, late summer days that was made for climbing apple trees. Looking higher in the tree, the boy felt the glow of the sun on his face in a special way; it was comforting, almost healing in nature. He could not remember ever feeling this way on any other day. The sky was the bluest of blues. The apples were such a bright enticing red! Why had he never noticed this before? It all seemed new to his eyes.

The family homestead was a place he loved to be. His parents had moved into the city when he was born, but he returned to his grandfather's farm whenever he could. It was only a few miles from his home, and he walked the short distance easily. The farm was in the open country without a lot of people rushing about, unlike in town where people hastily busied themselves coming and going. Here he could hear the bees, the frogs, the crickets, even the grasshoppers, and all the sounds which were lost in the din of the city. It was pleasant and comforting to him; it was a song played by nature herself.

Most of all, though, he simply enjoyed spending time with his grandfather on the farm. The farm had been in the family for three generations, since 1840, but his father had given it up to employ his skills in the carriage manufacturing business in town. The farm remained in his grandfather's hands for now, but he wondered if his father would return to the farm one day. It was his hope that his father would do just that.

His grandfather ensured that his grandson knew the family history and appreciated the work the family had put into the land over the generations. The boy thought it was fun when his grandfather would test him on his knowledge of the family history. Many generations back, the family had come to America from Ireland before America was even a country. He recalled their later travel from New York on the Erie Canal, their crossing of Lake Erie, and their overland trip from Dearborn, Michigan, to northern Indiana. The family had cleared the fertile land and established farms. They had also served as blacksmiths, even into his grandfather's day. He knew the names of distant aunts, uncles, and cousins. His family was close-knit and very supportive of one another.

He truly appreciated what his grandfather had taught him about the family history, but most of all, he enjoyed the time his grandfather spent teaching him about the crops and the plants and the animals of the area. His grandfather had taught him how to fish and hunt and trap. He taught him how to track the different animals, how to read the weather, and how to recognize plants that could be used for healing. His love of the outdoors and admiration for nature itself was certainly cultivated by his grandfather.

There were plenty of trees on the farm for a young boy to climb, but his favorite was this particular apple tree at the edge of the group of trees nearest the house that tried over the years to present themselves as an orchard. The grove of fruit trees had not been purposefully organized as such, but over the years it had grown on its own into the orchard. He had been told that his great-grandfather had planted this particular tree. It was fun to climb, and it provided the juiciest of apples to feast upon on a lazy summer day.

One particular apple caught his eye this day. It seemed as if the sun had directed its energy to this specific apple ripening it to an almost glowing perfection. It was just a little higher in the tree, so he reached out to the next branch and pulled himself up until he had a foothold to support his weight. He would have to climb out to the place where the branches split. He pulled himself along, scraping his stomach deeply on the bark as he went. He didn't seem to notice, however, as he was focused on his goal.

The splendid, glowing red object was now nearly in reach. One more push and a stretch, and he would have it. *Craaack!* The branch broke, and he tumbled down to the next large branch below him hitting his head solidly. The branch had stopped him for a moment, but then he fell to the next large branch with another blow to his head. This branch tossed him sideways. As he dropped farther down the tree, he hit his ribs very hard on a twisted limb. He turned his head and strained to see the ground, but he could not find it. He was falling from much higher than he thought he had climbed. How had he gotten so high that he could not even see the ground?! He had a sudden surge of fright as he hit the next branch, then the next. *Where is the ground?!*

The next blow was to the bridge of his nose. His eyes closed tightly and then immediately flooded with tears. Mucus poured from his nostrils. He hurt badly all over. As he threw his arms up to protect his head, he was brought out of his dream and returned to his senses, acutely aware of the pain that was being inflicted upon him by a railroad bull. There was a bright light in his face as he screamed, "What? Wait! Stop!"

But the bull was not finished working over the tramp trespassing on his train. The bulls were the railroad security police known for their brutality in dealing with the hobos riding the rails. He continued clubbing the boy until he stopped thrashing about. Still conscious but quite disoriented, the boy heard the voices of the two men who were in the freight car with him.

"What about the other one?" The bull swung his light around to the corner of the railroad car.

"I don't know. He isn't even moving. Could be dead for all I know. If he is, that's one less bum on my train." The second man was standing over the small boy in the corner.

He wanted to say something to the men, but he could not seem to make any words come out of his mouth. His mouth was filled with the taste of blood, and he couldn't seem to make his tongue form words. He could only force out muffled mumbling sounds that made no sense, and the men just ignored him.

"Well, grab him. I'll take this one," the first man commanded as he grabbed the boy's legs and slid him toward the opening of the freight car. As he glanced back, the boy saw the second man spit on the wooden floor then pull the smaller boy out of the corner and easily swing him over his shoulders, apparently ignoring the blood covering the boy's coat.

He must have passed out in the wagon riding from the railroad yard into town. He woke to find himself on a small bed in a room surrounded with bars. A jail. *Why am I in jail?* Confused, he tried to sit up but was immediately hit with sharp pains in his head, his ribs, and his left arm. It only took a moment for him to recall the beating that had rousted him out of his sleep on the train.

Sleep. He had been warned by the older hobos not to sleep in a dead car in a freight yard. It was the surest way to get caught, or worse, beaten and left for dead by the railroad bulls. Sleep. He had been up nearly the entire night. He knew it would be daylight soon, and he had tried to keep himself awake. He could not have been asleep for long before he was overpowered by the two bulls.

The boy. Where's the small boy? He had tended to him through the night. He was badly ill. He had tried to care for him as best as he could, giving him some water and trying to keep his head cool. The boy had a serious fever. He remembered now how the boy was coughing so badly. The boy had spewed blood all over the both of them with his coughing. Tilting his head down, it was obvious that his own blood was now mingled with the small boy's blood on his shirt and coat. *Where's the boy?*

He tried to sit up again. The pain was nearly overwhelming, but he pushed through it and was able to swing his feet over the edge of the bed. His head was spinning. He sat momentarily with his head lowered and waited for the room to come to a stop, which it eventually did.

"Hello?" He wasn't sure if he said the word aloud or not. He tried again, "Hello!" He knew the word came out this time, although not as loudly as he had tried to say it.

He heard a voice from down a hallway, "Frank, I think the boy's awake. I'll go check on him."

The man's boots sounded heavy on the wooden floor as he approached, "Hey, boy, you're alive. I bet you don't feel like it though." It was not said with sympathy, and the man laughed inconsiderately as he made the inquiry. "I'd say welcome to Dodge City, but we don't much care for bums squatting in our train cars."

Another man approached, again with heavy boots, nodded to the first man, and said, "Thanks, Henry, I'll take it from here."

"Where's the other kid?" He was able to ask the question with a little difficulty. He was not yet able to raise his head much, and it spun as he raised it to ask the question. He lowered his head immediately after asking the question.

"Don't you worry none about him, boy. You got plenty to worry about on your own. You got a name, boy?"

"Clay, sir." Raising his head to answer the question, the room spun a little less so this time.

"Got a last name, boy, or don't bums have last names these days?" The man had a grin on his face, but not a friendly grin.

Do they think all of this is funny? Frank is what the first man called him. He answered slowly, "Beckley, sir. Clay Beckley."

"Well, Clay Beckley, you're in the Dodge City jail. You were trespassing on the property of the Santa Fe Railroad Company, and you don't seem to have any money in your pockets either. Yes, boy, you are a bum, a trespasser, and a vagrant by the law. The judge'll see ya tomorrow about that." The man was very matter-of-fact.

Clay was still in a bit of a stupor. He was trying to understand what was going on. "Why am I in jail? Where's the other kid?"

"Don't listen so well, do you, boy. You are under arrest for trespassing and vagrancy . . . for now. Tell me about that other kid. Was he a friend of yours? Did you beat him up?" Frank sounded serious now.

"I only know that his name is Will. I was trying to help. He was awfully sick." The words came out slow and labored, but his head was beginning to clear a bit.

"How'd you know this boy, Will?"

"I only met him a couple days ago – I think it was a couple days – when I hopped the train. It was in Topeka. I didn't beat him up. I was trying to help him." He was trying hard to be understood, but he was still having a bit of trouble putting his thoughts together.

"I see." Frank paused. "What about all that blood?" Again, it was a very matter-of-fact question.

Clay looked down at his shirt, "I think it's from getting beat with a club last night." The events were coming back to him now. He could feel the crusted blood on his face. He touched the dried blood on his shirt.

"Not your blood, the blood on the kid!" Frank was not as matter-of-fact with his questioning now. He seemed to be getting very serious, and annoyed.

"I would guess for the same reason." The question did not make sense to Clay, and he answered as simply as he could.

"No, he was covered with blood when he was found. Did you beat him up and rob him? You could be in real trouble here, boy." The tone was now obviously accusatory.

"Beat him up? No, like I said I was trying to help him. He was awfully feverish, and he was coughing all night. He coughed so hard he began to cough up blood. I swear, I didn't hurt that kid!" Now frightened, his words came out rapidly as he realized what the man, Frank, was asking him.

"Well, we'll know soon enough. The doc will take a look at his body this afternoon." Frank stared coldly into Clay's eyes as he said this.

"W-w-what do you mean, his body?" Clay was clearly confused once again, and scared. "I don't understand." He was looking back at Frank but his eyes were searching for help, help which would not be found in Frank's cold stare.

"The kid – Will you said – is dead. He was dead when the railroad security men found him last night. He was covered with blood, so it appears someone may have killed and robbed him. We'll know for sure what happened after the doc does his autopsy. You might want to think long and hard about your story." He paused, this time to let his words sink in. "We'll get you something to eat soon. Looks like you could use a little water to wash up, too." He turned and walked away, his boots sounding heavier, even ominous, now.

Clay knew he had done nothing wrong, but he could not hold back the tears. He was hurt, confused, and scared. He had tried to take care of the small boy; he would never have hurt him. *Dead?! What had happened?*

Chapter 2

THE BEGINNINGS

Having washed up in the pan of cool water that the jailer named Henry brought to him, and having had a bite to eat, fourteen-year-old Clay sat on the edge of the hard bed feeling every ache in his body. The food, while not much, tasted good to him, and he felt a bit revived having filled his stomach. He was beginning to make sense of what had happened in the early morning hours, except for the death of the young boy, Will. The best Clay could understand was that he had been very, very ill and succumbed to whatever affliction was upon him. He was a thin, pale boy, appearing very young; maybe he was frail by nature and his body could not fight off his sickness.

Clay recalled the blood that Will had coughed up during the night. He tried to see in his mind if there was any blood on his coat or shirt when Clay first encountered him. In his mind he could not see any blood, or if there was any blood, it was in such a small amount that it was not noticeable. Had someone else done him harm before Clay jumped into the freight car? Again, he searched his memory for any sign that the boy had been assaulted, but he came up with nothing. He felt fairly certain that Will had just been a very sick kid.

Feeling a little better about his chance meeting with Will and his efforts to help him, Clay relaxed a bit and slowly laid back down in his bunk. For the first time, he noticed that the thin mattress was much more comfortable than the wooden floors of the freight cars he had been riding in.

Clay was very independent, and he had not had any feelings of homesickness up to now, nor did he have any at this moment. He could think about home in a good way and not be plagued by feelings or longings to be back there. His home, and family, had provided a solid foundation for him, one that now gave him strength and comfort.

His thoughts easily turned to his grandfather who had meant so much to Clay. His recent passing had left a hole in Clay's heart, but that hole was filled by the joy he found in the time he had spent with his grandfather. Clay was thankful that he had his grandfather to teach him so much about the joys to be found in hunting, trapping, fishing, and simply living in nature. He had taken the next step in life due in a large part to the influence and teachings of his grandfather. The fact that Clay was already trained in the art of taxidermy by his grandfather had been a help in procuring his job.

All of this did not mean that Clay was not close to his own father. As his grandfather had been, Clay's father had also worked as a wheel-wright and wagon maker when he was younger. His grandfather was a skilled craftsman who had patented several improvements to wagons, carriages, and cultivators. His father also had creative skills which ex-hibited themselves in an interest in science. Clay's father had blended his talents and interests together as a carriage painter, a well-respected occupation.

Clay had worked in his father's carriage factory where he became well aware of the knowledge and skill required of someone like his father. Clay's father had encouraged him to study and understand the science behind the things that interested him. Clay would always read as much as he could of his father's *Scientific American* magazine. Much of it was well beyond Clay's understanding, but what really caught his eye was anything to do with the science of nature.

So, the skills and knowledge he had learned from his father and from his grandfather greatly complemented each other and made him a well-rounded young man. He enjoyed finding ways to practice, or experiment with, the science he was learning from his reading and the nature he was learning from his grandfather. A good example was taxidermy. He was learning the art of the process from his grandfather while discussing with his father the science of what he was doing.

While he spent much time at the farm, Clay was also able to study nature around his home. Their neighborhood was near the south edge of town not far from the cemetery. It just so happened that near the cemetery was a large pond where Clay explored the plants and small animals that frequented the pond.

With each new animal he found, Clay took a specimen home to see if he was able to locate it in *The Illustrated Natural History*, one of his favorite books on his father's desk. When he was able to locate his newly acquired specimen in the book, he studied every page learning all he could about that particular creature. He then made a note in the book of the date and time he had found the specimen along with the size of each animal and any particularly interesting characteristics.

He had read articles in *Scientific Monthly* about how such details were recorded by those who collected specimens for science. He developed a real love for this blend of science and art with nature. He saw it as not unlike what his father had done in his own life with his blend of science and art within his own trade as a carriage painter.

Clay developed a good reading habit and began to follow the work of a few specific events and individuals. At the age of thirteen, Clay wrote a letter to Dr. Clinton Hart Merriam who was in charge of a division of the United States Department of Agriculture studying fish and mammals, and who had recently been one of a group of men to found the National Geographic Society.

Clay was surprised when Dr. Merriam responded to his letter. Dr. Merriam had been very encouraging to Clay and talked about his own interest in collecting bird specimens at a young age. In subsequent correspondence, Clay discovered that they shared many interests, including the practice of taxidermy. Soon, Dr. Merriam was guiding Clay in specific ways of preparing specimens to meet the requirements that he had set forth for the Department of Agriculture.

Clay was most excited when Dr. Merriam had asked Clay to send him some specimens of shrews. Dr. Merriam was having difficulty obtaining specimens of shrews and had reached out to several individuals around the country to see if they could provide them. Clay was able to locate some shrews near the pond at the cemetery, and after verifying that he did indeed have the proper mammal through his father's *Illustrated Natural History* volumes, he sent his specimens to Dr. Merriam having meticulously prepared them to the requirements set forth in Dr. Merriam's guidelines. The reply to Clay's submission from Dr. Merriam was, and Clay had the words memorized, "You have prepared your skins to the highest degree of perfection."

The next Clay knew, Dr. Merriam was looking for collectors to join him on a biological survey to be done in Arizona in 1890. Clay felt that the interest shown him by Dr. Merriam might go far in getting a place on the expedition team. Clay would be graduated from the eighth grade in time to be part of the expedition. So, he boldly wrote to Dr. Merriam offering his services. He had not approached his father about this, but he had discussed it with his grandfather who had encouraged him.

It seemed as if it took forever to get a reply from Dr. Merriam. Clay could not conceal his excitement the day he received the letter from Dr.

Merriam's office. His excitement soon turned to disappointment as he read the reply from Dr. Merriam. Dr. Merriam had indeed been on survey expeditions at a young age, but not as young as Clay at age fourteen. He would be unable to offer Clay an official spot on the team he was putting together.

Clay was devastated. He was about to put the letter down, but he felt he should read the rest of it. While Dr. Merriam could not place Clay on the team, if Clay could make his own arrangements to get to Flagstaff, Arizona, he could work within the team as a helper to the other members. He would be provided a place in the camp and provisions, but very little in the way of pay. Dr. Merriam told Clay that this was the best way for Clay to learn and grow at his age; he would be in a sort of an apprenticeship position. If he had a real passion for this work, he would find a way to Arizona and be personally taken under Dr. Merriam's tutelage. There was no doubt in Clay's mind – he was going to Arizona!

He was not sure how to tell his parents, but, of course, he did talk about the opportunity with his grandfather. The biggest concern was how Clay was going to get to Arizona. As Clay's grandfather did not have money to give him, he suggested that Clay work as much as he could at his father's carriage company to earn the money.

Clay followed his grandfather's advice and approached his father about working additional hours at the carriage factory. His father was concerned about Clay finishing his school studies as he would be nearing completion of the eighth grade in a few months. He felt Clay needed to focus on his studies. But in the end, he relented and let Clay work some additional hours into the evenings.

After a couple months, Clay could see that he would be far short of the funds that he needed. However, he talked with a number of the older men working nights who told him that he could easily hop the trains west. Some of them had, in fact, worked their own ways across the country doing just that.

Over the next few months, Clay learned all that he could about hopping trains. He learned routes and schedules from his home in Indiana to Chicago, then west on the Santa Fe Railroad to Kansas City and Dodge City, Kansas; Raton, Santa Fe, and Albuquerque, New Mexico; and then on to Flagstaff, Arizona. The best part was that he could begin his trek by jumping onto a freight car at his father's carriage business which shipped freight to Chicago on a regular basis.

The men would help him get on the car unseen. But most importantly, they were telling him what to do, and what not to do. They explained the best times and places to hop a train, what types of cars to look for and which ones to avoid, how to avoid the risk of an accident, where to find camps, and how to interact with other hobos.

After school was out, Clay was able to work more hours, but it would still not be nearly enough to provide for his transportation. He would have to stick with his plan to hop the trains. He felt bad that he was not able to spend as much time with his grandfather as he normally would have during the summer months. His parents were having difficulty understanding why Clay wanted to work so much. Clay had explained that he was saving the money to prepare himself to become a self-employed collector and taxidermist. They could not fault his eagerness to invest in his own future. And, he told himself that he wasn't really lying to them.

Everything was falling into place for Clay as the day of departure neared. Normally, the trip by rail would take about four or five days; however, hopping trains would take longer. He decided to allow himself two weeks, for he would be riding and camping while waiting to catch the appropriate freight train at key railyards along the way. His plan was becoming clear in his mind, and he was feeling good about it. Then the bottom fell out. Clay's grandfather died.

It broke Clay's heart that he had not spent as much time with his grandfather because of the extra hours he spent working to save money for the trip to the West. He felt like he had been selfish after all that his grandfather had given to him. He no longer felt like heading West to be a part of anything with Dr. Merriam. Clay just wanted to be with his grandfather, an option that was no longer available to him.

The day of the funeral, Clay cried like a baby. His parents knew how close Clay had been to his grandfather and understood his deep sorrow. They did the best they could to comfort him.

Over the course of the next several days, Clay left the house early each day and spent much of his time visiting the farm. Nothing about the farm had changed, but it was not the same place it had been just weeks ago. The sounds about the farm seemed to ring empty; the scents in the air left him longing for something more rather than providing a feeling of joy; and the world he saw around him was now less vibrant, as if the color had been drained out of it by some unseen force. Clay sought that deep feeling of contentment that was always aroused in him by merely being at the farm, but it was gone – it had died along with his grandfather.

Clay realized that there was no longer anything for him at the farm. Even more so, he realized that there was nothing left for him in his hometown. Sure, his family was there, and he loved them, but it was time for him to make his own way into the world. He knew it was what his grandfather wanted for him. He had helped Clay bring his plan together. He trusted the guidance he had received from his grandfather, and he knew that this trust was now stronger than it had ever been. He felt as if his grandfather was beside him inspiring him with strength and courage. Yes, there was nothing left for him on the farm, but the spirit of his grandfather was encouraging and guiding him to move forward with the life he had envisioned for himself. Yes, it was time to head West.

He finalized the plan to hop the freight train from his father's carriage business with the workers who had been helping him. Late the next night, he pulled a small bag from beneath his bed and finished packing a few small belongings along with a little food. From the bag, he removed the note that he had already written explaining his plan to his parents and saying good-bye to his two younger brothers. He quietly crept down the stairs and placed the note on his father's desk. He had signed the note, "C. M. Beckley." It was his way of saying to them, and to himself, that he was no longer the boy, Clay, but he was now a young man. He closed the front door silently behind him and stepped into the darkness of the early morning feeling as if the dawn would bring him forth into a new world in which he would be a man.

Chapter 3

RIDING THE RAILS

Clay had no problems getting out of the freight car in the Chicago railyard. He followed the directions provided by his co-conspirators, and although it took him a bit of time to gain his bearings, he eventually located the tracks heading West toward Kansas on the Santa Fe Railroad. He next left the railyard and found a hobo camp not far away. He had been cautious in making his way to the camp to ensure he was not followed. The few others at the camp were mostly lying in the sun either asleep or merely enjoying the warmth. There was not a lot of talk, but he did confirm that he had identified the proper track to follow. The others were all older than Clay, and they were kind enough in helping him while not being overly inquisitive about the nature of his travels.

A few days later, after similar time divided between noisy, uncomfortable train hopping and quiet time lounging in hobo camps, Clay arrived in Kansas City. As with Chicago, it had taken him a bit of time to locate the next route outbound to Topeka and points west. So far, the trip had been uncomplicated, and most of those he met had been helpful. Those who were not helpful were really just indifferent to him. He had not met any malice at this point. He had picked up some good tips from the more seasoned travelers.

While he never had a need to seek charity while traveling, the hobos filled Clay in on the best places to seek food. The first rule was to avoid the big houses. They said the rich people would simply not lend a hand; in fact, they said, they would likely call the local law to come pick you up. No, it was better to avoid any home that could easily be identified as to the wealth of its occupants. On the contrary, they had told him, the very poor could always be counted on. They never turn away anyone who is hungry. The very poor should always be the last recourse, but when asked, they will be charitable as they understand hunger. The exception to any rules were the homes with a simple sign that indicated food would be made available to the hobos. This was typically a sign set in a window that looked somewhat like a loaf of bread. These homes would always help a hobo in need of food.

The hobos taught Clay about the different types of cars. There were side-door Pullman cars known as boxcars, flat cars known as gondolas, and blind cars. Blind cars were typically mail cars built without doors in the ends of the cars. And, those that did have doors were typically kept locked. So, a hobo could jump on the platform of one of these cars, and no one could get to him without stopping the train. Of course, that could be problematic if the hobo had been seen and the train stopped while there was still daylight. This type of riding was best for nighttime travel.

Hopping the trains was never a lonely travel by any means. Some hobo camps had as many as twenty 'bos waiting to hop the next train.

Some of the men who had been riding for a long time had nicknames by which they were known – Boston Blackey, Yellow Belly, Texas Royal, Burley 'Bo, Ohio Fatty, and Blind Kid, just to name a few. They all had stories to tell late into the dark of night around the camp. Clay fell asleep under the stars to the tales of his fellow travelers on more than one night.

It was at the switching station in Topeka, Kansas, that Clay noticed the open freight car in the darkened morning. He heard himself running as his feet crunched the rocks of the rail bed. He was running in a straight line for the partially opened door of the boxcar. He hoped the sound he was making would not arouse the attention of anyone. At the opening of the freight car he deftly slipped up and onto the floor of the car. The wood floor was smoothed from the wear of freight being loaded and unloaded over time. As it was early morning and still dark, he could not see much in the car, but it did appear to have very little freight inside. He could just make out several large sacks stacked at the end of the car. Turning to the other end of the car, he saw similar bundles. The car had a mixed smell of grains or feed, old wet wood, and tar.

The train began to move causing him to lose balance momentarily. Having easily recovered, he picked up his bag and headed to one end of the car to look for a spot to settle in. The few large bundles contained cloth of some sort, so they were soft enough to lean into for a small bit of comfort in an otherwise uncomfortable wooden rail freight car. Any other freight must have already been unloaded. The remainder of the goods were obviously headed for a destination farther west.

As he settled into one of the bale-like bundles, Clay heard a sound from the opposite corner where there were several similar bundles. Cautious, he listened quietly. He then heard what sounded like coughing followed by low moaning. When the sound stopped, he remained where he was and again listened, this time more intently. More coughing. Clay tried to ignore the coughing which continued quite regularly, but after some minutes, he decided to investigate.

Crawling carefully along the floor of the clattering car, he made his way across the smooth wooden floor to the bundles in the opposite corner. As he neared the bundles, the coughing sound was less muffled and more distinct. He peered around the nearest bundle and saw the small boy sitting with his back against another loose bundle in the corner. Clay immediately knew that the boy posed no threat to him.

Clay moved toward the boy and tried to rouse him, "Hello?" He paused then said again, "Hello." The boy did not respond at first, but then slowly moved his head toward Clay. He was a fair-skinned young boy with cheeks that appeared red against a pasty white face even in the darkened freight car.

His lips looked very dry, and his words were parched as he said, "Dad?"

"No, my name is Clay. Your father's not here. Are you sick? What's your name?" Clay thought maybe that was too much for the confused boy to understand. He asked again, "What's your name?"

"Will." It came out dryly.

"Will, my name is Clay. You look real sick. What's wrong?" He waited as the boy gathered his wits.

The boy coughed several more times, then let out a long, slow moan. Clay was not sure what to do next. He reached out instinctively and felt the boy's forehead with his hand. There was immediately no doubt that the boy had a fever. The boy moaned and sounded like he was trying to get out some words, so Clay knelt closer and placed his ear near the boy.

There was a hard coughing fit that caught Clay by surprise. As it continued, Clay felt the wetness spew from the boy's mouth into Clay's face. Clay wiped his face with his sleeve, not noticing the blood. The boy then settled quietly back into the bundle. Clay noticed a canteen nearby and picked it up. He poured some water in his hand then slowly poured it over the boy's forehead. He remembered his mother had always put a wet cloth on the forehead for fever. He pulled a handkerchief from his pocket and soaked it with water from the canteen. He placed the wet cloth on the boy's forehead.

The coughing subsided, but the boy was breathing slowly with difficulty. Clay felt the boy's chest as it struggled to rise for each breath. He wanted to ask him more questions, but since the boy seemed to be resting for now, he decided just to remain at his side.

As daylight came, Clay became more aware of his surroundings. His own bag was on the other end of the car, and the boy's small bundle was at his side. He opened the boy's bundle and saw a partially eaten apple inside. He refreshed the cloth on the boy's head at regular intervals with cool water from the canteen. Despite Clay's efforts, the fever remained strong. Clay felt bad that there was not more he could do for the boy.

About noon, the boy awoke and spoke with some coherence, "Who are you?" His words were still slow and very dry. His face showed that he was in pain.

"Hi, Will. I'm Clay. Would you like some water?"

The boy slowly nodded, and Clay helped him sip some water from the canteen. After several slow sips, the boy sluggishly responded, "Thank you. How do you know my name?"

"You were pretty sick when I found you, but you were able to tell me your name, but that's about all. Are you feeling better?"

"Sorry," he said, and then he had another coughing spell. Again, it got worse, and his last heavy cough brought up blood which once again spewed onto Clay. Several quick subsequent coughs filled the air with fine red droplets. Clay again wiped his face with his sleeve. As the coughing subsided, Clay took the cloth and cooled it one more time.

"How long have you been sick, Will?"

"I dunno. I don't know what day it is. I've had the cough for a few weeks. I had it when I left home." The words had worn him out, and he laid his head back on the bundle.

"Be quiet for now. You can tell me more later. You have a fever, so I'll do what I can to try to keep you cool. We have a nice breeze coming through the doors. Maybe that'll help." But the breeze was nothing more than hot air blowing in through the open doors of the freight car.

Clay asked the boy if he wanted a bite of the apple that Clay found in his bag. The boy shook his head to indicate no. "Okay, well just rest while you can."

Clay crawled over to his own bag and reached inside grabbing a potato. He took out his pocket knife, cut the potato open and carved off a small chunk to eat. He still had an apple of his own from his grandfather's orchard, but he would save that for later. Just the mere thought of his grandfather's orchard offered him some comfort, and he leaned back against the bundle and soon fell asleep.

He was awakened when he felt the train coming to a stop. Now was a time to be cautious. He could tell by the time of day that he had not been asleep for long. They were likely stopping for water for the steam engine. Clay edged himself toward the door and ever-so-slowly poked his head out to confirm his thoughts.

They had indeed stopped at a small station. There was no one milling about at the station, and it appeared they were getting ready to take on water. He looked over and noticed that the boy was still sleeping. That was good; no one would be aroused at the sound of his coughing. Giving in to his caution, Clay buried himself between the bundles where he would remain until they were again in motion. He knew that if they were in a larger city he would have to get off the train and find a camp or hiding spot until he could re-board, but in a small watering station, there should be no problem.

It was not long before they were again underway. As they rounded a curve, Clay could read the name on the water tower: Florence, Kansas.

He should be in Dodge City by early morning. It was there that he would need to be alert to the railroad security officers, the bulls. He could not stay on this car when the train stopped, and he would need to be sure he found the proper line out of Dodge City to take him to points south out of La Junta, Colorado. It was there that he would take the train through the pass at Raton, New Mexico, as he continued south and west to his destination of Flagstaff, Arizona.

Once they were underway, the boy was awakened by the jerking of the train cars. It wasn't long before he was again coughing. Clay gave him some more water, but his fever had not broken. Clay told himself that he would help the boy off the train in Dodge City and try to get him to someone who could give him better attention. Before morning, however, was a long night trying to care for the boy as best as he could.

As the night crawled on, Clay knew that he could not fall asleep as morning was just mere hours away. The boy eventually quieted down, and Clay was doing all he could to remain awake. He thought about the apple from his grandfather's farm in his bag. Maybe he should eat that now. Yes … maybe … the apple …

Chapter 4

BEFORE THE JUDGE

Clay woke with a start. Thinking he felt the train car moving beneath him, he quickly sat up, felt the pain in his body, and realized he was in the jail. It was early morning with small slivers of sunlight reaching through the barred window in his cold cell. He heard a few coughs, throats being cleared, and spitting as other prisoners awoke. His stomach contracted in small cramps as he realized he was hungry. He had not had much to eat in the last two days. He thought of the apple from his grandfather's farm in his bag, but his bag was not with him.

He laid back down on the thin mattress and thought of the young boy, Will. Did they think that he had been responsible for the boy's death? He felt helpless as he thought of how he had tried to help the boy. His stomach again cramped.

Then he heard sounds from the front office of the jail followed by heavy boot steps in the hallway. The jailer was distributing food to the cells. Soon a pan was slid into Clay's cell, along with a tin cup of coffee. The pan was filled with a steaming congealed mass of hot cereal, but the smell of the coffee drew Clay's attention to it. He slowly moved to the door and reached down for the cup and the pan. The cup was still hot, but the pan of cereal was barely warm. He sipped the coffee carefully to ensure he did not burn his mouth. He was pleased that it was just hot enough to taste really good, but not so hot as to burn his mouth. He took a second, longer draft from the cup, then dug out a spoonful of the cereal and ate it. While the cereal was barely warm and unpleasant in appearance, it tasted surprisingly better than it looked. He quickly followed his first spoonful with two others.

As he took another swig from the coffee cup, the jailer, Frank, caught him a bit by surprise, "Hungry, huh, bum?" He did not wait for an answer, "I tell you what, why don't you take off that coat and shirt, and I'll have one of the ladies clean them up for you. It would probably be best if you saw the judge without all of that blood on you."

Clay looked down at his shirt. He had forgotten about the blood. He had washed himself last night, but his clothes were still covered with blood – a mixture of his blood and Will's blood. He placed the pan and cup on the floor then removed his coat and shirt. He reached out through the bars and handed them to Frank, "Thank you, sir."

"Finish your food, Clay." Frank grabbed the clothes and was about to leave.

"Uh, sir. I had a bag with me that had all my belongings in it. Can I have it?" Clay spoke quickly before Frank had a chance to head back down the hall.

"We have your bag. It'll be fine with us for now. No personal items in the cells. Sorry, kid." Frank walked away with his heavy boots.

The day passed slowly for Clay. After breakfast and a late small lunch, his clothes were returned to him with only some minor stains visible. He was pleased that nearly all of the blood had been removed from his clothing. He did not like the reminder of what had happened. And, as Frank had told him, he would probably look better in front of the judge with clean clothes.

It was after three o'clock in the afternoon when the other jailer, Henry, came to Clay's cell with a set of keys and opened the door. "Time to see the judge, bum."

While Frank had also called Clay "bum," Henry said the word in a much more derogatory fashion that upset, almost angered, Clay. Frank was stern in his approach to Clay, but Henry was simply cruel.

The courthouse was just a few doors down the street, and the short walk went quickly. Clay was surprised that he had shackles placed on his wrists. The few people on the streets stared at him and made him feel ashamed. He was confused since he felt he had nothing to be ashamed about.

The courtroom was spacious with a few scattered chairs in front of a large desk that was placed on a raised portion of the floor. Clay was told where to sit, and Henry remained by his side. The judge was making some comments to which Clay was not paying attention, until he heard his name called. Henry grabbed him under his arm and pulled him up as he said, "Stand up, boy."

"How old are you, boy?" The judge sounded disgusted as he asked the question.

"Fourteen, sir," was his too-quiet response while his eyes were looking at the dirty, tobacco-stained floor.

"Speak up, boy, and look at me when you answer my question!" His temper seemed short, and his demeanor suggested that he was annoyed by the whole process. To Clay his tone expressed that he was inconvenienced to even be here.

He lifted his eyes from the floor and looked straight in the judge's eyes, "Fourteen, sir."

"Old enough to know what stealing is then?" Clay could now see the judge peering over the top of his spectacles. His eyes were puffy, and his beard and hair were disheveled.

"Uh, yes, sir." Clay was puzzled by the question.

"And just how is it you decided to steal from the Atchison, Topeka & Santa Fe Railroad?"

Clay's eyes widened at the question. He didn't understand it. "Sir, I didn't steal anything from the train car. I was just riding in it when I –"

The judge cut him off. "Then you don't know what stealing is?!"

"Yes, sir, but I only hitched a ride in an empty freight car! I didn't steal anything!" Clay knew from the look that the judge gave him that he should stop talking.

"Boy, you didn't have a ticket to ride on that train. Riders on the Santa Fe Railroad give their hard-earned money for tickets to ride the train. Shippers pay for those freight cars so their goods can be delivered in a timely manner to people willing to pay for those goods. It is these good folks who keep the Santa Fe in business. Boy, you thought you could ride for free! Well, the railroad will not put up with that! This is why you were pulled from that freight car and brought to jail. Do you have anything else to say for yourself?!" The judge was obviously agitated.

Clay was quiet. He was not a thief. How could the judge not see that? He kept his head up as he searched for something to say. But he could not get any words out. He simply stared in disbelief at the judge who looked upon Clay with disgust.

"Guilty! Take him back to the lock-up. And, boy, I don't ever want to see you in Dodge City again."

"Yes, sir," spat from Clay's mouth as the law officer grabbed him by the arm and dragged him toward the door.

When Clay was able to gather himself as they walked back to the jail, he asked Henry, "What about Will? You said he was dead and that I was in trouble for that, too. Why didn't the judge ask me about him?"

Henry was very matter-of-fact, sounding almost a little bit disappointed, "The doc said that boy died of natural causes. There was no sign that you, or anyone else, had attacked the boy. The doc said the boy died from consumption."

Clay was familiar with consumption from some of his father's scientific magazines. He knew it affected the lungs and that blood could be coughed up. That explained about the blood that the boy had spit on Clay. Clay did not know the cause of the disease, but he was sorry that a small boy like Will had died from it. There was little comfort in the fact that the authorities were aware that Clay was not responsible for the boy's death. He arrived back at his cell and laid down on the thin mattress.

Chapter 5

ON TO ARIZONA

The days in the jail went excruciatingly slow for Clay, and he longed so to be outdoors. His mind turned to the work for Dr. Merriam that required Clay to be in Flagstaff soon. He spent many days just staring out the window of his cell looking off into the distance where he could see trees, hills, and grass. He allowed his imagination to take him beyond those hills to a freer, open space that longed to be hunted and studied. After five tedious days, he was set free, his bag was returned to him, and he was told in no uncertain terms to leave town and not come back. The jailers were stern with Clay, but Frank gave him a warm pat on the back and wished him well as he left the jailhouse.

Clay knew he could not hop the train here, so he was going to have to spend some of the money he had hidden away in a slit in the bottom of his bag. He would buy the cheapest ticket he could to the next nearest town on his way to Flagstaff. So, at the railway station he purchased a ticket to La Junta, Colorado. He knew that he should be able to hop a train from there with no problem. As bad as he had felt in jail, he knew that he had no other option to get to Flagstaff, and he was already nearing the day he was supposed to be there and meet up with Dr. Merriam and the expedition.

It was nice to ride in a passenger car, but he was actually less comfortable in the fancy car than he was sitting on the floor of a freight car. He felt the eyes of many passengers gazing at a young man with a bruised face who actually looked like he should be riding on the floor of that freight car. He decided to ignore their stares and closed his eyes to take a nap.

He arrived in La Junta in the late afternoon. Locating a small camp, he settled in among the men as he made his plans to catch the next train south to Raton. By early evening, not a single train had arrived at the station. Many of the men began to talk about the trains not running. It made no sense to Clay. Then, late in the evening, an engine pulled into the station with what seemed like more cars than usual. The passengers exiting the train were all abuzz with talk about this overcrowded and late leg of their journey.

Eventually, some of the 'bos from the train made their way to the camp. It was then that they learned that the railroad was on strike. Apparently, all over the country, trains were no longer running. Clay did not understand about strikes. He listened carefully and eventually put it together. Because of a dispute about wages, the railroad switchmen refused to handle any Pullman cars. Apparently, thousands of workers were taking part in this strike, and the railroads were virtually shutdown across the country. The men had heard the rail workers at the La Junta Station announce that there would be no trains running to Raton.

It did not make a lot of sense to Clay for the workers to stop work-ing because they wanted more pay. In Clay's mind, if you wanted more pay, you worked harder. To Clay, this action seemed to be hurting a lot of people. Clay, still a bit puzzled, decided he would see what the morning would bring, and he went to sleep.

Nothing had changed in the morning. No one seemed to know when the trains might start running, so Clay decided to walk to Raton. He had to keep moving, and he saw no other option at this point. He gathered his things together, replenished his water supply, and left just about sunrise.

Fortunately for Clay, there were station houses with water tanks along the railroad route, so Clay was able to rest at regular intervals. The land was flat and dry and sparse. It was a monotonous journey that seemed to have no end, just two rails always coming together in the distance, a point always beyond Clay's reach. Then, a handcar came along, and Clay was able to get a ride for which he was very thankful. After two days, Clay arrived in Trinidad, Colorado, only about 20 miles north of Raton.

It was the next day, the Fourth of July, that Clay witnessed fire-works of a different sort. A large crowd of strikers had gathered at the station as a train pulled in from the south. The group of men jerked civilian armed escorts from the train and took their weapons. Clay did not see how this could come to any good as he watched from a safe dis-tance.

Shortly thereafter, a second northbound train pulled into the sta-tion. Out of this train emerged a full company of United States Army soldiers. The officers quickly lined the soldiers up facing the growing crowd of strikers and sympathizers. The soldiers were ordered to raise their weapons and march toward the crowd. The crowed moved back, slowly at first, and then quickly dispersed, dropping clubs and rocks as they left.

When a few men still remained, the soldiers were ordered to fix bayonets. They again marched straight at the remaining group which quickly made for safer ground. There was no doubt that Uncle Sam was now in charge of this station.

Clay learned that the train would be running the next day. He now had no time to lose. He was going to be late getting to Flagstaff as it was. It took most of the rest of his money to purchase a ticket from Trinidad to Flagstaff, but he would finally be on the way to his destination in the morning.

After several stops and route changes, Clay arrived in Flagstaff two days later. His delay in Dodge City meant that he was now three days late for his meeting with Dr. Merriam. Unsure what to do, he went to a local hotel and asked for Dr. Merriam. While Dr. Merriam's party had left the previous day, Clay felt he should be able to catch up to them. He had just enough money for a small meal and an old burro that had seen its better days packing in the mountains. With not much in the way of supplies, Clay felt the old burro should be able to carry him along without any problem, or at least he hoped so. This burro was quite unlike the well-attended mules on his grandfather's farm.

Clay also purchased a new hat as he had nothing to keep the sun off his head having left his tattered wool cap on the train. The two of them made quite a pair as they left town – a ragged young boy with black, bruised eyes in a too-large new hat and a sway-back, half-blind, too-small old burro. Out of town they went, leaving behind stares and chuckles. They were headed north toward the San Francisco Peaks where Clay hoped to catch up to Dr. Merriam's expedition within a couple of days. He expected easy traveling the first day with more difficulty as he approached the base of the mountains, but he felt surely he should come upon the expedition by the second day, even with the old worn-out burro as his companion.

Clay did not mind traveling alone through the open country. He was happy to be off the railroad and out of jail. He was finding that he had to make himself keep moving as he wanted to stop often to observe and study the land around him. It was all so very different than Indiana. The old burro did not seem at all to mind when Clay would make an occasional stop to get a closer look at some of the plant life. Clay had an eye for searching out the smallest of details in the barren land. He could not wait to arrive at Dr. Merriam's camp and go to work.

After a night spent in the foothills of the mountains, Clay was up early the next morning and moving along the trail. The old burro, while slow, was able to move at a steady pace with little in the way of a load.

As the burro plodded along, Clay was able to enjoy his pipe. He had been introduced to pipe smoking in the hobo camps. Having shared a pipe a number of times in the camps, one older hobo by the name of Boulder Joe had given Clay a pipe of his own. Clay enjoyed the smell of the tobacco as it reminded him of his grandfather and father, both of whom smoked pipes. His father also smoked cigars, but Clay found the taste and smell of the pipe to be much preferred. It was a popular form of relaxation in the hobo camps and seemed to encourage thoughtful conversation.

He was pleasantly surprised to come upon the camp late that afternoon. As he approached the camp, he saw a number of tents set up and small groups of men engaged in activities nearby. Clay was walking the old burro as he entered the camp. Several men noticed him right away as they looked once, then twice, at the young man in the oversized hat with two bruised purple and yellow eyes. Several of the men poked at others nearby to get their attention for what they perceived as a rather odd spectacle. Within no time at all there was contagious laughter all around the camp. Clay and the old burro stopped as one of the men approached them. "And who might you be, young man? Are you lost?" Clay was a bit of a puzzling site in the mountains.

"My name is Clay, Clay Beckley, sir. I'm here to work for Dr. Merriam," he said confidently as he stood large and tall. He was large for his age, so that was an advantage at this time. His bruised face also helped to belie his age.

"Here to work for Hart, huh? And what about that old pack animal? I don't see much work coming out of him. How was he even able to make it up here?"

Clay was comforted by the innocent humor he sensed in the man's comments. "Oh, he got us up here just fine. He didn't cost me much."

The man laughed, "Well, I'm sure he didn't. My name is Vern, Vern Bailey. I'm the field agent for this area." He removed the glove from his hand and reached out to Clay, "Welcome to the camp, Clay. Hart was wondering what had happened to you. We expected you to arrive in Flagstaff several days ago."

Clay took his hand firmly and gave it solid shake. "I ran into a few problems along the way." He tried to be as matter-of-fact as he could in his reply hoping to avoid any further discussion on his delay.

"It definitely looks like you 'ran into a few problems,'" and again he chuckled with his comment. "Do you need the doc to take a look at those eyes?" He lifted Clay's chin to get a better look at his face.

Clay was comforted by the real concern he detected in his voice. "No, this happened more than a few days ago, and I'm fine." Clay tried the best he could to quickly put the topic aside.

"Okay, then, let's get you settled into your quarters." He took Clay's bag, "Oh, tie that old burro to the log on the near side of that clearing. The cats and bears might see him as easy prey and make a quick, albeit rather small and stringy, meal of him." He seemed to have a way of lightening the conversation with his laughter. Clay liked him already.

Chapter 6

WORKING THE EXPEDITION

After getting settled in his tent, Clay spent some time with Vern meeting some of the other members of the expedition. Everyone had a very specific job. He noticed that all the men referred to Vern as "Boss," so he figured that he would as well. He wondered where Dr. Merriam was, and since Vern had not said anything about him, Clay asked, "Where's Dr. Merriam?"

"He's out in the field right now. He and the others should be returning soon." He paused for a moment before continuing, "I can assure you they will not miss supper. No one goes hungry around here. I hope you have a good appetite. We do eat well. Nothing beats fresh game, and we have no trouble procuring what we need."

Not soon after completing his tour of the camp and meeting the other men, he heard riders nearing the camp, and moments later four men on horses appeared through the break. Clay did not know what to expect of Dr. Merriam, and he could not identify him among those in the group. None seemed particularly outstanding in any way. None were large men, and all had the weathered look of men who had spent many years in the mountains. They dismounted their horses and took them to the small makeshift corral that had been set up. They each tended to their own saddle and gear. Clay thought that perhaps someone would take care of Dr. Merriam's horse for him, yet they all took care of their own animals.

A short time later, one of the smaller men approached Vern who was standing next to Clay. "Well, Boss, none of the traps had even been approached. We freshened up some of the bait. We'll see what tomorrow brings." He turned his head to Clay and continued, "Who's this black-eyed fellow?" The man looked straight into Clay's eyes. The rough looking character had a large bushy mustache, as did several of the men, but his seemed especially long and full.

"Why, Hart, this is the long-lost Clay Beckley from Indiana." He turned to Clay with a smile and said, "Clay, meet the man responsible for all of this, Hart Merriam."

Dr. Merriam already had his hand extended, and his bushy mustache lifted as he smiled at Clay. "Welcome, young man. I certainly hope your eyes don't always look that way; otherwise, we may have to look at you as some new species of raccoon." He laughed at his own joke as he gave Clay a hearty, welcoming handshake.

"No, sir, Dr. Merriam. I mean I had a little trouble, but my eyes are fine." Clay was nervous meeting a man that he admired so thoroughly.

"Okay, Clay. And call me Hart; everyone does. But, Vern here is the Boss who keeps this outfit working together. He's a stickler for detail, and lots of it. That's the way I like it." Clay noticed that he was still smiling. "Let me get cleaned up, and we'll talk more at supper." He walked away with an air of confidence that separated him from the other four men. Clay thought he should have noticed that and made note of the importance of keen observation.

At supper, Clay learned more details of the expedition than Dr. Merriam had been able to summarize in his letters to Clay. This area of the West had yet to be studied with regard to the plants and animals of the region. Clay learned that a vast amount of the West was still in such need of surveys just like this one to study the vegetation and mammals of the area. It was important to the U.S. Government in Washington to have the Western frontiers fully explored and understood. New species of plants and animals were being found at an astounding rate. Not only the government, but also the general population in the eastern part of the country could not get enough information about the vast West.

Clay was on the forward edge of an undertaking that had begun not that many years ago when explorers had opened the West to trade and opportunity. In the early 1880s little was known of American mammals. With trains now bringing people West at an alarmingly rapid rate, the job of Dr. Merriam's organization at the Department of Agriculture was to do a full and complete study of the West from the low, barren deserts to the highest mountain ranges. They needed a sound assessment of potential use of the land for agriculture. This included not only what plant life was in abundance, but also what animal life existed. The mammalian species were being evaluated both as a food source and as a potential problem for agricultural endeavors.

The work that had been done up to this time was spotty at best. Specimens were poorly prepared and little data had been provided about the specimen at the time of its collection. Mammalian specimens were few and far between as most collectors had been focusing on birds. This was changing with Dr. Merriam. He was a perfectionist who was exacting in the type and amount of detail to be provided for every specimen. This very detailed type of work was expected of every collector who worked for Dr. Merriam. No bit of detail was to be left unturned, from geographic data, to measurements, to colors, to variations, and to differences in males and females, mature specimens and immature specimens.

Dr. Merriam – Clinton Hart Merriam – was a medical doctor educated at Yale University and Columbia University. His heart, however, was in collecting and studying birds and mammals. At the age of sixteen, he joined the Hayden Geological Survey of 1871 which explored the region of northwestern Wyoming that became Yellowstone National Park in 1872. While still a medical student, he organized ornithology clubs. By 1885, he had given up his medical practice and accepted a position in the Department of Entomology at the U.S. Department of Agriculture. He expanded the position in 1888 to include the study of mammals. It was in that same year that he and thirty-two others, a diverse group of geographers, explorers, teachers, lawyers, cartographers, military officers, and financiers, formed the National Geographic Society. All shared an interest in scientific and geographical knowledge, as well as an opinion that in a time of discovery, invention, change, and mass communication, Americans were becoming more curious about the world around them.

Dr. Merriam was currently working on the development of a Life Zones concept that he was finalizing on this expedition. His Life Zones concept defined a belt of vegetation and animal life that is similarly expressed with increases in altitude and increases in latitude. The concept recognized the similarity between their vertical distribution and the north-south distribution of similar plant and animal species from other areas. This means of describing areas with similar plant and animal communities recognized the relationship between latitude and altitude.

Clay was fascinated by all of the information that was flooding him. He pledged himself to be fully immersed in learning every bit of collecting expertise that Dr. Merriam expected. He felt the contagious enthusiasm that Dr. Merriam displayed as a trusted leader. Clay found, over time, that Dr. Merriam was patient and generous in teaching new recruits, but he could be impatient and hard on those in his group who were experienced naturalists. His attention to detail and organizational skills were evident at every turn of events. Clay found his own inquisitiveness and awareness of the world around him being both challenged and expanded with each new day.

There were days, however, when Dr. Merriam was busy working on his Life Zones concept and seemed to have no time for anyone, including Clay. It was these days that Clay found himself at the side of Vern Bailey. While most of Clay's time with Dr. Merriam was spent learning how to collect data and prepare specimens, his time with Vern was spent in the field learning the finer points of hunting and trapping mammals of every type. In the mountains, they were capturing everything from rodents and beavers to mountain lions and bears. Just as Clay was dedicated to learning from Dr. Merriam, he was also dedicated to learning techniques for capturing large mammals from Vern. He felt he was becoming well-rounded with the guidance from both men.

As they were riding into the mountains one morning, Vern asked Clay, "So, Clay, Hart has told me a little bit about you, but why don't you tell me how you managed to get yourself into this outfit of his? You're fairly young to be out on an expedition like this." Vern turned toward Clay awaiting an answer.

Clay felt the need to immediately go on the defensive in his reply to Vern, "I'm not that much younger than Dr. Merriam, uh, Hart, was when he went on his first expedition. I read some about him in my father's science magazines. I've always had an interest in being a naturalist from as early as I can remember while spending time with my grampa on his farm back in Indiana." Clay held his hat and ducked as he rode under a low hanging branch. "I guess I just never knew there was such a thing as a naturalist."

"You obviously did a little taxidermy work before coming out here."

"My grampa taught me how to do that. I have some ducks and squirrels and a raccoon back on his farm." Clay's voice trailed off as he realized his grandfather was no longer on the farm. "Except that he died not too long before I came out here."

"Sorry to hear that, Clay. Seems he taught you well." The two of them continued down a saddle along the ridge line they were following. He changed the subject for Clay. "I was a little surprised that Hart consented to having you come out here. How old are you?"

"Fifteen. Well, almost fifteen. I will be fifteen before the year ends, so I say fifteen."

"So, Clay, you're only fourteen years old?"

"I guess, but not for long."

"Hart has given you an amazing opportunity, Clay. I hope you understand that and appreciate it."

"Oh, yes! I know I'm not a full expedition member, more of an apprentice, but I'm really excited about this. Hart seems even nicer in person." Clay had a broad smile on his face.

"You know, I was kinda young when I went to work for Hart, although not as young as you. He has a good eye to see something in people that they don't always see in themselves. He's a good man, but he can be tough. The more you learn, the more he expects. Give it your best, and you'll be just fine."

"Yessir, I'll give it my best. I want to learn." He still had the smile on his face. He enjoyed having this conversation with Vern.

"Okay, so how did you convince Hart to take you on?"

"Well, I wrote him some letters about my interest as a naturalist and the work that he was doing. I mentioned how I had been collecting at a young age just like he had. He eventually asked me to send him some specimens." Clay paused as he remembered the letter he got back from Dr. Merriam. "He was real pleased with my work." He looked over at Vern to see how he reacted. Vern had a pleasant smile on his face as they continued to plod along. "Then when I learned of this expedition, I got real brave and wrote him asking if I could join."

"And he said yes?"

"Not quite. He told me he couldn't offer me a full position, but if I could get out here, he'd provide a place for me. And here I am." Once again he was smiling with the realization of his place with the group. He couldn't have been more proud of himself.

"And your parents were fine with all of this?" Vern was a bit serious now.

"Well," Clay hesitated as he tried to figure out how to answer, "I didn't really tell them what I was doing. I did leave them a note when I left. I saved up some money working at my father's carriage factory and headed west."

"Have you written to your parents since you left?" Vern's tone turned fatherly.

"Yes, I explained everything. My father has always encouraged me to follow my dreams, so he was okay with it. I made sure I finished the school year before I left as I knew that was important to him."

"Good. Be sure to write to them regularly." It was fatherly advice.

They continued along the ridge line until they came to the next saddle where the bear trap had been set.

Many weeks passed with Clay sharing his time between Hart and Vern and balancing his activities between preparing specimens in camp and riding trap lines in the mountains. He was absorbing everything he learned like a sponge that could not be filled. He also became good friends with Ed Goldman, a young naturalist only four years older than Clay. He was an assistant to another naturalist on this trip, Ed Nelson, in much the manner that Clay was becoming to Vern.

Weeks turned into months as they moved farther up the mountains topping out at Humphrey's Peak. It was quite a bit colder at the top of the mountain, and the plant life was completely different at the upper ranges. Hart explained the changes in the plant and animal life at the higher altitudes through his developing theory of Life Zones that he was hoping to publish within the following year.

It was a particular morning when the weather was changing that Clay woke up with a cough. He had been quite tired the night before and had not rested well. It took all of his energy to get up and going this day. The cough lingered throughout the day, but he tried to suppress it as best he could since he was riding a trap line with Vern and two others. As the day wore on, all Clay could think about was getting back to camp and sleeping.

After the men had taken care of their mounts, Vern pulled Clay aside, "Are you feeling okay, Clay? You haven't looked too well all day."

"Just tired. I didn't sleep well last night." Clay tried to appear fine, but he was not.

"Get some grub, then turn in. If you're still feeling poorly in the morning, I'll have you stay in camp to get some rest. You can prepare some specimens."

"Sure," Clay tiredly answered as he moved off toward his tent, no longer able to suppress his coughing. He went to bed without eating, but his sleep was fitful at best.

Chapter 7

CONSUMPTION

When morning came, Clay slowly woke from a restless dream soaked with sweat, and coughing hoarsely. He felt that if he got up and ate a good breakfast, he would feel better. He splashed himself with some cold water and slowly made his way to breakfast.

"How're you feelin' this mornin', Clay?" asked Vern as Clay approached.

"Oh, better, I guess," although he really didn't feel better at all. "But, maybe I should stay in camp today and work on some specimens." He tried to sound as strong as he could, but his reply was followed by a brief bout of coughing.

Vern stared at Clay and agreed, "Yep, stay in camp today. See Ed about specimens you can work on." Vern stared at Clay longer than Clay realized. "We might just keep you in camp for a few days and let you rest some."

Clay nodded and sat down to eat. As cool as the weather was, he felt that he should not be so warm. He wasn't really hungry, but he forced himself to eat a good, full breakfast.

The day was a long one for Clay. It was difficult to stay awake and remain focused. He just felt so tired, and the coughing would not go away. His work on the specimens was slow and difficult. His energy was low, and the coughing interrupted his work.

Immediately after supper, Clay retired to his tent. He was no longer warm; he now felt chilled. This night's bout of coughing was worse than the previous night's had been. He did all he could to control his cough so no one would hear him. His chest was now beginning to hurt from the coughing, mostly on his right side. By morning, he noticed that a small bit of blood had been expelled with his coughing. His mind immediately flashed back to the small boy on the train who had coughed up blood all over Clay during the night in the railroad freight car. But, surely he was not that bad; it was just a little bit of red in his coughed up phlegm.

"Clay, you okay?" It was morning, and Vern was peering into his tent. "You darn near kept the whole camp awake last night with that cough. Maybe you better have the doc take a look at you." Vern had a caring tone to his voice.

Clay squeaked out, "Yeah," and then broke into a fitful cough and grabbed at the right side of his chest.

"Stay here, and I'll get the doc," Vern said with concern as he disappeared from Clay's tent.

Moments later, the camp doctor returned with Vern. "Sit up, Clay," ordered the doctor. He took Clay's wrist with one hand to check his pulse while placing his other hand on Clay's forehead. "Well, you have a fever for sure." The doctor reached into his bag removing his stethoscope. He asked Clay to remove his shirt, and placed the stethoscope against his chest. Clay tried to suppress a cough as the doctor listened to his chest, but he could not stop it. "Take in a deep breath for me, Clay," the camp doctor said as he placed the stethoscope on Clay's warm back. Clay took a deep breath, but instead of exhaling, he coughed hard and long. "How long have you had the cough, Clay?"

"I don't know. I guess it actually started a few weeks ago. It wasn't too bad at first. It's only gotten worse in the last few days."

"And, the fever?"

"I'm not sure. I've been awfully tired."

"Okay, lay back down, Clay." He reached into his bag and pulled out a small bottle. Opening the bottle, he poured some of the liquid into a spoon, and lifted Clay's head so he could swallow. "This should help some with the cough. Stay in bed for the next couple of days. You seem to have a real bad cold, and we don't want it to get any worse. A little rest and time should take care of it. I'll give you some of the cough medicine a few times a day. That should help you rest better." He paused, looked at Clay, and smiled. "Any questions?"

Clay shook his head and rolled over in bed. After some time, the coughing was better controlled, and Clay fell asleep. He dreamed of the small boy on the train. Only, in the dream, the boy's coughing spread to several other small boys who were all coughing and spitting blood all over Clay. The coughing grew louder until Clay woke in confusion and a cold sweat.

Several more days passed in a similar manner. The doctor's cough medicine was helping control Clay's cough, but he was not feeling any better. His fever was not breaking, and he was still very tired. His night sweats were leaving him drenched by the time morning arrived. The doctor entered Clay's tent and asked how he was doing. Clay no longer tried to hide his real feelings; he was miserable. The doctor added some more medicine to help fight the fever, and he left.

For two more days, Clay was in and out of a confused state. The third morning, Dr. Merriam entered the tent with the camp doctor. It was Dr. Merriam who asked Clay if he had coughed up any blood. Clay showed him a handkerchief that was now well-covered with blood. Clay had not realized how much blood he had coughed up. Dr. Merriam listened to Clay's chest with great intent and then asked, "Clay, does your chest hurt at all?"

"Yes. It hurts a lot on the right side."

Dr. Merriam once again listened to Clay's chest, especially his right side. He thumped Clay's chest numerous times, listening carefully. Clay wasn't sure what he was doing. "Lay back down, Clay." Then Dr. Merriam and the camp doctor left the tent without saying anything else.

Late that afternoon, Dr. Merriam returned to the tent and found Clay awake but looking miserable and tired. "Clay, I've taken a good look at your symptoms and everything the doc has done for you. We've discussed your illness in some detail. This is not a simple cold." Dr. Merriam paused long enough to ensure he had Clay's attention. "Clay, we need to send you back to New Mexico where you can get better treatment. There's a nursing home there that has recently begun to pro-vide care and comfort for people with your condition so that you can recover. You'll need a lot of rest."

"What condition?" Clay weakly and quietly asked. "The doc said it was just a bad cold." By now he was whispering his words.

Dr. Merriam again paused and looked Clay in the eye, "Clay, I think you have consumption." Another momentary pause to let his di-agnosis sink in. "Do you know what consumption is, Clay?" Dr. Mer-riam's tone was caring and sympathetic.

Do I know?! Yes, it's a death sentence! Clay tried to hide the thoughts that were filling him with fear. "I helped a small boy on the train. He had consumption." Clay paused as he found the courage to say the last part of his thought, "He died." Clay began to sob as Dr. Merriam put his arm around Clay's shoulders.

The next morning Clay was loaded into a small wagon, and one of the camp men began their drive back to Flagstaff where Clay would board the train and head to Las Vegas, New Mexico. Clay remained wrapped in blankets in the back of the wagon, where he slept fitfully, but at least slept, thanks to the doctor's medicine to control his cough.

The doctor had provided a small bottle of laudanum for Clay to take with him for his cough.

Dr. Merriam wrote Clay's family to let them know that Clay would be cared for in Las Vegas, New Mexico, at a newly opened facility where Clay would receive good care from a Catholic charity organization. Dr. Merriam also offered to help with the cost for Clay's care at the home. He knew that recovery could take many months, but he was more than willing to assume the obligation to assure Clay's full recovery.

The next few days were mostly a blur to Clay as he fought fever and chills, slept fitfully, and coughed regularly. Clay had been placed on the train, and the conductor kept close watch on him to ensure he would get off at his stop in Las Vegas. A carriage from the sanatorium was waiting for him at the train depot in Las Vegas when he arrived.

Mostly incoherent, Clay had to be helped into the carriage. The ride to the sanatorium was short, but the last hazy memory Clay had was of being helped into the carriage. He slumped over in the seat as the driver walked the horse away from the depot.

1891

Chapter 8

RECOVERY

C lay could not even remember the first weeks that eventually dragged into months at St. Anthony's. When he became more alert, he was very despondent as all he could think of was the small boy who had died from the disease that had now grabbed Clay in its tight grip. Clay was fortunate, however, that Dr. Merriam was familiar with the disease and had kept up with developments in the care and treatment of its victims. The Sisters of Charity of Leavenworth, Kansas, had opened a care facility in St. Anthony's Parish in Las Vegas, New Mexico, that had only recently begun offering care for consumptive patients, and Dr. Merriam had family connections that allowed him to get Clay into the custody and care of the Sisters.

Clay's early days were spent sleeping, eating, and getting plenty of fresh air. Clay had lost some weight by the time he was admitted for care, and now his meals were well-prepared and strictly scheduled. He ate very well, six times a day at first and then, later, four times a day, with an abundant, nourishing diet plentiful in milk, eggs, and meats. Clay never drank so much milk as he did during his recovery.

Between meals, there were exams on a most regular basis with all the statistics being carefully recorded and charted, especially Clay's weight. The rest of the day was spent in defined rest periods in bed where the activities consisted of light reading or letter writing. Clay was under the very strict supervision of Sister Anne who, while very kind, was also a tough disciplinarian. His schedule seemed to be monitored to the minute, and deviations were simply not tolerated. As Clay understood more about recovery from consumption, he learned to follow Sister Anne's tight control.

Sister Anne checked on Clay one afternoon during his rest period. Clay was sitting up in a chair reading. "Clay Beckley, you get back in that bed right now!"

Sister Anne could scowl her face in a way that rivaled the face of any railroad bull that Clay had run into. Clay looked up from his reading and began to plead his case, "Sister, I . . ." He was immediately cut off from adding even a single word.

"And I am here to see to it that you get well. I will not have you up and moving around when you should be lying in bed!" She stood tall over Clay and pointed her left arm at the bed while still looking intently into Clay's eyes. "Back in there, young man!"

Clay obeyed, of course, but he knew he was to move slowly and deliberately, not showing any signs of exertion in moving to the bed. He climbed into the bed, and Sister Anne placed his bed covers up on his chest. Clay still had his book in his hand. Sister Anne retrieved it from him before he even knew it happened.

"Now, you will stay in bed until the call for supper. You will not get up to get that book. You will not get up to sit in the chair. You will lie still in bed. Do you understand me?" She had paused after each command to be sure it was completely clear to Clay. Then, she added that scowl to her face and waited for an answer.

Clay knew there was only one correct answer, but he couldn't help but be amused by Sister Anne's demeanor. They had had this same conversation on several other occasions. Clay fought back a smile and responded in a most apologetic manner, "Yes, ma'am."

"Fine, then. I will be back at the call for supper." She turned and walked stiffly out of the room, but Clay was sure he saw a slight smile on her face as she turned away.

As his condition improved, but still with most of the day spent in rest periods, Clay was able to extend his time for reading, and he devoured every article and book on the subject of consumption that he could get his hands on. Whenever possible, he engaged many of the Sisters in conversation about the disease, its causes, and the treatment. Only recently had the disease been identified as a bacteria named *M. tuberculosis*. The bacteria invaded the lungs and seemed to almost "consume" its patients from the inside out, hence the common name of consumption. As fluid filled the lungs, the patient had to spit constantly. A severe infection in the lungs and constant heavy coughing caused the patient to spit up blood as well, just as Clay had been doing when he was sent to the facility by Dr. Merriam.

Starting about 1880, New Mexico became known as a significant area of care and healing for those who were beset with the leading cause of death in America. By Clay's time, the state was well-known for the qualities that most physicians said were the keys to treating the illness. The Sisters of Charity was operating a small nursing home in a donated house in Las Vegas caring for consumptives when Dr. Merriam approached them on Clay's behalf. While the home cared for fifteen patients when Clay was admitted, The Sisters of Charity organization was planning a new sanatorium hospital to be constructed on additional donated property nearby.

The present medical regime for the treatment of consumption consisted of nutritious food, fresh air, and rest, preferably in a high, dry and sunny place. New Mexico with its high elevation, dry climate, and abundant sunshine was considered an ideal location for healing and cure. It was this environment that was bringing so many patients from the East to New Mexico for treatment. When the railroads were built out into the West, the opportunity for travel from the East greatly increased for those with the money to do so. This era was a boom time for the health industry in New Mexico.

Clay had two factors working for him to overcome the extreme boredom of such a care regimen. First of all, since he loved to read, he devoured every book and magazine he could get his hands on. Through correspondence that continued with Dr. Merriam, he was able to obtain magazines and books to continue his study of the natural world including plants, insects, and mammals in particular. Dr. Merriam also kept Clay informed of his work and the standards he would expect of Clay when he was well again. Clay was extremely grateful for all that Dr. Merriam had done for him. He had only known him personally for a short time, but had grown close to him.

The second thing that helped Clay was his love of the outdoors. At least twelve hours a day were spent outdoors on the large porch that surrounded the house. In fact, on very many of the nights the patients slept in their beds placed on the porch to ensure maximum exposure to the pure, dry air of New Mexico. From the western side of the house, Clay could look out to the mountains, knowing that only about forty miles beyond them was Santa Fe. He was well aware from his letters from Dr. Merriam that much of the mountain region of New Mexico still needed to be studied by the naturalists. He would wander over the mountains in his mind's eye searching all the time for new plant and animal specimens to collect. He looked forward to the day that he was cured of this affliction and could begin anew his field studies.

Clay's easy-going nature also helped him overcome the boredom of his situation. He was able to talk with the other residents, not all of whom, however, were willing to share their stories. Many of those recovering were from wealthy families from the East and were not ready to open up to complete strangers whose "destitute position in life" had contributed to their disease – at least that is what Clay had overheard two of the patients discussing. But, he had no time for such nonsense and provided cheer to others where he could, even though all were older than he was. Maybe they just tolerated him because of his youthfulness, but, either way, he didn't care.

Clay was tall for his age and had previously had a good weight for his height, but he was losing weight when he entered the nursing home. As he improved, his charts showed that he was gaining weight while also growing taller, and that was a very good sign according to Sister Anne. She let him know that he was fortunate to have been in good, youthful health when he was struck with the disease as that should help him in making a relatively quick recovery. At the same time, she was always blunt with Clay about the serious nature of consumption and his need to strictly adhere to his recovery program. She tightly monitored Clay's carefully prepared meals and his controlled rest periods and sleep patterns, while checking his charts many times each day.

As his recovery progressed in his latter months at the home, Clay wandered from the large porch into the surrounding countryside where he began to collect plant specimens from the area. The walks were a part of the recovery process that were greatly welcomed by Clay. His cough was now gone, his chest was feeling better, and since he was gaining weight, the next phase of his recovery was outdoor exercise. It was something Clay eagerly looked forward to each day, unlike some of the patients who seemed to prefer being pampered.

Sister Anne accompanied him for the first several weeks to ensure that he was well enough to be out on his own. He used the opportunity to share his knowledge of the natural world with her. She was attentive to Clay's words, and she noticed the emotion and comfort in his voice and his demeanor. These outings were helping Clay grow in confidence in his own abilities as a naturalist.

Clay was one of the very fortunate patients to recover from a serious case of the bacterial infection. As he learned later, nearly half of all consumptive patients did not recover. He was thankful that he did not know this earlier as it might well have affected his outlook and attitude about recovery.

Finally, the day came when the doctor announced that Clay was symptom-free and could leave the nursing home. He cautioned Clay to take good care of himself, continue to eat well, and get plenty of rest, but his youth and general good health at the outset had helped him to achieve a recovery from the dreaded disease.

Thankful to Sister Anne and the rest of the staff, and to Dr. Merriam, Clay was ready to be on his way. But to where?

Dr. Merriam had published his results of the biological survey of the San Francisco Mountains in the *North American Fauna* series produced by the Department of Agriculture. It was noted that between 1889 and 1890, Dr. Merriam had discovered an unprecedented seventy-one new species of mammals. The report also included a discussion of the Life Zones that Dr. Merriam was working on. He, of course, had provided a copy to Clay for his reading during his convalescence in Las Vegas. Clay read it with great interest, recalling some of the specific specimens and places that Dr. Merriam wrote about.

Since then, Dr. Merriam had organized a larger expedition into Death Valley, and, of course, Clay had been unable to participate. Dr. Merriam had cut short his own time with the expedition as President Harrison had appointed him as a Bering Sea Commissioner to study the life of fur seals in Alaska. Many of the men who had tutored Clay in the San Francisco Mountains were now serving on various expeditions in the West, as well as in Mexico.

With less frequent correspondence from Dr. Merriam, Clay contacted Vern Bailey, who was in California at the time. Vern responded and let Clay know that the Division of Ornithology and Mammalogy, as it was now known, was spreading itself thin. He was still interested in additional specimens from New Mexico, but he had no one to work that area at the present time. He could not offer Clay a permanent position in the organization, but he did offer to pay Clay for any specimens of new species that he could find, both plant and mammal. Vern let Clay know that the organization was especially interested in the Sangre de Cristo Mountain Range in northern New Mexico.

Clay was champing at the bit to be in the field again. His physical health was much better, but there was one problem. While Dr. Merriam had been kind beyond understanding by paying for Clay's stay at the care facility, Clay was broke with only a few dollars to his name.

1892

Chapter 9

THE AZUELA FAMILY

Clay made some contacts and found that the Raton Land and Cattle Company located just east of Raton, New Mexico, was looking for workers in their stockyard at the railroad station in Raton. Raton was on the northern border of the New Mexico Territory about one hundred miles from Las Vegas. Clay wished he had the old burro to get him to Raton.

But fortune once again smiled on Clay. When Sister Anne heard of Clay's plans and his lack of funds, she was able to obtain a train ticket to Raton for him. As he accepted the generosity of the Sisters of Charity, he had a smile that reflected his good health, his good fortune, and his great thanks. Sister Anne said her good-bye to Clay, and he was off to catch the train.

Clay had not been sure what kind of work he would be doing in a railroad stockyard, but he was soon to find out that it wasn't what he had expected. The job he was offered was actually working for the railroad in the railyard at Raton. He was to begin at the bottom rung of the ladder as a wiper. A wiper worked long shifts cleaning the engines with wads of greasy waste. It was a dirty, greasy, hot chore often comprising an eleven-hour day. It was far from what Clay thought he would be doing working with cattle in a stockyard, but it was a paying job.

Clay was able to talk a local stable owner, Mr. Ludwig Wendt, into hiring him part time in exchange for a place to stay in the stable. This allowed him to be around the animals, which he enjoyed. By the end of each long day, Clay was so tired that he could have slept anywhere, so a small tack room in the stable was just fine as far as he was concerned.

A small Mexican boy helped out in the stables in the mornings. He was smaller than Clay, and Clay noticed scars on his hands that indicated to Clay that the boy had been working hard for most of his young life. He was a good worker with a serious nature about him. Clay went out of his way to engage the boy in conversation. He introduced himself on the third morning that he saw the boy at the stable. "I've seen you here every morning for the past three days. Do you work here every day?" The boy looked up at Clay and did not immediately respond, which made Clay wonder if he spoke English. "Do you speak English?"

"Yes, I speak English," he replied in fairly good English. "I come here in the mornings to help in the stables. Then, I go back to my family's farm to work." He looked down again and continued with his work.

"My name's Clay. What's yours?" Clay smiled and reached his hand out to the boy.

The boy looked up again and stared at Clay's hand momentarily before reaching out. "My name is Carlos. Carlos Antonio Azuela." He finally had a bit of a smile on his face as he shook Clay's hand.

"Well, Carlos Antonio Azuela, nice to meet you. I am Clayton Martin Beckley, but call me Clay." He gave Carlos a broad grin. "I help out in the evenings after my job at the railroad. I'm a wiper at the railyard. I usually leave early in the morning, so I guess we won't see each other much."

"I know. Mr. Wendt told me about you. He says he hopes you will be a good worker. He is not sure about you because you work at the railroad." The boy continued working as he talked to Clay.

"What do you mean 'not sure' about me?" Clay asked with a look of concern on his face.

"He says they work you very hard at the railroad. He hopes you do not let him down in your work here." He was serious for a young boy. "He likes you."

"I won't let him down, Carlos. I'm a hard worker, and I need this job." Clay found himself being defensive toward the young boy but realized that it was not the boy who was questioning Clay's work ethic. "Sorry, I just really need the job."

"Then do the work Mr. Wendt wants you to do. He is a fair man."

They left their words at that as Clay had to get to the railyard to begin his day there.

Over the next several weeks, Clay felt his strength fully returning. The work was as difficult as he had expected the first day, but it was helping him to develop the stamina he would need to head into the Sangre de Cristo Mountains. He was eventually moved to a job known as engine watchman. For the engines in the yard, Clay had to keep water in the boilers and enough fire going in the firebox to move the engines about the yard. It was hot work, and dirty in a different way than his job as the wiper had been. He was usually covered with soot by the end of the day.

Clay got to know Carlos a little better over time. He resolved to take time each day to talk with Carlos. Once in a while, Clay was given a day off. He typically got as much rest as he could on those days. Then one day, Carlos asked Clay if he would like to visit the farm where he lived. Carlos told Clay that his mother would welcome him for dinner with his family. Clay was quick to accept the invitation. He welcomed a change of scenery . . . and the thought of a home-cooked meal.

The Azuela family lived in the foothills of the Sangre de Cristo Mountains, so Clay was anxious to get a look at the area as he thought about field collecting in those mountains.

As they neared the farm, which Carlos referred to as *La Granja Azuela*, Clay could see in the distance a large adobe house with several outbuildings. The house appeared to have had several additions made over time. There was a large corral and a decent-sized stable. There were a few cattle grazing about in the distance. As the two approached nearer to the house, Clay also saw a chicken coop. Farther in the distance, Clay saw the main crops, fields of potatoes and corn.

"This farm is our homestead. Our family has been here for many generations. Our ancestors traveled up the El Camino Real and settled in this area." While his tone was still serious, it was also full of pride. Clay noticed that Carlos lifted his shoulders taller as he spoke.

"What is El Camino Real?" Clay questioned, truly interested.

Carlos seemed to know his history well. He explained that the full name of the trail is *El Camino Real de Tierra Adentro*, or the Royal Road to the Interior in English. It was a 1,500-mile trade route that began in Mexico City, Mexico, and ended just north of Santa Fe. Spanish explorer Juan de Oñate blazed the northern portion of the trail into what is now New Mexico Territory in 1598, and claimed the land for Spain. He took 500 soldiers and settlers and 7,000 head of cattle on a 1,000-mile, six-month journey to Espanola, New Mexico. This trail was used by emigrants from Mexico and brought thousands of Spanish and Mexican colonists to the New Mexico Territory.

Carlos' ancestors left Mexico for Nuevo Mexico about 1719 following the El Camino Real all the way to Espanola. The Azuela family eventually moved farther north into the Sangre de Cristo Mountains just west of what is now Raton where they were farmers. More recently, however, following the end of the Mexican-American War in 1848, they had lost much of their land to raiders ready to drive the Mexican immigrants out of New Mexico Territory. The family started over on a portion of the original family settlement along with some newly-acquired land. They all thought of themselves as New Mexicans and had spoken English for at least two generations.

Clay and Carlos arrived at the house and were greeted by two younger children and Carlos' mother. "Hello, Mama," Carlos said respectfully. The two younger children held onto her legs and peered from behind her at the tall young man with Carlos. This is Clay Beckley from the stables."

"Hello, Clay. I am Carlos' mother, Señora Azuela."

"Hello, ma'am. Thank you for having me to your home. Carlos has told me a lot about your family." Clay smiled as he held his hat in his hands.

"Come on in, boys. Let me get you some water." They sat down at a large table.

Carlos had a younger brother and a cousin who were working in the fields with Carlos' father. The two younger children, a boy and a girl, who had met them at the door, were helping their mother around the house. Carlos' older sister and older cousin were in another room where they were making blankets. Carlos told Clay that the two older girls and his mother made blankets which they sold in Raton.

The home was clean and comfortable. It was surprisingly cool inside considering how warm it was outside. The adobe structure with numerous windows provided for a comfortable setting.

Since it was Sunday, Carlos' father and the younger brother and cousin in the field would be in soon. "Carlos, why don't you and Clay bring some wood in for the stove and then get two chickens ready for us." The two younger ones were clinging less tightly to her legs now.

As Clay and Carlos rounded up a couple plump chickens, the two younger children stood in the doorway watching, and now giggling. One at a time, the boys took the chickens, calmed them with their heads on a weathered stump of wood, and quickly chopped off their heads. They waited while the headless chickens flopped around with blood spurting from their necks. The two younger children approached from the doorway to watch the spectacle.

Having dispatched the chickens, they placed them in a pot of water hot water for a few minutes. Pulling them carefully out of the water, they proceeded to pluck the feathers from the chickens to the giggling of the two smaller children.

Carlos' father, brother, and cousin came in from the fields and washed themselves outside. Carlos father then approached Clay, "Hello, I am Antonio, Carlos' father, and you are?"

"I am Clay Beckley, sir." Clay extended his hand to Señor Azuela.

"Clay Beckley, hmmm. Looks like you know your way around a chicken. I hope you are hungry. Carlos' mother is a wonderful cook." He smiled a broad, welcoming smile.

"Yes, sir. We had chickens back home. I am sure hungry, too." Perhaps he sounded too eager to eat. He felt a bit embarrassed by the way he responded.

"Where is back home, Clay?"

"Indiana, sir."

"Indiana? Where is that? Is that some Indian territory?" He was curious.

Clay had not thought about how far he was from home. "Well, it's back East, but not all the way to the east. It is pretty far from here. It's not Indian territory, just so-named, I guess." Clay had never really given any thought to the name of his home state.

"Carlos tells me you work in the stables and at the railroad. It sounds like you are an ambitious young man."

"Yessir, I'm saving up some money so I can get back to being a naturalist," Clay said with a sense of pride in his voice.

"A naturalist? Well, Clay-from-Indiana, what does a naturalist do?" Antonio seemed to be in wonder of Clay.

"I go into new areas that haven't been much studied as far as the plant and animal life, and I collect specimens for the United States Department of Agriculture." Now Clay was really feeling his pride.

"I guess there must be some reason for that, but all I know is we have corn and potatoes and cattle and horses and sheep and chickens. That's plenty enough for us." He laughed politely not really understanding what Clay was saying.

"Well, the government wants to know all about the types of plants and animals that live in the West. They hope that the things they learn can help farmers better control their crops and livestock." He was proud with his answer.

But, Señor Azuela just looked at him and changed the subject. "Let's get these chickens to your mother, Carlos." They all went in together.

It was the best meal Clay had eaten since he left the nursing home. He was trying to eat well in town, but he was also trying to save as much money as he could. After the meal, they sat and talked while the younger children played. It reminded Clay briefly of home, but he quickly put that out of his mind. The two older girls, especially Carlos' cousin, were paying a lot of attention to Clay.

Carlos' cousin had not gone unnoticed to Clay. He found himself feeling things that he had not felt before when he looked at her long black hair and dark brown eyes. He had looked at her several times during the meal, and their eyes had met a number of times. The cousin, Analena, finally crossed the room and sat next to Clay. She was very inquisitive about Clay, and he answered many of the same questions he had answered for Señor Azuela earlier.

Before it got too late, Clay excused himself as he knew he had to be up early in the morning. He expressed his deep appreciation to the family for their kindness as he headed for the door. Analena quickly walked up next to him and touched his arm as he made his way out. Clay politely said good-night to Analena and headed back into Raton on the burro that he and Carlos had borrowed from Mr. Wendt. Analena was all Clay could think about on the ride back to Raton.

Chapter 10

ANALENA

Clay and Carlos spent more time together as they worked out a good plan for taking care of the stables that made both of their jobs easier. Clay was happy to have met Carlos and developed a friend-ship with him. Clay learned that he was about two years older than Carlos, and Carlos' cousin, Analena, was only about six months older than Clay. Carlos, however, was not very forthcoming about his cousin, and it seemed to Clay that Carlos was not pleased with Clay's growing interest in Analena.

It was two weeks later when Clay was back at the Azuela ranch with the opportunity to get to know the family better; in particular, he was looking forward to seeing Analena. Señora Azuela had once again prepared a great meal, and the family relaxed in the cool, dry adobe house after eating. Clay appreciated the closeness of the family. He especially admired the Azuelas for taking in the children of Antonio's brother after a fire destroyed the brother's house and barn, and also took the lives of Antonio's brother, his wife, and one child. That had been over three years ago, and the cousins were now simply a part of their new family as if they had always been so. All of this made Clay briefly long for his own family, but he was becoming more independent of them with each passing day.

As the oldest child, Analena missed her family more than the younger children as she could best remember her parents. Clay observed that Analena was very carefree and happy except when she talked about her family. She was then somber, and he could tell she did not want to think about their death, let alone talk about it. So, Clay avoided being overly inquisitive about her life prior to moving in with her cousins.

Analena took Clay aside in the next room where she made blankets with her cousin and Señora Azuela. She sat at the loom and showed Clay how it worked. Clay admired her hands moving deftly back and forth across the loom. She then stood up and said, "Now, it is your turn," and smiled at him with those gorgeous big brown eyes.

Clay was surprised at her request. "Me? I've never done anything like this." He was suddenly fearful of making a fool of himself in front of Analena. He could feel the redness rising in his face.

"Sit down," she ordered as she pushed him into the chair in front of the loom. Her long black hair swept against Clay's neck as she eased him into the chair. Clay offered no resistance yielding to her charms.

"Look, you've got to show me again. I can't do this. Your hands moved so quick. I couldn't do what you just did if my life depended on it!"

"Here, place your right hand here," and she placed her hand over his as she gently moved his hands into the proper position on the loom.

Clay forgot about the loom and the room and the ranch. All he could think of and see was Analena. Was he dreaming? He was like a rag doll in her hands as she moved him about, working the loom. She laughed as she worked the loom through Clay's hands. After some moments – and Clay wasn't even sure how long – she moved away.

"There! Look what you made." She smiled with a pride for Clay, and politely laughed.

Before him he saw a short bit of colored pattern of material in the loom. His heart was pounding, but he dare not show it. "Yeah, well, I think I better stick to working in the railyards. I'll never make enough money trying to make a blanket on my own." Then they laughed together as he looked into her eyes.

Carlos walked into the room. "I don't think you'll make a weaver of Clay. He's much better at cleaning the horse stalls at the stable." Carlos laughed, Clay smiled, but Analena glared at Carlos.

"Don't be so mean, Carlos." She was stern, the smile gone from her face.

"It's okay. He didn't mean anything. Just having some fun." Clay was embarrassed, but he did not show it as he tried to let Carlos off the hook from his older cousin's anger. "I better be going anyway."

"Let me walk you out," said Analena as the smile reappeared on her face. Clay noticed that she even smiled with her eyes. Clay also noticed that Carlos was frowning at him.

Clay said his good-byes to the rest of the family and thanked the Azuelas for their kind hospitality. Then, he and Analena went outside and headed for the stables where the mule was tied up. As Clay unhitched the mule, Analena caught his hand. Clay looked down straight into her eyes, those beautiful brown eyes. As she moved in closer to Clay, Clay leaned into her and their lips met. Her lips were soft and warm upon his. As he once again wondered if he was dreaming, he hoped he was kissing her correctly for it was his first kiss. As they drew gently back from one another, Clay was about to make some comment about his kissing ability, but Analena quickly leaned in again with her creamy lips and kissed him once more. This time, she wrapped her arms around him, pulled him close, and held him tightly. Instinctively, Clay placed his arms around her thin waist and pulled her closer. Clay was sure this was a dream, as anything this wonderful had to be. They ended the kiss at the same time, and they quietly gazed into each other's eyes.

Her normally large, joyful smile was replaced by a soft, gentle smile that made Clay feel warm and comfortable. "I have to go, but I can't wait to see you again. Thank you for making this such a wonderful afternoon." There was a tenderness in his voice that Clay did not know he had. He had been experiencing many new feelings in these last couple of weeks, and they were all good.

"Be safe, Clay. Come back as soon as you can." She gave him one more quick kiss and then turned and ran off to the house.

1893

Chapter 11

THE HALLS PEAK EXPEDITION

The weeks passed quickly for Clay as he spent more time with the Azuela family, in particular with Analena. Clay and Carlos talked a lot about Clay's plans for his collecting expedition. Clay shared with him the letters he received from Dr. Merriam and Vern. Clay also showed Carlos how to prepare specimens with some mice and gophers. In fact, in the process of teaching Carlos, Clay had run across a type of gopher that he had not seen before. Found at the ranch, the gopher was used to show Carlos all of the careful preparation work as well as documentation that had to be prepared for a specimen. After all preparation was complete, they mailed the specimen to Dr. Merriam. By teaching Carlos, Clay was able to continue to sharpen his own skills.

Clay was pleased with how well Carlos was learning. Perhaps he had been too encouraging, as one morning Carlos approached Clay asking to go with him on his expedition.

"Clay, you have taught me many things about collecting specimens. You have said yourself that I am a fast learner." He hesitated before continuing. He lifted his head and stood as tall as he could. "I would like to go with you on your expedition into the mountains." He now spoke quickly as if he would not be able to get all of his words out. "We can collect more by working together, just as we did at the stables. I can help with preparing the specimens and with setting traps, and you know I can cook and care for the burros. I will not be a burden, but I will be a good helper." He stopped suddenly and just stared at Clay.

Clay stared back at Carlos. He was surprised as he had not expected Carlos to ask to join him. "I don't know what to say, Carlos." He thought about his words carefully. "You've learned quickly, and you are a very good friend. You, however, have your family, and you have your farm to work. They need you. Besides, I have only planned for this undertaking on my own. There would be additional supplies and much more to consider for two people." He knew that Carlos was going to be very disappointed.

"I know, but I can help out," Carlos pleaded.

"Look, Carlos, I'll be ready to leave soon. I've planned this for nearly a year, and you can't make a decision like this when you have your family to consider. You understand, don't you?"

"I know, but . . ."

"No, Carlos, I can't take you with me this time." While understanding, Clay was now being firm with Carlos. In his heart Clay wanted to go alone. It was another chapter in his growth as a man, and he needed to proceed as he had planned.

"But, Clay . . ."

"I'm sorry, Carlos." Clay thought for a moment, unsure of what to say next. "Look, I'll tell you what, while I'm away, speak with your family about making an expedition with me. After I complete my survey of the Halls Peak area, I'll come back up to Raton, and then we can talk about the next part of the survey farther into the eastern slopes of the Sangre de Cristos. If you are still interested, and if your family supports it, you can join me. How does that sound?" He ended with an encouraging tone in his voice.

"I understand, Clay." And then excitedly, he said, "But I will be ready! You will see!"

"Alright, Carlos, then we have a plan for a future partnership." Clay reached out his hand to Carlos, and they shook hands, both smiling.

Vern had passed along instructions from Dr. Merriam about the areas he would like Clay to survey. He was to head to the Halls Peak area and work the canyons and mesas in that area. He could then trek farther west into the eastern slopes of the mountain range before heading farther south along the eastern slopes of the mountains.

Clay planned to work the area around Halls Peak and then make a first approach farther west to the eastern side of the mountain range before returning to Raton. He planned to replenish supplies at that time anyway. It would be a minor change in plans to return to Raton instead of Cimarron as he had originally planned. Anyway, maybe he would welcome a partner by that time. He felt very good about his plans.

Finally, an evening came about four weeks later when Clay was reviewing the list of items he needed to purchase from the local stores in order to be ready for his expedition. He had priced all the items, including the burros he would be buying from Mr. Wendt. He felt good about the final list of gear and supplies that he had continued to winnow down to the absolute necessities over the last few weeks. He pulled out the secreted stash of money that he had so carefully scrimped and saved over all of the past months of hard work in the railyards and at the stable. There were so many days, especially early on, that he had been exhausted at the end of the day and wondered how he could continue on in this manner. But tonight, his grueling efforts had finally paid off – he had enough money to purchase everything on his list. He smiled to himself with pride and immediately thought of his grandfather. He had not thought about him for a very long time. His death seemed so long ago now. Somehow, though, Clay felt his presence as he was about to begin on this next phase of his growth as a man. Tomorrow, he would let Mr. Wendt know that he would be gone in a week.

This also meant he would need to tell Analena that he would be gone very soon. He had prepared himself to say good-bye to her, but now it seemed as though it would not be as easy as he had thought it would be. Just as quickly, he told himself that there would always be time for girls in his life, but he would not always have before him the opportunity to be a part of the study of the natural history of the Great American West. He felt he had a real purpose in his life. He knew that this was what he wanted to do; he had known it since he was a young boy. But something was different now. He felt he was a part of something bigger than himself. It was no longer just about himself, but rather it was about some greater good that he could be a part of.

The work excited him just as it always had, but now there seemed to be a calling about it that was drawing him in an even stronger manner. It was as if a new life had opened right before his eyes, asked him in and welcomed him with great joy. He could not wait to begin his quest.

By the end of the week, Clay had his outfit put together – tent, bedroll, and camping gear; boots, hat, gloves, and new clothes to replace his old clothes that had become rags; a Winchester 1886 rifle that Vern had recommended, a Colt 45 1873 Model P revolver, and ammunition; tools, knives, and preparation equipment and chemicals for specimens; bridles, saddle, and pack gear for the burros; and personal items and miscellaneous supplies. Clay had bargained with Mr. Wendt for three burros, two of which he had had his eye on and was pleased to acquire from Mr. Wendt at a very fair price.

The railroad was not too interested in Clay's new undertaking. If anything, his foreman seemed a bit angry at Clay that he was leaving what the foreman referred to as a "great future on the railroad." Clay was cordial with him and thanked him for the job, but let him know that there was a different future for himself. His foreman looked at Clay and said with disgust, "Well, piss-off, then!" He then turned and walked away from Clay.

Carlos had eagerly helped Clay acquire his gear and pack it. On the morning Clay was to leave, Carlos helped him pack everything on two of the burros. The third would be used to rotate the load over time while serving as Clay's transportation when needed.

Carlos and his family had been very helpful to Clay showing him on the map where other family members and acquaintances had farms in the mountains. Clay planned to follow the old Santa Fe Trail along the railroad south out of Raton for about five or six miles before taking the more westerly route that was closer to the mountains. This trail was originally used by ancient dwellers of this area, and it was the route that the Azuela family ancestors had taken into the area of Raton. It later became known as the Mountain Branch of the Santa Fe Trail. Although not traveled much since the arrival of the railroads about ten years ago, that road would be easy-going and Clay should make good time. He felt he could possibly be in Cimarron in two days, two-and-a-half days at the most. He would then scout the area for a bit to locate a good place to set up camp. He was feeling very good about his plans.

Clay and Carlos finished packing the burros and checked that everything was secure. Clay reached his hand out to Carlos, "Thank you for everything . . . but especially for being a good friend. Your support has meant a lot to me." Clay held onto Carlos' hand and then pulled him and gave him a bear hug. Clay had grown taller over the past year, but Carlos seemed to be at a standstill in his growth. Clay easily engulfed the younger boy and picked him up off the ground.

Carlos moaned as if he were being crushed by Clay and then laughed. "Well, you needed the help. Your weaving skills were better than your stable skills!" And, he laughed some more. He was in a good mood despite the situation of a few weeks ago when Clay had turned him down for the trip.

"At least I know how to properly pack a burro," said Clay as he reached out to check a strap on one of the animals.

Clay had never had a friend like Carlos, and he greatly appreciated it. They slapped each other on the back, then Clay grabbed the reins of the first burro, gave Carlos a big smile, and turned his small pack train west. Clay wanted to look back at Carlos as he left, but he decided not to. Clay's very first stop was, of course, the Azuela ranch where he would say his good-byes to the family . . . and to Analena.

When he arrived at the ranch, everyone was busy with their ranch duties. Clay went first to the barn where Antonio was working. He told Señor Azuela how much he had appreciated his time at the ranch and what a good friend Carlos had been to him. They shared a solid hand-shake, then Señor Azuela went back to work.

Clay entered the house and went straight to the back room where the women were working on their blankets. Señora Azuela saw Clay first and rose up from her loom to greet Clay. "Clay, we have been waiting for you." She grabbed him and hugged him. "Now, remember, you are welcome here any time. So, if you need a place to come back to rest, please come here to the ranch." She held him at arm's length and smiled at him with pride as if he were her own son.

Clay smiled. "Thank you very much. You and your family have been more kind to me than I could ever have expected. I'm very grateful." He shared a warm smile with her.

Clay's eyes then turned to Analena who was now standing just to his right. They gazed at each other, and Clay could see the moisture building in her eyes. He took her hands in his. "I will miss you very much." He paused to say more, but no words came to him.

Analena threw her arms up around Clay and hugged him, and Clay hugged her back. He was completely unaware that Señora Azuela was still in the room as he pushed Analena back just enough that their lips could meet in a kiss. It was a warm, comforting kiss that Clay knew he would miss. Analena was now crying. "You better go," she said.

Clay shook his head. "Good-bye." He lowered his eyes as he turned toward the door and left the house. As with Carlos, he wanted to look back but knew that he shouldn't.

Burro reins in hand, Clay passed the barn and corn fields as he turned southeast so that he could intercept the road out of Raton. Before him the clear blue skies and beautiful unspoiled mountains called Clay over a threshold to a new life, a life of unknowns, surprises, and adventures.

Chapter 12

ON THE TRAIL

Clay moved along at a steady pace on the flat road. It felt good to be out of town, and especially away from the dirty railroad job that he had come to deeply resent. He had struggled every day for the past eight months or more working at the railroad. He had to force himself to look at the job as a means to an end. He knew that at some point he would be on the very path that he was walking on this day. He felt great joy as he viewed the expanse before him. It was quiet and warm with only the sound of his own feet and those of his burros who were following nicely. As he listened to his own footsteps, he became aware of the other sounds of the land around him. He heard insects buzzing and occasional birds calling.

The road was flat for hours before some long low hills rolled out before him. Clay was in great physical condition from his hard work, and easily continued on. The burros seemed comfortable with the pace, and the loads were sitting fine on them. The land was quite barren with only a few small scrub bushes scattered out along the plain. The low mountains, about two miles to the west, rose abruptly out of the high desert floor and immediately displayed their cover of pine trees. Clay ached to be in those mountains.

Clay knew he would need discipline for the first few days of travel as his eyes kept searching everywhere for plants and animals. The mountains just off to his west called to him, and he wanted so much just to head into those mountains and begin his exploration. He was sure there would be something new just over the next hill or around a turn in a direction that would take him off his planned path. He had wanted this so badly that he could hardly control himself. He had to turn his thoughts to words from Dr. Merriam about the need for discipline as a field collector. He had to have a goal and a plan and stay with it. So, he kept his objective in mind and continued his trek along the old trail.

Clay had not covered as much ground as he had hoped he would on his first day. He started late as he and Carlos packed and re-packed the burros until Clay felt the loads were just right. Then, he had not figured in the short diversion to the Azuela ranch and his time saying his good-byes.

As evening neared, Clay knew it was time to make camp. With some concern for his safety along the road at night, Clay made his way west toward the mountains to ensure that he would not be seen by any nighttime travelers who might mean him harm. He had been cautioned about this as he neared Cimarron, and although he was still a long way from there, he decided to be cautious anyway. He led his burros over a nearby hill into a small depression that would place him just out of sight of the road. He felt that he could even have a fire without it being seen from the road.

He took care of the burros before starting to set up camp. The burros had been named by Mr. Wendt: Gustav, whom Clay called Gus, Oskar, and Jake. It was Gus and Oskar that Clay had had his eye on and was pleased to purchase from Mr. Wendt. The third burro, Jake, was provided at such a good price by Mr. Wendt that Clay could not refuse. Jake was a bit smaller than the other two burros, but Mr. Wendt assured Clay he made up for his size with his intelligence. Clay trusted Mr. Wendt, and so far none of the burros had been any problem at all.

Clay decided not set up his tent tonight, rather he would sleep on the ground near the fire in his bedroll. With the animals cared for and a fire going, he prepared a supper for himself. He sat back and felt joy in being out in the open in new surroundings. He looked up as the stars began to appear and felt a deep sense of contentment.

His thoughts turned to his grandfather and the time spent on the farm with him during his formative years. His grandfather had been the first to encourage him when Clay took an interest in the natural world about him. Clay had displayed a curiosity with everything that nature presented to him. It started when Clay discovered the simplest of creatures around him – worms, butterflies, grasshoppers, birds, snakes, rodents. Clay, at times, nearly drove his grandfather crazy with question upon question.

But, Clay could only recall his grandfather being patient and providing great detail about each creature or plant that Clay's eyes set upon. His grandfather had not been scientifically educated in any manner about nature; rather, everything he shared with Clay was based upon life experience, including the practicality of making his own living off the land. Clay's appreciation of his grandfather's teachings grew nearly as fast as his knowledge of nature.

Under the guidance of his grandfather, hunting and trapping were to become as natural as breathing to Clay. By the age of eight, Clay had his own shotgun provided from his grandfather's collection. It wasn't long after that he was hunting the land shooting various birds, and, depending upon the time of the year, deer, squirrels, groundhogs, and coyotes. He also trapped muskrats and beavers with his grandfather.

He was especially excited a few years later to be taught the art of taxidermy by his grandfather. Clay had admired a few stuffed specimens that his grandfather had mounted. He eventually learned that his grandfather had performed taxidermy services for others in the area. When Clay asked to learn the art, his grandfather was quite pleased to teach it to him. His grandfather had always told Clay that he was a quick learner. While his grandfather taught him well in so many ways of nature, Clay was also encouraged by his grandfather to learn what he could find in books.

As with everything else his grandfather had told him, Clay eagerly pursued the knowledge available, asking his father to guide him into his areas of interest in the scientific journals that his father subscribed to. This interest in education pleased his father, and he helped Clay find articles of interest. Clay later heard his father telling his mother that he had subscribed to some new journals just for Clay's benefit. Clay recalled how good that had made him feel.

As Clay drifted off to sleep, he found himself near the creek where he and his grandfather trapped. It was a sunny, yet cool, early autumn day with a few high clouds slowly drifting above. He and his grandfather were sloshing along the shore of the creek setting beaver traps. As they went along, his grandfather told him about the time when beaver pelts were more highly valued than they currently were. He told Clay tales of mountain men who spent months in the West harvesting the pelts for the buyers in the East. Clay loved the stories of these men spending months on their own in the wilderness country relying on themselves in an area of potential danger from bears, mountain lions, and Indians. Clay fell soundly asleep with a smile on his face.

Packing the burros in the morning was a little more difficult without Carlos' help, but Clay managed fine and was soon back on the road heading southwest. He accepted that he would not make Cimarron by the end of the day. He moved along thinking less of drifting off his path and into the mountains.

His mind was already organizing his camp near Halls Peak. He was really looking forward to spending several months in the area gathering specimens. He knew he would have it much easier than those mountain men his grandfather had told him of, but his sense of adventure and the structure of science blended together and made him feel as a brother with those earlier men.

This day proceeded much like the previous day, and he had not seen any other travelers on the road. That was somewhat expected as this road was not used as much as the route farther to the east, and that was just fine with Clay. He was enjoying the company of his burros as they trudged along in line, and he frequently shared his expectations with them.

His thoughts were now under more control as he planned for his time at Halls Peak. While still eager to get started, he was interested in assuring that his plans were firm. While his grandfather had taught him so much about nature and taxidermy, his father had taught him a good deal about planning and organizing and the scientific method. His father supported him in collecting specimens and taught Clay that there was more to do than just collect the specimens. Through the scientific method, his father taught Clay about observing the specimens in their natural habitats in order to study their patterns of behavior. He had the same advice from his grandfather, but it was to improve his hunting skills rather than to gain scientific knowledge.

When Clay collected specimens, his father taught him how to weigh and measure them as well as how to make field notes about the location and environment in which the specimens were collected. Through his grandfather and his father, Clay had learned a beautiful blend of the old ways and the new ways of natural art and science. It was while walking along the road at this place in this time that Clay actually came to that realization, and it made him appreciate and love his family that much more.

Clay was thankful for his family and all that they had provided for him. He liked that he had a close family with aunts and uncles and cousins, and, of course, his two younger brothers and his new baby sister. The family had always helped each other with the farming, with building homes, and with any troubles that any of them faced. They were a close, true-hearted family with a strong work ethic and many accomplished skills and trades. There was a core character within the family that Clay felt good about.

He drew strength from his family, a strength that had provided him the courage to leave home and head West on his own. There had been no doubt in Clay's mind that he had made the right decision in setting out to work for Dr. Merriam. He saw his bout with consumption as a mere minor setback, one that had actually afforded him the opportunity to grow even stronger, both physically and mentally. He was thankful to now have the opportunity to work as a collector on his own for Dr. Merriam and the Department of Agriculture.

He had learned from Vern that the work now being undertaken was to assist the farmers in their efforts to develop the land, care for the land, and improve their crop production. Clay would survey the local plants, insects, and small mammals to provide information that would support the agricultural efforts in the West. His survey would also help to support the Life Zones concept that Dr. Merriam had developed. These elements combined throughout the West would be extremely valuable to the agricultural economy of the United States. And, in a very personal way for Clay, it would help families like the Azuelas as they eked out a living in this arid land of the Territory of New Mexico, a land that Clay imagined would one day become a state.

Chapter 13

BLACK JACK KETCHUM

Clay held Jake's reins loosely in his hand as he led him along the road. It seemed as though Jake was a natural leader to Gus and Oskar as the other two burros wanted to follow wherever Jake led. The travel seemed easiest with Jake leading the other two, and Jake was the easiest for Clay to lead. As Mr. Wendt had told him, Jake was an intelligent burro, and it seemed that Jake respected Clay as the boss.

"Jake, you're a darn good burro. Mr. Wendt knew you well. I want you to know I appreciate the way you lead those other two." Jake gave a short whinny as though he understood what Clay was saying.

Clay turned his head and looked back at the other two burros. "And thanks, Oskar and Gus, to you two for staying in line there and following your buddy Jake. If you guys keep up the good work, maybe I'll have some carrots for you when we get back." There were no sounds from Oskar and Gus. Clay laughed to himself.

Clay was getting closer to the mountains as he continued traveling southwest along the dusty old road. He found plenty of opportunity to water the burros, just as Carlos had told him. The work did not seem difficult for the burros, and they were easily satisfied with the available water and sparse short grasses.

With the afternoon getting late, Clay began to think about camp for the night. Saltpeter Mountain was less than a mile from the road, and the foothills would make a good place to camp out of sight. Stopping now would mean that the next day's travel should easily put him in Cimarron in the afternoon.

"Whaddya say, boys, shall we head over to the foothills? You'll likely have a little more grass than you'll have right here." Clay pulled Jake's reins to the right, and they headed toward Saltpeter Mountain.

Señor Azuela told Clay that there could be miners in this area of the mountains, but that they should pose no problem as long as they did not feel Clay was trying to steal their silver. There were also farms in the valley where the Vermejo River flowed just beyond Saltpeter Mountain where Clay could stop if he needed. Clay felt he would be just fine in the foothills overnight. He would not be going into the valley, and so should not run into any miners. He certainly did not want to appear as any type of threat to anyone.

Clay headed toward an opening between two small hills at the base of the mountain. As he passed through the opening, he found himself in a bowl surrounded by the hills and the mountain. Were it not for the dry, high desert climate, the bowl would have been the home to a nice meadow, but in this location all it offered was a bit more of the short grass for the burros. It would make an ideal location for camp. The burros could be hobbled without a need to range any distance for grazing on the grass.

Since he was well off the road and situated in the bowl, Clay had no concern about a campfire. So, after setting up camp, he had a nice fire going and cooked himself a satisfying, hot supper. As with the previous night, he was feeling good and thinking again about all that he had learned from his grandfather. The fire reminded him of sitting around so many campfires with his grandfather back on the farm in Indiana. He found the fire comforting in both its physical warmth and its peaceful memories.

As Clay was lighting his pipe after supper, he was suddenly stirred by the sound of horses approaching through the opening to the bowl. He looked up to see four men on horses approaching in the twilight. The man on the horse on the left hailed Clay, "Say there, fella, I guess we're not the only ones who saw this as a good place to bed down for the night." The four men pulled closer, reining in their horses just in front of Clay's campsite, and the man continued talking, "I sure hope yuh don't mind sharing this nice spot with some company. Looks like yuh might have a little coffee yuh could share." Clay could make out a grin on his face in the fading light.

"Sure, there's plenty of room for everyone and some decent grazing for your animals." Clay was wary, but as a normally trusting individual, he had no real hesitation in welcoming the strangers into his camp. "I only have a bit of coffee, but I can sure make some more real quick." Clay got up to get some coffee from his supplies.

The man spoke up quickly and a bit loudly, "No, that's fine. We don't want yuh to go to any trouble. Just sit back down there by your fire."

Clay stopped in his tracks and looked up at the man. He hesitated momentarily, then returned to his spot by the campfire. "Okay, suit yourself." Clay puffed slowly on his pipe pondering the situation.

There was a long silence, then the four men dismounted from their horses. Clay noticed that the horses all appeared to have been ridden hard. The men looked like they had been on the road for quite some time. As they dismounted, they shook the dust from their hats and coats. Two of the men approached Clay's boxes of supplies while the other two advanced in Clay's direction. No one said a word except the first man.

"Are yuh from around these parts?" He stared coldly into Clay's eyes in an unfriendly manner for a friendly question.

"No, sir, I worked in Raton for awhile, but now I'm headed south," Clay replied, but he was now feeling like he needed to be a bit more cautious. He had good instincts about people, and he was not feeling good about these fellows.

From over by his supply boxes one of the other men now spoke. "So, whaddya got in all these boxes, kid?"

"Mostly just supplies for my trip." Clay was not feeling at all good about these men and kept his answer short.

The same man continued, "Yeah? What kind of supplies? It looks like an awful lot of provisions." This second man had the same cold stare as the first man.

Clay did not respond immediately, and the first man spat his words out at Clay. "Yuh wouldn't be out here mining silver, now, would yuh?" The man had now placed his right hand upon his gun holster. If it was meant as a gesture to intimidate Clay, it was certainly successful. Clay could not help but notice the man's deep dark eyes.

Clay set his pipe down and stood as tall as he could. "Why no, sir. I'm on a collecting expedition for Dr. Merriam." Clay was hoping the name of Dr. Merriam might bring some credibility and strength to his reply. In Clay's mind, Dr. Merriam was well enough known that certainly even locals in these parts would be familiar with him.

The first man was now only a few feet away from Clay. "Oh, a collecting expedition for – who was that – Dr. Marion? What type of collecting are yuh doin'?"

Clay was going to correct the man on Dr. Merriam's name, but he decided to try to avoid even a hint of confrontation with the man. "My name is Clay, Clay Beckley, and I'm collecting plants and animals for the survey that Dr. Merriam is doing of the West."

"Well, then, Clay, yuh wouldn't mind us takin' a look at some of your collections, now, would yuh?" Although it was a question, Clay could feel that it was more of an order, maybe even a threat.

"Well, Mr. ... uh, what's your name again?"

"I'm sorry, I didn't introduce myself, did I, now. How very inconsiderate of me. Clay, my name is Ketchum, yuh may have heard of me, Black Jack Ketchum." The man had that grin on his face again, only bigger now. "This here is Ben, and over by your boxes, that's Sam and Bronco Bill." He turned his head to the two men standing by Clay's supplies. "Say howdy to Clay, boys." The men only continued to stare coldly in Clay's direction.

The blood drained from Clay's face. He had heard of Black Jack Ketchum. Most everyone that Clay knew in Raton had told him of Black Jack Ketchum. The workers at the railroad had said the most about him. He and his gang had robbed the Santa Fe Railroad just outside of Nutt in the southern part of the New Mexico Territory. Clay had been told that the gang had been seen everywhere from Des Moines and Folsom in the northeast corner of the territory to Elizabeth and Cimarron not far from Clay's present camp. Others had told Clay tales of Black Jack Ketchum murdering those who crossed him, or those he simply did not like. Clay had not taken any of the stories too seriously . . . until this very moment. Those black eyes now seemed to reveal to Clay every bit of evil in this man.

"Now, Clay, tell us again about your 'collecting supplies.' Perhaps yuh do have a little silver from your efforts. We'd just like to take a look at it. And, maybe yuh could let us know where your mine is located. Yuh know, just in a friendly sort of way, now."

The grin and the dark eyes were ominous. Clay knew he could be in trouble, but surely when he let them know he had no silver and no mine, the men would be on their way. "Truly, sir, I have no silver, and there is no mine." Clay could hear the desperation in his own voice.

"Well, then, we'll just take a look in those boxes." The man glanced over to the two men standing near Clay's supplies. "Tear 'em open, boys!" His eyes quickly returned to Clay as a hawk to its prey.

Immediately, the other two men started tearing into Clay's supply boxes while Black Jack Ketchum and Ben hovered over Clay, guns now drawn and pointed at Clay. Clay saw his supplies being tossed around. As the men got to the boxes with his preservation chemicals, they thought they had something.

"Hey, Tom, I think we found something. Look at this."

Black Jack told Ben to keep an eye on Clay while he went over to the other two men. Clay was confused when the man called him Tom, but this whole ordeal was confusing. They pulled out Clay's preservatives and carefully looked at the bottles and cans.

"What is this? Is this for testing for silver?" Black Jack, or Tom, seemed impatient now.

"No." Then Clay choked briefly as he tried to speak. He finally got his words out. "Those are preservatives for the specimens I collect."

"What specimens! I don't see any specimens here! Where's the silver?!" His impatience had built to anger as he threw a can to the ground.

"I haven't collected any specimens yet. I'm headed farther south to do that." Clay's voice broke as he got out the words. He realized it did not sound good. Here he had told them he was collecting specimens, yet he had none. Fear overtook him.

"Look, kid, where's the silver?!" He nodded to Ben who then punched Clay in the stomach.

Clay doubled over and fell to the ground, his breath knocked out of him. He heard the men now tearing everything to pieces. Just as Clay regained his breath, Ben order him to stand. Clay slowly brought himself erect. He looked at Ben with pleading eyes. "Please, I have no silver!"

Clay did not see the nod again from Black Jack, but once again Ben delivered a severe blow to Clay's stomach. This time, however, before Clay could hit the ground, Ben delivered a second blow from underneath that caught Clay's chin and sent him backwards and onto his back. Clay lay moaning on the ground as the men finished tearing up every piece of Clay's supplies and equipment.

"Well, Clay, it looks like you're right. There's no silver here." He paused and raised the grin on his face. "I would suggest yuh take us to the mine or to the place where yuh've hidden the silver. And don't lie! Yuh'll tell us one way or another." He nodded to Ben again.

Ben easily lifted Clay off the ground and straightened him up. Clay stood rather limply as Ben delivered a devastating blow to Clay's ribs. This was followed by several more blows to the ribs as one of the other men stepped in to hold Clay up.

Clay was now in tears. "I don't . . ." Two more short jabs to his ribs brought Clay to his knees and then to all fours. He had not felt such pain as this. He could not breathe without sharp stabbing pains in his side. He knew he must have some broken ribs. He could not make sense of what was happening to him. Ben picked up a bucket that was half-filled with water and threw it on Clay.

"Stand up, boy," ordered Ben.

Clay struggled to stand. Ben reached down and pulled him up. Clay tried to double over because of the pain in his side, but Ben forced him to stand. The pain was excruciating. Tears streamed down Clay's face.

Black Jack now stood in front of Clay. "You're not making this easy, boy. Tell us what we want, and we'll be on our way. Yuh can rest and heal and be none the worse for wear. But, if yuh don't tell us where the silver is, it'll be much, much worse for yuh." He paused to let his words sink in. "Somewhere yuh must have a mama who would like to see yuh again. Think of your mama, kid."

"I swear, there is no silver! If there was, I'd tell you! Please, just let me go." He barely got the words out through his tears. He felt a gun barrel against his head and heard the hammer click followed by an evil laugh.

"There's no silver!" Clay shouted as loudly as he could muster with his broken ribs.

This time it was Black Jack who used Clay as a punching bag. Once on the ground, he kicked Clay with his boots in the ribs and the back and the stomach, and then he went for Clay's face. Clay did what he could to try to cover his face and head with his hands, but the kicking continued until Clay lost consciousness.

Chapter 14

RETURN TO THE TRAIL

Clay awoke just after daybreak, although the sun had not yet peered over the hills surrounding the bowl where he had made his camp the day before. He opened his eyes slowly with great caution. *Are they still here? Am I in for more beating?* He wasn't sure what time of day it was at first, as the light in the bowl was not much different than it had been last evening. He was having trouble seeing, and he realized he was only seeing out of his right eye.

He very slowly moved his head to try to get a better look around him. The movement made him very aware of the pain in his face and jaw, as well as in his neck. It was all he could do not to make a sound, but he did not want the men to know that he was awake. Peering as best he could with one eye, he did not see any of the men in his immediate vicinity. He then listened carefully, and the only sounds he heard were a few birds and some buzzing insects. Still, he lay quietly for several more minutes.

Finally gaining some courage, Clay turned himself and tried to sit up. It reminded him of the time he tried to sit up in the Dodge City jail after being beaten by the railroad bulls, only this was much worse. He was groggy, but he easily recalled the events that left him in his present situation. He remembered thinking that his ribs were cracked, and he was even more sure of it now. He tried to pull himself up on a nearby rock, but his head began to spin as he did so. He lay back down and felt awful.

He continued to look around as best he could, now feeling confident that he was alone. He saw remnants of his supplies and equipment scattered about the campsite. He saw his canteen near the ashes of his campfire and longed for some water. He tried to sit up again, and while his head once more began spinning, he managed to get himself propped up against the rock. He closed his eyes hoping the spinning would stop, but when it didn't, he vomited, retching with intense pain because of his broken ribs. When the pain subsided, he sat still leaning against the rock and, in his mind, went over the events from the previous evening. As he thought about his treatment, he became angry. He was angry with the men, but he was also angry with himself for letting them get the better of him. He let his anger pass as he realized he needed to take care of himself and get back on the road. He recalled that Señor Azuela had told him of the farms in the valley that was not far from his camp just on the other side of Saltpeter Mountain. So, he made getting to that area his objective.

As he looked about, he saw that the gang had left his burros; they were obviously more interested in horses, which turned out to be a good thing for Clay. He called to Jake, and though hobbled, Jake obediently made his way over to Clay. "Good boy, Jake. I can always count on you," Clay mumbled from his swollen face. It was a struggle, but Clay was able to remove Jake's hobbles.

Clay tried to stand, but the pain and dizziness made him sit back down against the rock. He coaxed Jake closer to his side, and reached up for his halter. Clay would have to endure the pain if he wanted to get on Jake, get out of the bowl, and head up into the nearby valley. He managed to pull himself up using Jake and stood very weak-kneed, head spinning. Placing his arm around Jake's neck, he managed to lead him and shuffle over to where the canteen sat. Fortunately, the canteen was on a rock where Clay had left it, and he was able to crouch slightly and retrieve it. He drank deeply, but choked at the first attempt to swallow. He spit the water back up and saw that it was dark pink from his blood. He took a smaller sip and rinsed out his mouth spitting more of the dark pink liquid and blood clots to the ground. He then took several small sips that he was able to keep down. Clay felt as if he had not had a thing to drink for days, and the cool water satisfied him deeply.

Every move was painful, but Clay knew he had to push through the pain. He shuffled closer to the rock and brought Jake up next to him. Leaning on Jake, he managed to get on top of the rock and then swing himself onto Jake. As he did so, the pain and dizziness caused him to momentarily lose consciousness, and he slumped forward on Jake. Good fortune seemed to favor him, however, as he managed to remain on Jake's bare back.

Rousing, Clay urged Jake forward toward the entrance to the bowl, and Jake dutifully obliged. Clay gently nudged Jake along out of the bowl and straight to the road. Clay was not sure of the exact location of the farms in the valley, but he felt sure it could not be more than a few miles following the Vermejo River up the valley. He kept Jake on the road until he came to a trail near the river that led into the valley. He coaxed Jake onto the trail before he again lost consciousness.

Clay had flashes of the encounter with the Black Jack Ketchum gang and of his efforts to get himself onto Jake and on the trail up the Vermejo River. He was half-awake and half-asleep as he saw images of himself being pulled off the burro and taken into an adobe house. He saw many faces, but they were all a blur and unrecognizable. Then, he again lost consciousness.

He awoke with a start, feeling his pain and finding himself in a bed. A Mexican lady was beside him and smiled at him as Clay came out of his half-sleep state. She placed a cool, wet cloth on his head as she spoke, "You just stay still. We are taking care of you."

"My burro, Jake?" Clay was still a bit dazed and confused, but he wanted to be sure Jake was okay.

"Your burro is fine. He is enjoying some good feed which he must have earned getting you here."

"Thanks. Where am I?"

"You are on my husband's farm in the Vermejo River valley. My husband is Señor Miguel Montero, and I am Señora Isabella." Her voice was gentle and kind. As with the Azuela family, she too seemed to speak quite good English. "And what are we to call you, young man?"

"I'm Clay Beckley." His voice did not sound like his own, and he hoped his words came out clearly as his swollen face and sore ribs made it difficult to speak.

"Well, Clay, get some rest. It looks like you have had a difficult time recently."

He still felt awful, but he did not want to rest without explaining to her who he was. He also realized that he knew the name Montero as one of the families that Señor Azuela had told him about. "Please, let me explain," he pleaded. "I want to tell you what happened."

She easily observed that he needed to talk about his ordeal and asked him to proceed. As briefly as he could, he told her about the Azuelas and about his trip. He then choked a bit as he told her about his confrontation with Black Jack Ketchum and his gang. Even with one eye, he saw that she listened closely, and when he finished he was relieved to have gotten everything out. It felt good to be able to tell someone.

"This Black Jack Ketchum is a very bad man. It is said he has been in Cimarron not far from here. The stories of his brutality are too well-known in the New Mexico Territory. You mentioned that the other men called him Tom. His given name is Tom Ketchum. There are wanted posters for him placed in Cimarron." She paused briefly and looked into Clay's eyes. "Clay, you must have been blessed by God to have gotten out alive," and she made the sign of the cross.

Clay rested and slept, awakening periodically to find there was always someone attending to him. He was very grateful for their care and hospitality. He caught sporadic bits of conversations and thought he heard mention of the Azuelas in some of their discussions. He eventually fell into a deep slumber.

Clay had a fitful dream in which he was mauled by a bear. He had stumbled upon the bear while hunting in the mountains. The bear came upon Clay from behind, trapping him in a small blind canyon. His gun misfired, and the bear was quickly upon him before he could at least draw his pistol. In his dream, Clay watched the bear attack as if he were standing to one side as a spectator. He saw every movement and defensive action taken, but the large animal was nimble and strong, easily bringing his prey to the ground. The bear ripped into his victim tearing away the face so that Clay could not tell for sure that it was even himself. The bear then picked up the body with his massive jaws and swatted it to one side with his giant paws. The body hit a tree and became lifeless as well as faceless. It was a horrific sight that terrified Clay as he continued to observe off to one side. He screamed loudly as he woke from his nightmare.

There before him, he saw the startled face of Carlos! Clay tried to sit up, but as before, he was hit with sharp pains. "Carlos!" He cried out and reached for Carlos.

Though startled at first, Carlos immediately placed his arms around Clay's shoulders to support him. "It's good to see you, Clay!" It was Carlos with as big a smile as Clay had ever seen on his face.

Immediately comforted by Carlos' presence, Clay smiled back, but he wasn't sure how well he smiled since his face was so swollen. "Carlos. It sure is good to see you!" He immediately felt his spirits lifted at the sight of Carlos, and he forgot about his vision-like nightmare.

After telling Carlos of his ordeal, Clay asked Carlos if he would be able to take someone to his campsite and collect his things for him. Clay was especially concerned about his collecting supplies and wanted to recover as much as possible. He was also concerned about the other two burros, Gus and Oskar, and asked Carlos to find them and see that they were taken care of. Carlos was more than happy to oblige Clay.

Over the next several weeks, Clay began to heal, but his ribs seemed to heal the slowest. This made it difficult for Clay to perform any activities that were too strenuous. His facial swelling had diminished, but the deep, dark bruising remained and was now beginning to take on a yellow tint. He was also just beginning to be able to eat normally again. As his condition improved, his appetite grew as well. Señora Montero and her family saw to it that Clay was well-cared for and well-fed. He could not imagine how he could ever repay them for their generosity.

Having gone through the items recovered from his camp, Clay was pleased that the bulk of his preservation chemicals were still good. Some of his papers had apparently been burned, and, not to be unexpected, his rifle, pistol, and ammunition were all gone. Most of his other camping equipment had been recovered.

It was obvious that the Ketchum Gang had been after only items of great value, especially the silver, of which Clay had none. The money he did have had been placed in a money belt around his waist, and the men had not seen that, so he would be able to get most of what he needed with his remaining funds. This would be a bit of a hardship, however, as he proceeded with his collecting trip. He would need to count on the payments from his specimens to keep him going, and he was already behind in his commitments to Dr. Merriam and Vern.

A few weeks later, Clay was ready to be on his way. He would stop in Cimarron to re-supply what he must, and then continue south to the Halls Peak area. Carlos stayed with him the entire time at the Montero ranch where he seemed to provide enough work to the family to support the both of them.

Carlos had already approached Clay again about joining him on the expedition. Clay felt that he simply could not refuse him this time after all he had done for him. Carlos jumped for joy when Clay told him that he could join the small expedition. Carlos then left to go home and gather his supplies for the expedition. He would also pick up a few other things for Clay in Raton before returning to the Montero ranch. And, Clay made sure that Carlos would tell Analena how much he missed her. Carlos still seemed unhappy about Clay having an interest in his cousin, but he finally agreed to relay the message to her.

A week later, Clay and Carlos were on their way together, now with a fourth burro, one by the name of Calvo that Carlos brought from his father's ranch. Now, Clay had picked up plenty of Spanish in his time spent with Carlos and the Azuelas, and now with the Monteros, but he was unfamiliar with the name Calvo and asked Carlos about its meaning. Carlos pointed to the bit of gray on the top of the burro's head, the only bit of light color on the black burro. "See, he looks like a balding old burro. Calvo means bald!" The two of them laughed together as they headed down the trail.

Chapter 15

HALLS PEAK

By early that afternoon, the two young men and four burros arrived in Cimarron. The town seemed unfriendly to Clay, and Carlos confirmed that it was not the best place to spend a lot of time. His uncles had told him the stories of the conflicts in the area, and the farmers in the mountain valley spent as little time as possible in the town.

The Colfax County War had ended not too many years ago, and there was still a lot of hostility between various factions. Carlos told Clay the story as it had been told to him. A man named Maxwell had founded the town and eventually sold his land to a group of investors who tried to push off many of the early settlers, miners, and farmers.

The governor of the New Mexico Territory eventually brought soldiers in to try to keep peace between the settlers and the land owners. But things escalated, and after nearly fifteen years and 200 deaths, the new owners won with the backing of the government. As a result, many of the original settlers had to leave the area.

Without any delay, the two took care of the business of replenishing their supplies, and then moved south out of town as soon as they could. No one at the general store had really been friendly to the two; if anything, they looked suspiciously at the pair. They proceeded out of town as far as they could travel before needing to make camp for the night. Clay was overly cautious because of his encounter with Black Jack Ketchum and his wariness of being so near to Cimarron. He and Carlos took turns keeping watch throughout the night.

The next day, the two made an early start as this would be the day to get onto Rivera Mesa to the south of Rayado, a much smaller town and one unlikely to present any problems for Clay and Carlos. The terrain remained unchanged until they passed Rayado and turned to the west toward the mesa. The few small hills gave way to an ever-increasing incline. They searched along the base of the mesa for a route to top the mesa. They were able to spot a little-used footpath that looked to be the best way to the top.

The footing was easy, and, by late afternoon, they were atop the mesa and ready to make camp for the evening. The next day started easily enough, but, after a short time, they were into the pine forests of the mountains. This made the travel a bit more difficult as they had to work their way through both the tall pines and the large dead pine trunks on the ground. Pushing hard, they eventually came to an opening in the forest which presented a lake to them. They rested and watered the burros here.

The group proceeded past the lake and followed an old footpath around a rise and into a small valley which routed them west to a larger valley that took them past Cooks Peak. They entered the small valley between Cooks Peak and Halls Peak and looked for a place to set up a permanent camp. This looked like a well-protected area with easy access to Wheaten Creek to the northwest, so they found a nice flat place just beneath the slope of Halls Peak near the tree line and began preparing camp. For now, they would prepare for the night and make a more permanent camp in the morning.

Clay was well-pleased to finally be ready to begin his collecting expedition in earnest. He had sent a few small rodent samples from the Montero ranch area to Dr. Merriam. They were not much, but he was already far behind in his schedule for Dr. Merriam and wanted to show him that he was working in the field. He explained that he had had some delays without going into detail about the attack upon him by Black Jack Ketchum. From here going forward, he would show Dr. Merriam how productive he could be.

The next day was spent making the camp more permanent. Logs were used as a base for a more secure tent structure. A cooking area was set up, and, most importantly to Clay, he set up a place to work on specimen preparation. Carlos was proving himself to be a very good partner for Clay, and at the end of the day they both smiled as they looked around their camp.

The next weeks passed quickly for Clay and Carlos as they went about collecting specimens on and around Halls Peak and Cooks Peak. Though the land had been in a drought condition for the past few years, things were improving, and hunting was good enough to support the two. There were enough deer and rabbits in the area to keep them well-supplied, and local farmers were most generous in selling them potatoes. Most of their time, however, was spent on collecting duties: surveying the area to understand the terrain, measuring altitudes surrounding Halls Peak with an aneroid barometer, placing traps to capture small to medium-sized animals, preparing the specimens, and packing the specimens for shipment. They were also collecting flowers and grasses of the area for the survey.

Each specimen they collected was well-documented. Clay was very specific about the need to see that the documentation was complete and accurate, just as he had learned from Dr. Merriam and Vern.

Carlos continued to be a fast learner, and he was now handling a lot of the final packing of the specimens. Clay also worked with Carlos teaching him how to prepare the variety of small mammals that they were collecting. The smaller specimens proved to be the most challenging to prepare due simply to their tiny body parts. With a fine touch, Clay still handled most of the tiny specimens, and while Carlos was doing a respectable job on the larger specimens, Clay did most of the preparatory work and then allowed Carlos to complete the specimen by stuffing it with cotton and sewing it up.

Mammals had to be skinned as soon as possible after the blood had coagulated in the body. The first step in preparation was to measure and document each specimen. All measurements and identifying characteristics were written, along with a detailed description of the exact date, time, and location of collection. After all the data was recorded, the mammal was placed on its back and pulled taut while an incision was made from the breast bone to the base of the animal. The legs were then bent inward from the outside until the leg was visible through the incision. The leg was then cut at the knee and the skin was removed from around the leg. Sawdust or corn meal was used to keep the skin clean while undertaking the skinning process.

The skin was now worked loose from the body. The tail was a little tricky at this point. The end of the tail was held tightly with one hand while the other hand was used to pull the tail vertebrae out of the tail skin without tearing the tail skin from the body skin. Clay had learned the "touch" to this process from his grandfather. He recalled the many times he had ripped the tails from mice while attempting the process. This was also where Carlos was having a problem.

The remainder of the body skin was removed working forward on the specimen. Care had to be used not to stretch the skin thus distorting the shape of the mammal. The front legs were removed in a manner similar to that of the hind legs. The skin was then freed up to the base of the specimen's ears. This now entered the most difficult part of the process.

The cartilage of the ears was carefully cut away from the skull, being cautious not to damage either so that the skin of the head could next be removed up to the eyes. A cut was made as close to the eyes and skull as possible. Done properly, even the eyelids were undamaged. The skinning was continued to the snout, and the lips were the next to be freed. With only the nose now holding the skin in place, the cartilage at the base of the nose was cut with care to not damage the nasal bone or skull.

A deft touch was required for all animals to achieve a nicely prepared specimen, but the process was especially difficult for the tiny mammals. Clay, having been taught in the discipline by his grandfather at a young age, had already mastered the process. He was most willing to teach Carlos, but he also needed to ensure not only a perfect preparation but also a timely completion in order to get his delayed specimens to Dr. Merriam. Carlos seemed to understand, and he was a patient student.

The final preparation included removing any noticeable fat, loose tissue, and flesh from the raw side of the skin. The skin was then preserved with a mixture of powdered arsenic and powdered alum. The entire inner surface of the skin was dusted with the powdered mixture. The specimen's lips were then sewed together with a needle and thread. Turned right side out, the skin was then carefully cleaned and dried. Rolled up cotton batting was next placed into the skin in a manner that approximated the original size of the animal. Forceps were generally used to ensure that the stuffing occupied the entire length of the specimen.

Finally, the leg bones were inserted into the leg holes and wrapped with cotton. A small wire wrapped with cotton and dusted with the powdered mixture was placed into the tail skin. The incision made through the abdomen was then sewed up taking care to ensure that the proper body shape was retained. Additional cotton could be added as needed to fill any voids.

The skull being an important part of the specimen, care was taken to ensure it was not damaged. It had to be thoroughly cleaned of its contents and any insects, and completely dried before final storage.

A specimen label was attached directly to the skin before final packing for shipment. Once again, the specimen had to be carefully examined to ensure it had retained the proper shape, and final adjustments were made as needed.

There were also very specific methods of preparation for mid-sized and larger mammals including mountain lions, wolves, coyotes, deer, elk, and bears. Not having any experience in Indiana with some of the larger specimens like elk and bear, Clay had valued his time with Dr. Merriam's party in Arizona to learn the proper methods for these. The larger specimens were fairly well documented in the mountains of the Southwest, and Clay's assignment was to focus on the small and medium-sized mammals of the area. For the farmers, as an example, it was often the rodents that were a larger problem for agriculture.

Additionally, flowers and grasses were collected in order to identify those plants growing wild in the area. Of particular interest, again of the farmers, were grasses that could sustain their cattle and sheep herds, as well as those that might compete with their crops. After detailed identification and documentation, the plants were pressed in paper and tightly packed after thorough drying.

After about six weeks, Clay was ready to send a shipment of small mammal specimens as well as a nice set of plants to Dr. Merriam. He was anxious to get the results of his first expedition into Dr. Merriam's hands. The burros were packed with the boxes of specimens. They would only be gone three or four days, so they left the camp intact after cleaning and securing everything that would be left behind.

The trip into Rayado was uneventful, and the boxes were set for shipment. Clay and Carlos took the rest of the day to get a bath and enjoy a nice beefsteak dinner. Having left an address for himself at General Delivery in Rayado, Clay was happy to see that a letter had arrived for him. It was from Dr. Merriam. Clay was a little hesitant to open it as he feared Dr. Merriam was likely to express disappointment in Clay's efforts to date.

He opened the letter before they went to dinner. Dr. Merriam noted that he was happy to see that Clay had made some progress in his efforts, but he hoped for more progress to come. Clay smiled broadly, however, as he read further down the page, "Dr. Meek never ran an expedition on so little money." And, enclosed was money to cover two month's expenses. Clay was completely thrilled!

After feasting on their beefsteak dinners, the two left Rayado and headed back toward Rivera Mesa where they camped for the night. Clay enjoyed his pipe after dinner, and Carlos worked on a bird carving. Clay enjoyed watching Carlos carve and felt it was a good activity to improve the deftness of his hands that was important in preparing the smaller specimens. Carlos had several carved birds at the stable where they had worked, and Clay now recalled seeing some of them at the Azuela family home as well.

Later in the evening, Clay and Carlos enjoyed lying on their backs and looking up at the sky. In no time at all, they saw a shooting star. Carlos told Clay that shooting stars were a good omen.

1894

Chapter 16

WORKING THE EXPEDITION

Clay and Carlos continued their routine over the next weeks that turned into months, and about every six-to-eight weeks they returned to Rayado to deliver their most recent collection of specimens, receive their payments in the mail, and have a hot bath. The length of their trips to Rayado varied depending upon how far they had traveled from their original main camp location.

With fall closing in quickly, they made a trip to Rayado Canyon where trout were plentiful. The pair climbed a rough ridge on a good trail, crossed over a beautiful mesa, then dropped into the box canyon of the Rayado on the steepest trail they had yet to cross. As they

trekked the canyon, they enjoyed the fruits of the local small game including some dusky grouse which they prepared for supper.

The following day, they camped at the bend where the Rayado
Creek turned north toward its headwaters, while the canyon they
planned to follow was to the west along the Agua Fria Creek. They decided to take advantage of the river and try for some fish for dinner. It
took them about an hour to get their first bite, but they caught some
medium-sized trout that would make a fine supper. Cleaned and pan
fried, the trout was a fine meal to finish out the day. They went to bed
after cleaning the cook pans, and fell quickly asleep thinking about the
next day's travel.

Leaving the larger Rayado Creek behind them, the pair headed
west the next morning. Over the next two days, they carefully followed
the map as there were many canyons that all looked alike. They
checked the compass heading often to ensure they were on the right
route. Their burros were proving to be as good as Clay had hoped as
they followed without hesitation.

On the third day, they made their way up to a small plateau at an
elevation of about 8,000 feet. It offered a nice view of the canyon they
had traveled, and it would make a good place to set up a camp from
which they could explore the area. There were mountain farms another
day or two to the west, so this was a good centralized area to study the
animals that would affect future agriculture in the area.

Clay and Carlos established a camp that would provide them nicely
for several weeks. The next day, Clay unpacked his Cyclone traps. Dr.
Merriam had shown him these traps in Arizona. Made of tin and wire
springs, the traps were very portable, collapsing to only two-inches
square when folded. The new design provided an inexpensive and very
usable trap for small mammals such as rats, mice, shrews, moles, chip-
munks, and ground squirrels. Clay also had some leg traps for larger
specimens such as beavers and raccoons.

Clay's first priority was the small mammals that Dr. Merriam and
Vern had asked him to find. So, he set out with his burro and traps in
the morning setting up a circuit out about two miles away from camp.

Traps were placed in locations that Clay felt might be habitable by such small mammals. In some areas of fallen and rotted timber, Clay saw evidence of small animal presence and took particular interest in such areas. A wide circuit would provide plenty of variety for the area. He blaze-marked his trail as he went so he could easily find his way back to the traps.

These small traps were baited with bits of food, mostly meat. This was all much easier to manage than some of the homemade traps that he and his grandfather had made back on the farm. He was becoming appreciative of some of the more modern methods of trapping.

The leg traps were different. He had used these on the farm for coyotes and foxes. This type of trap had not changed, and Clay was easily familiar with them. They simply varied in size depending on the size of the animal one was trying to trap. Clay was not after any large game, like bears, so he had no large traps. He looked for signs of raccoons in the area as he went, but he did not see any. After completing the high area, he rode back down into the canyon near a creek where he looked for signs of raccoons or beavers. He found a promising location and placed two leg traps. He also placed a number of Cyclone traps in various areas near the creek and up to the foot of the cliff. Satisfied with his trap lines, he returned to camp to make some notes in his journal.

As late afternoon approached, Clay rode out to some areas where he had seen evidence of deer. He tied his burro to a tree and headed into an area that looked like a good prospect for a deer. Backing himself into a small group of shrubs, he settled into a nice overlook of a game trail where there were fresh deer tracks. With his traps all placed and with time available, Clay settled in for a hunt. Deer hunting was something he had engaged in often with his grandfather, and he looked forward to the familiar feel of it.

He had not waited more than an hour when a small doe appeared along the trail. He watched as she ambled along nibbling here and there. She eventually turned to provide him a good target, and he easily took her down with a single shot. He quickly went about gutting the deer and cutting it up to take the meat back to camp. He and Carlos would eat well tonight. It was a common mule deer and not anything Clay would need as a specimen. This was all about providing nourishment for the two collectors.

The steep sides of the canyon were forested with sizable spruce trees. Here, they found a small red squirrel in abundance, and specimens were obtained. There were fresh beaver cuttings along the stream, but trapping for three nights yielded no results. The two had a lot of fun catching and eating trout, which they found truly delicious when fried fresh from the stream.

Days turned quickly into weeks, and their collections were abundant. They moved back down the canyon of Rayado Creek as they made their way back toward their main camp at Hall's Peak. Having eaten the last of their bread and coffee for supper on the second night, they decided to return to the main camp under the light of a bright full moon. Topping the canyon rim and starting over the mesa, it was nearly as light as day. The animals knew where they were headed with no need for urging.

Clay, in the lead, was almost asleep riding the burro with his bedroll. He was suddenly startled by the loud voice of a man, "Halt! Stick your hands high! Where in the hell do you think you're going with my beef?!"

Clay was instantly brought back to the encounter with Black Jack Ketchum, and a chill of fear ran up his spine. He and Carlos followed orders to the very letter, then Carlos called out hesitatingly, "Juan, is that you?"

The cowman said, "What? Carlos?" The man was in the dense shadow of a big pine tree but Carlos knew his voice. Just hearing that it was not Black Jack Ketchum brought Clay back to the present, and he immediately relaxed.

Juan and Carlos gave each other a firm handshake, and Juan pulled Carlos in for a hug. Carlos introduced Clay to his uncle. Juan told them that someone had been killing his beef and packing the meat out of the country at night.

Juan asked, "What are you two doing out here at this time of the night?" As with most of the Mexicans in the area, Juan spoke English quite well.

Carlos explained their reason for being in the area. Juan invited them back to his camp where they enjoyed some coffee and biscuits before continuing on to Halls Peak.

As time moved forward, their explorations took them continually farther west into the Sangre De Cristo Mountains. After completing a thorough study of the lands immediately surrounding Halls Peak, they moved west over the Ocate Mesa and into the more difficult terrain of mountains and canyons on the eastern side of the larger mountain range.

Several weeks later, winter quickly set upon the mountains. As they made their way on the circuit of their traps this particular morning, they found a large wildcat and a coyote in their traps. Bagging the animals, they headed back to camp as the snowfall became heavier, and the wind strengthened. By the time they reached their camp at the small meadow surrounded by pine trees, they found their specimens had frozen solid. In no time at all, the weather continued to worsen and became a full-blown blizzard.

The two sheltered in their tent as the powerful storm continued relentlessly. Their supplies were running low, but travel back to their main camp at Halls Peak was not possible in such a storm. They had plenty of the potatoes provided by the area farmers, but not much else to eat. With nothing but boiled potatoes to fill their stomachs over the next three days, they longed for some real food.

Carlos was the first to suggest the frozen specimens, "That wildcat is plump, and the meat is white. I believe it would taste good." He looked at Clay questioningly.

Clay rose to make his way to the frozen cat, and Carlos stood to follow. Then, Clay stopped in his tracks and turned back to Carlos. "There must be something else we can do. That cat really has no appeal to me, and I can only imagine that the coyote would be far worse." Carlos nodded his head in reluctant agreement.

Fortunately, the next day dawned clear and bright; the blizzard had ended. They were able to make their way outside of camp with some difficulty and capture some small game. The meat was a much-welcomed change to their diet.

In early April, spring seemed to make an unexpected arrival. Birds began to appear with joyful songs. As the weeks moved forward, even some of the trees were beginning to bud. They were as delighted as the birds at this welcomed relief from winter. They moved farther up the mountain to the point where they made camp at the edge of the treeline. For miles above them, there was nothing but grass and rocks.

Clay found himself awed at the wildlife with each new specimen. While they trapped specimens of animals with which Clay was familiar, they were all quite different than the species in Indiana. There were black marmots living in rock piles as the ground hogs lived in burrows in Indiana. Mice came in varieties of size and shape that Clay had not previously seen. Clay was particularly taken by a bushy-tailed wood rat with a tail that was tipped with a large tuft of white hair. He could not wait to get these specimens to Dr. Merriam.

Carlos decided to make his way down into a canyon for a deer hunt. He had been gone most of the day, and near sundown Clay heard the sound of two gunshots well to the south. He knew this meant that Carlos had managed to get some meat for them and that he would not be back that night. It meant that Carlos would find a safe place to bed down and return in the morning.

Comfortable that Carlos was safe and would have meat in camp in the morning, Clay crawled into his bedroll for a good night's sleep. They had placed a tarp over their bedrolls as protection should it rain. The early spring was warm, but there was always the chance of a shower. Tired, Clay quickly drifted off to a sound sleep.

It was not yet dawn when Clay heard a sound that awakened him. It was something hitting the tarp. Putting his hand out, he realized it was snowing a heavy wet snow. Even in the early morning darkness, Clay noted the snow would prevent him from seeing much beyond his immediate camp. The early spring that had been so welcomed had taken leave; winter had returned.

Clay decided to remain under the shelter in his bedroll until daylight. After all, he was dry, comfortable, and warm in his present situation.

At daylight, Clay stepped out from under the tarp to check on the burros. It was then that he discovered that the snow was high above his knees, well over two feet deep in his estimation. All the camp equipment and food was buried beneath the snow that was continuing to fall.

Clay recalled a log cabin that he had seen on the way up to this camp. It had appeared to be a summer cabin for cattlemen, but he remembered that smoke was coming from the chimney at the time. He estimated it to be about four miles downhill to the cabin. So, foregoing breakfast, Clay decided to abandon camp for a more favorable refuge that would likely be warm and protected.

While he was concerned for Carlos, he decided that Carlos would likely head for the cabin as well. In fact, it should be a shorter walk for Carlos. As Clay set out, the snow stopped, and the sun shone brightly over the snow-covered mountain. The clear blue sky lifted Clay's spirit as he trudged through the deep snow.

It was difficult walking in the deep, wet snow, but as Clay entered the timbers, the trees offered enough cover to make the walking easier. Clay traveled about a mile when he came across a cattle trail that he figured would likely take him near, if not right to, the cabin. He was again out in the open where the sun shone brightly.

The glare of the sun on the snow became painful to Clay's eyes after some time. While the air did not feel extremely cold, Clay was now wet from his thighs down, and his feet were very cold. He struggled on for several hours until he finally saw the shelter in the distance. He noticed that his eyes were burning as he strained to bring the cabin into focus.

The cabin was occupied by the local cowmen who had holed up there during the storm. A blazing fire kept them all warm and comfortable. They welcomed Clay as he knocked on the cabin door. The cowmen immediately recognized that Clay was suffering from snow blindness and covered his eyes with a cold compress. They offered Clay food and hot coffee which he gladly accepted.

About two hours after Clay had arrived and explained his situation, Carlos was welcomed into the cabin. Carlos related that he had made a log camp under a large spruce tree where he was able to keep a fire going through the night. Having shot a mule deer, Carlos broiled the liver and so kept himself satisfied through the night. Having left his camp at daybreak, Carlos made a trek that was uphill from the canyon in which he had spent the night.

Clay experienced a painful snow blindness for the next twenty-four hours. He was thankful to the cowmen who provided for him and Carlos during this time. His feet were badly swollen and tender for the next few days, but from this, too, he recovered fully. He was grateful that otherwise he was fine and that Carlos did not suffer from anything other than exposure to the cold. Clay's body was warmed and his spirits were lifted with plentiful food, hot coffee, a warm fire, and his pipe.

The next day, two of the cowmen left on well-fed horses and retrieved Carlos' deer. They had fresh meat that night and enjoyed the cheerful fire. For a week, they played cards, told stories, and cooked and ate with plenty. Clay had no means of repaying the men for their care and kindness as he had left his supplies back at the camp so he could travel light and quick. He did have tobacco for his pipe with him and so was able to share this with the men who had only chewing tobacco. They seemed to accept his offer with an understanding of his situation.

As the weather once again began to warm, Clay and Carlos made their leave. Handshakes and hearty hurrahs were shared by all as the pair left the winter haven. Most of the snow on the southern slopes had melted where it was exposed to the warming sun. The ground was again visible, and the buds on the trees had survived. The only struggle in their travel was the thawing ground that challenged their footing.

Back at their camp, everything was in order. The storm had done no damage to their equipment. The burros grazed on the young shoots of grass that were appearing, and they seemed to have no ill affects from their time left alone at the camp.

Clay and Carlos packed up their camp, loaded the burros, and headed back down the mountain. They returned to Rayado to mail their specimens to Dr. Merriam, enjoy a nice meal, and re-supply themselves for their next trek higher into the mountains. With spring in its fullness, the travel was pleasant for the pair and their animals.

Chapter 17

CERRO DEL OSO

Clay and Carlos planned to make their way back into the mountains where they had spent the winter, and then push farther
south along the mountain ridges to gather specimens. This was the area
that Dr. Merriam had directed them to study. One goal was to gather
specimens similar to what had previously been collected in order to examine them for any differences compared to those that had been found
to the north.

Rested and resupplied, and with their spirits lifted by the spring in
full bloom, they easily made their way back into the mountains. Clay
was comforted by the greening of the mountains. The winter snows

had provided plenty of moisture to bring the land back to life. Streams were filling with melting snows providing needed irrigation for the farmers in the dry lands below. The cold water provided a welcome refreshment for their journey.

As they traveled, Clay explained to Carlos why they were studying this particular area assigned to them by Dr. Merriam. Clay had been provided the basic information by Dr. Merriam, Vern had filled him in with more detail, and Clay was able to read some of the previous survey records provided to him by Vern.

The area had been surveyed and mapped as early as 1874. This was a part of what was called the Wheeler Survey made for the United States government. Lieutenant George M. Wheeler organized and carried out the early surveys. They conducted topographic surveys for maps and some limited scientific surveys of the flora and fauna. It was the Wheeler Survey to which they owed thanks for the maps that were available to them.

The area had not, however, been well studied when it came to the plant and animal population of the area. So, Clay explained, it was he and Carlos who were providing specimens for Dr. Merriam to complete a study of the area from a scientific perspective. Clay told Carlos, "You're now a real scientist – one of Merriam's Men!"

Carlos grinned and looked puzzled at the same time. "Well, Clay, I do not think that I am a scientist. I am only able to do what you have taught me in preparing our specimens." He paused as though searching for a thought. "And, what do you mean by saying that I am one of Merriam's men? I have never met your Dr. Merriam."

Clay chuckled, "Carlos, you've learned very well the process of preparing specimens. The small mammals are the most difficult, and you've done very well in working with them. You've learned the scientific method! Yes, you and I are becoming skilled, scientific collectors. Dr. Merriam and Vern have been pleased with our collections."

"But, how am I Merriam's man? I have learned from you, not from Dr. Merriam." Carlos still had that puzzled look on his face.

Clay looked closely at Carlos. He had changed a lot since they first met. Carlos always carried himself in a manner that belied his young age, but now Clay could see a maturity in his face and in his actions. "Well, let me tell you about Dr. Merriam and Merriam's Men," Clay replied as he began to share what he had learned about Dr. Merriam from his talks with Vern, as well as from his own direct experience with Dr. Merriam.

He told Carlos that Dr. Merriam had taken an interest in the natural world at a young age, just as Clay himself had. In the early 1880s, little was known of the world of the American mammals. Of the few specimens available, most were ill-prepared, imperfect, and lacking in details. It was about this time that Merriam met Vernon Bailey, another young man interested in the natural world, and especially in mammals. The two worked closely in creating a growing mammal collection.

As Dr. Merriam's reputation continued to grow, he eventually became the head of the Division of Economic Ornithology and Mammalogy for the U.S. government. By this time, Vern was employed as a field agent for the organization and was ranging the West. The manner of study and the descriptions of specimens prepared by Vern were well received by Dr. Merriam.

Zoologists around the country began to adopt Dr. Merriam's strict standards in pursuing the classification of mammals. In 1890, it was Dr. Merriam's expedition with Vern into the San Francisco Mountain region of Arizona to study the distribution of mammals, birds, reptiles, and plants where Clay met the men. This expedition solidified Dr. Merriam's position, and it was also during this expedition that Dr. Merriam developed his Life Zones concept, which Clay slowly and carefully explained to Carlos.

Clay had given Carlos quite a bit of information as they ambled along the trail with their burros. He noticed that Carlos had been very attentive. Clay paused to see if Carlos had any reaction to his history of Dr. Merriam.

"Clay, you are the scientist to know all of this. I appreciate all that you have taught me, but I have much to learn if I am to be a scientist as well." Carlos paused and had that puzzled look once again. "I still do not understand what you are telling me about Dr. Merriam's men."

"This has all been background leading up to that, Carlos." And, Clay continued with his story.

Dr. Merriam gathered around him a close group of naturalists and collectors and dispatched them in all directions. In 1891, he organized a larger expedition into the mountains and deserts of California and Nevada. He had planned to study mammals from many points of view. Not only would they be classified with noted distribution, but the specimens would also be examined with regard to anatomy, ecology, nomenclature, and specialized regional study. Those who worked with Dr. Merriam found him to be a perfectionist who had difficulty trusting anyone with the detail he expected. His say was final on all publications from his organization.

With an ambitious list of projects, Dr. Merriam eventually had to rely upon his staff to carry out his plans. Once he had taken this direction, he freely gave advice and assistance, spending many hours revising manuscripts of younger men or carefully reviewing their materials with them. His standards were high, and his methods were worked out with extreme care. In effect, he founded a school, and the work of Merriam and Merriam's Men, as they were eventually known, was generally admired and respected.

In the field, Vernon Bailey was an extended hand of Dr. Merriam. It was through his field work that he advanced the standards of Dr. Merriam. Vern's work in the field was as exacting and detailed as Dr. Merriam's own work. He was the first of Merriam's Men, with his personal work only enhanced and broadened with the guidance and support of Dr. Merriam.

"We are Merriam's Men because we follow the strict standards for collecting and preparing our specimens that were set forth by Dr. Merriam and Vern. What I have taught you is what I was taught by Vern himself. We are well-trained scientists, Carlos!" Clay finished his discourse and waited for Carlos' reaction.

"Clay, if you say I am a Merriam's man because of your teaching, then I must accept it as you say. You are a good teacher, and I am sure Dr. Merriam would say so himself." Carlos held his head high and grinned.

After supper, Clay enjoyed his pipe while Carlos worked on a bird carving with his small scarred hands and his pocket knife. Clay felt good having Carlos with him on this expedition. Carlos handled the specimens well, but Clay realized that Carlos was held back by his lack of ability to read and write.

Several weeks of travel brought them deeper into the Sangre De Cristo mountain range and higher in elevation. Thick forests opened to occasional meadows. Water was plentiful, hunting was bountiful, and their specimen collection was broadening. They were currently pro-ceeding along the western ridge of the mountains toward Cerro del Oso, or Hill of the Bear, a peak of 11,255 feet.

As they walked along toward their next camp, Clay began to think about Analena. He had to say her name out loud; he needed to hear it. "Say, Carlos, what do you think Analena is doing about now?" It was not much of a question, but he did hear himself say her name.

"What do you mean, Clay? She is working making blankets to sell in town. What else would she be doing?" Carlos seemed to be annoyed by the question.

"I just meant that . . . well . . . you know . . . I was just thinking about Analena." Clay stumbled over his words, and realizing it, he felt his face turn red. Fortunately, Carlos was not looking at him.

"Why are you talking about my cousin? I think you were too close to her when we were back in Raton. Surely, you are not thinking of her as more than . . . than a friend." Carlos' voice rose in volume. "There cannot be more than that between you and Analena. You should forget about her." Carlos was direct and pointed with his words.

Clay was taken back a bit by Carlos' words. He thought that Carlos was pleased that he and Analena had become close. "Carlos, I don't un-derstand what you're saying. You know that Analena and I were close to each other back at your ranch. Why are you acting this way now?" Clay did not recognize his own voice rising as he spoke.

"You and Analena cannot be! She is of the Azuela family, and you . . . you are a gringo. There can be nothing between you!" Carlos now glared at Clay.

Clay had never seen this side of Carlos, and he was quite surprised. "Carlos, how can you say that about me. You and I are friends."

"Yes, Clay, we are friends, and there cannot be anything more than that with you and Analena. It will not work! You and I come from different worlds; you and Analena come from different worlds." Carlos stopped and turned toward Clay. He now spoke slowly while looking Clay directly in the eyes. "You cannot be involved with Analena. You must forget about her." He did not take his eyes off Clay.

Clay was confused by this reaction. He had not seen this side of Carlos. He closed his open mouth and looked up at the bits of blue sky peeking through the trees. He did not know what to say, and he felt tears rising in his eyes. It wasn't at the thought of not having Analena, but more at the way that Carlos felt.

They had both been distracted and unaware of the nervousness of the burros. They trudged along both in their own thoughts now. Suddenly, out of a thicket of trees a bear charged from no more than fifteen feet away. It lunged at Carlos, knocking him to the ground before Clay even knew what was happening.

As the bear reared to come down again on Carlos, Carlos managed to roll away from under the bear. The bear's right front paw tore a bit of Carlos' back as he rolled away. Carlos screamed, "Clay!!"

Clay, stunned, stared for what seemed like minutes at the scene before him. He was not even sure this was real. *What's happening?!*

A second scream from Carlos brought Clay back to reality. Clay screamed at the bear in an attempt to distract it. But, he only saw the bear rising again as it pursued Carlos, who had now scrambled to his feet. Clay turned to get his rifle from the burro, but there were no burros to be found. The presence of the bear had spooked the burros who had turned back down the trail. Without a weapon, Clay quickly scanned the area around him for a large stick. Not wanting to lose sight of Carlos, Clay looked up to see the bear swat Carlos with one paw and send him flying into a tree.

"Clay! Help me!!" It was a wild, savage scream that immediately ceased as Carlos hit the ground.

Clay picked up a large downed branch as Carlos got to his feet and ran further into the timbers trying to get away from the bear. The bear pursued Carlos, easily crushing small trees as it made a straight line for Carlos. Clay chased after the bear waving the stick and his hands while screaming. He was trying to get the bear's attention away from Carlos, but the bear seemed focused on nothing but Carlos.

The bear easily reached Carlos and took another swipe at him. The large claws tore open a gaping wound in Carlos' back as he fell to the ground. Carlos managed to get to his feet one more time as Clay got closer to the pair. Carlos looked up as the bear's next blow struck across his face. Clay stopped as he saw blood, bone, and raw flesh where Carlos' face had once been. He no longer heard any screaming, only the deep growl of the bear.

Carlos was now completely still on the ground. The bear ripped at Carlos' torso, then took a large bite from Carlos' small belly. Clay looked in horror as the bear ripped Carlos' intestines from his abdomen.

As Clay stood motionless, the bear looked back at him and roared while rising to his hind feet. Clay did not move. He was ready to die. *It should be me, not Carlos!* He dropped the stick and waited for the bear to charge.

The bear pounded on Carlos' body as he came back down. He swatted at the lifeless human form on the ground. He then grabbed one of Carlos' legs in his mouth and dragged him away deeper into the forest. The bear was gone; Carlos was gone.

Clay was not aware of how long he stood there in silence.

The sound of birds brought Clay back to the world around him. He started shaking and could not stop. He fell to the ground and cried. He had never experienced anything like this in his life. He was confused and troubled and scared. "Carlos," he softly whispered, "Carlos." He curled up in a ball and wept. He thought of home and family. He wondered how his own family would feel knowing he had been killed by a bear. He thought about Carlos' family and their loss. He thought about Analena. *What have I done to the Azuela family?!* He pounded the ground. "No, it should have been me!"

Chapter 18

LOSS

Finally getting to his feet, Clay tried to think sensibly, but it was not easy. He needed to find his burros; that had to be done first. He stumbled back to their trail and walked in the direction that the burros had retreated. He wasn't even sure how far he had gone before he found the burros in a small meadow enjoying the grass as if nothing had happened. They were all there together, and their loads were all intact. Clay retrieved his rifle from Gus.

Gathering the burros, Clay proceeded back up the trail to the place where the bear had attacked Carlos. He was nervous and cautious and kept his rifle ready. He listened carefully as he walked along with deter-mination.

When he arrived at the point in the trail where the attack had oc-curred, Clay knew what he had to do next – he must locate and retrieve Carlos' remains. It would be important to the Azuela family that this be done. Clay was driven by a sense of duty to the family as well as a deep sense of guilt. How could he have let this happen? He should not have been arguing with Carlos; he should have been paying more atten-tion to their surroundings, for he knew they were in bear country.

Clay tied all the burros to small trees with the exception of Gus. He would need Gus to carry the remains of Carlos. Clay retrieved a small tarp and some rope from the burros, and then he transferred Gus' load to the other burros. Gus seemed a bit nervous as they turned off the trail, but Clay coaxed him on.

The trail that led into the dense forested area was easy to follow. Clay was repulsed by the amount of blood splattered on the ground. The smaller trees and scrub brush had been easily trampled down by the bear. Then, Clay came upon the site of the worst of the slaughter by the bear. Away in the bushes were the remains of Carlos' intestines. Clay retched until his stomach was empty.

The bear had turned east from this point, dragging Carlos and leav-ing a clear path. Clay continued cautiously easing Gus as they moved forward following the decimation that created a trail through the trees. Gus was definitely not comfortable as they moved along. Clay pro-ceeded with his eyes scanning for any sign of the bear's presence.

About one hundred yards into the forest, Clay saw a glimpse of white near the base of a tree. His heart pounded as he approached what remained of Carlos. Clay stopped about thirty feet away. He told him-self to be strong; he must do this for Carlos. He stepped slowly toward the gruesome remains. Clay was able to see Carlos' legs and arms, but his torso was simply not there. The bear had consumed all he could of that part of Carlos' body.

Again, Clay stopped in his tracks. He scanned the area and listened intently. It was likely that the bear was long gone by now, having eaten his fill. After several minutes that seemed like an eternity, Clay approached the remains.

Clay took the tarp from the mule and spread it out on the ground next to Carlos. He again had to stop and prepare himself for what came next. He carefully straightened what remained of Carlos' legs and positioned his arms downward. He then slowly moved the rest of Carlos onto the tarp. While the remains of the body were covered with blood, there was no longer any bleeding. Clay folded the tarp over the remains and tightly wrapped it. He used some of the rope to secure the tarp. He next turned to Gus who was still nervous. Clay did his best to calm him, and then he lifted the bundle onto Gus' back and secured it with the rope. He was fortunate that Gus accepted the load.

Clay had never prayed for anyone before. He realized that he had to do this for Carlos. He removed his hat, and bowed his head as he closed his eyes. "God . . . I don't know why this happened . . . I feel like it is all my fault . . . I'm so sorry." Tears now welled in Clay's eyes. "But, this isn't about me, it's about Carlos. He was a good friend to me. He cared very much for his family, and I'm sure he loved you, God." Clay trembled as his tears flowed freely. "He was so young. He did nothing to deserve this. I just pray that he is now in Heaven with you where you can care for him. Thank you for letting me know Carlos . . ."

Clay stood silently until he heard Gus bray. He lifted his head quickly and looked around, momentarily unsure where he was. He put his arm around Gus' neck and hugged the burro. "Thanks, Gus," he whispered to him.

Back at the trail, Clay took a map from Jake's pack. He needed to find the shortest way to get to Mora where Carlos had told him he had family. Studying the map, Clay decided to work his way down to the Tres Ritos area and then follow the valley of the Pueblo River until it split to form the Alamitos Creek. The Alamitos would take him just to the west and above Holman. He would finally drop down through Holman and finish the short route to Mora. It looked to be a two-day trek, but Clay would travel night and day to get to Mora much sooner.

He neared Mora the following afternoon. He did not know where Carlos had family in the area, other than it would be a farm about three or four miles northwest of town. The area was sparse with a few scattered adobe homes within view. Clay guided his burros to the nearest house. In his best Spanish, Clay was able to determine that there was an Azuela family located just to the west about three miles on Encina Creek.

The local Azuela family was a cousin to Carlos' father, Antonio, and they knew the family well. They were very welcoming to Clay, but he had difficulty explaining to them why they had been in the mountains and the events leading up to Carlos' death. In the end, they were caring and comforting and sent for the priest from Mora to handle the burial.

Clay spent two days with the family and thanked them deeply for all they had done. He assured them that he would write a letter to Carlos' family and mail it from Mora the next day. They bid him safe travel and sent him off with some fresh biscuits and fried chicken in his pack. Passing Carlos' grave while leaving the farm, Clay pulled a small item from his pack. It was the bird that Carlos had carved just days ago. Clay placed it on Carlos' grave, bid him his last good-bye, and headed toward town.

In Mora, Clay found a place to stable his burros and give them a deserved rest and some good feed. He found a room and busied himself making final preparations for his specimens for shipment. He kept himself occupied with his tasks while he put off writing the letter to the Azuela family in Raton.

However, after getting his specimens packed and shipped, Clay realized that he had to complete his letter to the Azuelas. He started it several times, but he could not get it right. Eventually, he simply poured his heart out onto the page. He apologized to the family, but he avoided making the letter about himself. He told them how Carlos had grown to become a good scientist and what a hard worker he had been. He let the family know just how much Carlos' companionship and friendship had meant to him.

He wanted to share some personal thoughts with Analena, but this was not the time for that. Clay thought of the exchange he had had with Carlos about his relationship with Analena. Perhaps Carlos was right, and there was no future for the two of them. He dropped the letter at the dry goods store where it would be picked up and carried to Raton.

Back in his room, Clay finally opened his mail. His needed funds were in there, and a letter from Vern. Clay was to head south and meet Vern in Albuquerque where they would take a party into the Mogollon Mountains on an expedition for Dr. Merriam.

Chapter 19

UNBURDENED

Vern's letter had only recently arrived in Mora. Clay and Carlos were not supposed to reach the town for two more weeks, so Clay was reading the letter earlier than Vern had anticipated. Since it would be nearly four weeks before he was to meet Vern, Clay had plenty of time to rest up and make his plans.

Vern told Clay in the letter that they would be meeting in Albuquerque. Vern would make all the preparations for transportation and supplies; all Clay had to do was show up with his personal effects.

From Albuquerque, they would continue by rail to Magdalena where they would make final preparations and continue west along the

Magdalena Trail. Magdalena was the end of the trail for the cattle ranchers who brought their herds from as far away as Arizona. Vern told Clay they would be following the trail into the mountains north of the Mogollons and travel south through the territory.

There were several large cattle ranches in the area to be surveyed, and they would be studying the current state of the plant and mammal populations of the region. Dr. Merriam was especially interested in observing any negative effects that the cattle ranches had on the natural resources in and around the Mogollon Mountains.

Clay made a couple of decisions. First, he would spend few a days relaxing and enjoying some hotel-cooked food. He was in need of a little change in his diet, and he looked forward to a nice beefsteak dinner. Secondly, since he had plenty of time before he had to meet Vern, he would make a side trip to Las Vegas where he would visit Sister Anne at the sanatorium where he had made his recovery from consumption. He was still quite grateful for her help in his recovery, and he wanted to let her know that she had meant a great deal to him. But, deeper down inside, he hoped he could talk to her about Carlos' death and his own feelings of guilt. He needed to talk to someone about his feelings, and she would be perfect for that.

At the end of the week, Clay was ready to leave. He sold two of the burros and purchased a small wagon. He did not need anything large as he only had his pack of personal items, bedroll, and small camp outfit. Gus and Oskar would do fine pulling the buckboard. The terrain would be fairly even for the trip to Las Vegas and so an easy chore for the burros.

As he headed east out of town, Clay's thoughts turned to Carlos. He felt like he was abandoning him. He also felt the intense loss of not having his friend along with him. His reflections on Carlos turned to Analena. He knew that Carlos was right; any relationship with her was over. He still had not found the courage to write to her. He hoped that his time at St. Anthony's Parish with Sister Anne would give him the courage and the words to compose the letter.

Clay followed the Mora River through the valley, then turned his small team to the south across the Mora River near a farm keeping the ridge to his right. Looking out over the desert to the east, Clay was finally able to let go of his thoughts of the Azuela family. He stared at the trail ahead and felt a glimpse of the joy that the land around him brought to him. It was one of those points in time when he felt alive in the present moment.

Clay knew what it was to be alive. He knew that there was something larger than himself that was providing for him. There was comfort in these thoughts, and he felt like maybe this was what God was all about. Was it God's presence that was caring for him? He was not sure. He had not really learned much about God. Church had not been a big part of his time growing up. Sure, his family had attended church, but it seemed to be a lot of singing and the droning on by a pastor who used a lot of big words and occasionally yelled at everybody about how sinful they were.

He seemed to learn more about God in some of the words that Carlos had shared with him. The Azuela family was Catholic, and their religion was important to them in an everyday way, not just on Sundays. It made Clay feel good to think that maybe Carlos was still there – somewhere – perhaps looking down from heaven?

Late in the afternoon, Clay arrived in Las Vegas. He went straight to St. Anthony's, which had been relocated to a new structure to the east. He stopped about 100 yards from the three-story building and observed the large wrap-around porch. He could make out numerous beds sitting out in the open air. It was a much larger facility than the house he had stayed in when he had been a patient here. He thought it must be at least triple the size of the house where he had convalesced.

He felt a bit of unease, now, about stopping at the sanatorium. It had been nearly three years since he had been admitted here. His early weeks had not been comfortable, but it was here that he had healed and then regained his strength. He needed healing again, but in a different way. It wasn't physical this time; he needed healing from his guilt over Carlos' death. Would Sister Anne be able to help him?

After several minutes, Gus brayed, getting Clay's attention. Clay allowed Gus and Oskar to move forward. Pulling up to the sanatorium, Clay tied the pair of burros outside the fence. Getting out of the buckboard, he dusted himself off. He took a long draft of water from his canteen. While making sure all of his equipment was in place, he realized that he was just busying himself to avoid going up to the front door. He turned, opened the gate, and walked toward the porch under the quiet stares of many dark, desperate eyes.

He was greeted at the front door by a woman in a nurse's uniform. She asked if he knew where he was. Clay related to her about his time as a patient at the former facility. She was pleasant as she listened and then openly welcomed him back to St. Anthony's. She immediately followed by asking him if he were feeling alright or if he were ill again.

"Oh . . . no!" Clay quickly responded. "I'm quite fine. I'm on my way to Albuquerque, and I wanted to stop by to see Sister Anne. She was so kind to me and helped me in my recovery."

"I see," the kind nurse replied. "Won't you come in." She opened the screen door and showed him into the large foyer. "Please have a seat here while I find Sister Anne and let her know she has a visitor. It was Clay, correct?"

"Yes, ma'am. Clay Beckley. I was here a little more than three years ago, and I hope she remembers me." He had not thought that she might not remember him. She surely had many patients to care for since he had been here. He was almost fearful for a moment and thought about leaving.

"I am sure she will remember one of her patients who has recovered so well." Her words encouraged Clay. "Would you like a glass of water while you wait?" Her voice was filled with a kindness that put him at ease.

"No, thank you. I'm just fine." He paused as if he were going to say more. She looked at him, then turned and left the foyer. Clay stood after she left. He had been sitting all day, and it felt good to stand for a bit. He noticed a hat stand and placed his hat on it.

Only a few minutes passed before the nurse returned. "Sister Anne is finishing up some work, then she will be down to see you." She motioned to him and said, "Follow me. You can wait in the drawing room."

"Thank you once again, ma'am."

The nurse had gone, and Clay was now seated in a stuffed chair unlike anything he had seen for quite some time. The clock on the wall ticked loudly as Clay sank deeply into the soft, plush chair. Alone in the room, Clay was sure that the clock ticked slower and slower while growing louder and louder.

After a few minutes – minutes that seemed like hours to Clay – he heard footsteps coming from a hallway at the far end of the large foyer. Sister Anne rounded the corner and gave a broad smile from beneath her habit. She quickened her step and reached her hands out to Clay who was now standing.

Sister Anne took Clay's hands in hers and warmly welcomed him. "Clay Beckley, what a nice surprise to see you here! When the nurse told me it was you, I was sure she had made a mistake." She stepped back and looked over Clay. "You look healthy, indeed. Are you feeling well? You are not here because you are sick are you?" And a look of concern overtook her smile.

"Oh, no!" Clay quickly replied. "As I told the kind nurse, I'm on my way to Albuquerque, and I wanted to stop by and see how things were with you and with the hospital. I owe so much to you that I just had to stop by on my way." He paused to be sure she understood he was not ill.

"Well, that is certainly good news," she interrupted with a sense of relief. "It is getting late in the afternoon. Will you be able to stay the evening here, or do you have plans to be elsewhere? We can certainly make up a private room for you. As you can see, we have a much larger building now, and we are able to accommodate family visitors. We certainly have room for you, Clay." She smiled brightly.

"Well . . . I would very much appreciate it if I could stay." He was having trouble getting out the remainder of his request. "Sister Anne, I was hoping I could stay for a few days. I'd really like to talk to you about some things that have happened to me recently." He looked down at his feet, for some reason feeling embarrassed.

"Clay, you can stay as long as you want. Why don't you gather your things while I have a room prepared? We have a new stable out back that you can use. Go around the south end of the building. Come back here, and someone will show you to your room."

Clay could hear the concern in her voice, and he felt that maybe he was making too much of things. He kindly thanked her and went to the wagon to retrieve his bag. After dropping the bag in the foyer, he took Gus and Oskar and the wagon around the south end of the building to the stable. After caring for the animals, Clay returned to the foyer where he was taken to his accommodations. In his room, Clay suddenly felt exhausted, laid down on the bed, and fell fast asleep.

Clay woke later than usual the next morning. He did not hear much activity as his room was near the far end of the second floor. As he made his way downstairs, he was met by a young lady who offered to show him to breakfast. He dutifully followed and ate the best breakfast he had had in many months. He had forgotten how well they were fed at the sanatorium.

As he was finishing his meal, Sister Anne appeared in the doorway. She informed Clay that she would be busy the rest of the morning, but she had cleared her time in the afternoon to meet with him. Clay thanked her, and she quickly disappeared. From where Clay was eating breakfast, he could hear the activity of the patients finishing morning exercises and readying themselves for a large breakfast with plenty of milk. The sounds brought back a familiarity to Clay that was both comforting and a bit distressing at the same time. He was truly grateful for his treatment here, but he was also glad not to be here as a patient. His time as a convalescent had not been easy.

That afternoon, Clay and Sister Anne sat in a small, but comfortable, room where they could talk in private. Clay told Sister Anne of the Azuela family and of his friendship with Carlos and with Analena. Once he began talking, he could not seem to stop. He finally got through the encounter with the bear in the mountains and his feelings of guilt over Carlos' death. He finished his story with the burial of Carlos in Mora. He had tried not to make the story of Carlos death too explicit for Sister Anne.

As he finished, Sister Anne reached out and gave Clay a warm hug. It was only then that Clay realized that he had tears running down his cheeks. Sister Anne retrieved a handkerchief from one of her deep pockets and gave it to Clay.

"Clay, you are guilty of nothing. You have feelings for the loss of a good friend. That is all completely normal." She looked at Clay with compassion. "You could not control the actions of a wild animal any-more than you could control the weather. It is obvious that one reason you feel so badly is that you and your friend were arguing before the bear attacked. But, Clay, nothing you did or said – did *not* do, or did *not* say – would have stopped a bear charging at that time of the year in the mountains." She spoke slowly and with a deep tenderness.

They continued talking late into the afternoon. Clay wiped away his tears several times. But, Sister Anne was now pulling him up out of his well of guilt. She made a sense that Clay could not refute, and she was slowly and surely uplifting his spirit. She had a special way that Clay recalled from his time as her patient. She explained to Clay how God will use our worst circumstances to teach us. She told him that he was a loving God, and he was not punishing Carlos or Clay. She asked Clay to think about the good of his relationship with the Azuela family, and even more so, to think about what God wanted him to learn from his experience. She finished by saying a blessing over Clay:

"Dearest Jesus, who wept at the death of your friend
and taught that they who mourn shall be comforted,
grant this young man the comfort of your presence in his loss.
Send Your Holy Spirit to direct him
lest he make hasty or foolish decisions.
Send Your Spirit to give him courage
lest through fear he recoil from living.
Send Your Spirit to bring him your peace

lest bitterness, false guilt, or regret take root in his heart.

The Lord has given.

The Lord has taken away.

Blessed be the name of the Lord.

Amen."

Clay held his head still for a moment, then looked up into Sister Anne's eyes and said thank-you to her with his own eyes. She smiled in understanding.

"Clay, I know you told me before that you do not have much church background, but perhaps it would do you good to talk to the priest. The priest can forgive you of all your past sins. I think it would help you to confess your sins to the priest. It will lift the burden that you carry on your heart." She let the idea sink in.

"Think about it, Clay. The priest will be here in three days for mass. Stay until he arrives." Her tone lifted as she reached out to Clay, "And, I will put you to work around here until you are ready to leave." Her tone now tried to lighten the mood, "After all, we expect a lot out of healthy young men like you. There is plenty of work in the garden. It will keep your hands busy and your mind occupied."

"Well, I would like to stay a while longer, and I'm surely ready to work for my keep." He found himself smiling. "And, I will think about talking to the priest; will you show me how to prepare to talk with him?"

"Yes, Clay, yes."

Chapter 20

LUZ DE ORO

Clay sold his burros and wagon in Las Vegas. He used some of his funds for new clothes and a few personal items, and he updated his camping outfit. Comfortable on the train heading for Magdalena, Clay thought of some of his early transportation on the trains. "Riding the cushions" was certainly more comfortable than some of the other places he had stowed away on trains.

He was comforted by his time at St. Anthony's with Sister Anne. He followed up on her advice and confessed his sins to the priest on Sunday. She was right; it had helped relieve some of the burden he carried. He was now feeling much better about proceeding on to meet Vern in Magdalena and heading into the Mogollon Mountains.

With the help of Sister Anne, Clay found the strength to compose a letter to Analena. Once he started writing, the words poured out from his heart. He expressed his remorse for what had happened to Carlos. He told her how kind the Azuela family in Mora had been, and how they provided for the burial. He expressed his great appreciation for the kindness of Analena's family to him in Raton. He finally told Analena how much she meant to him, but that he had to move on with his life as a field collector. His work as a naturalist would keep him wandering over the remote areas of the country. It would be no life that he could expect her to be a part of. He did not tell her of the conversation that he and Carlos had had over his relationship with her. He ended by saying that he prayed for Carlos and Analena and the entire Azuela family as they dealt with the loss of Carlos. He signed the letter, "Como Siempre, Clay."

The train was scheduled to stop in Lamy before going on to Albuquerque where Clay would meet Vern. Vern would have four other men with him for this expedition, making six in all with Clay on this undertaking for Dr. Merriam. Clay was looking forward to working with Vern once again. While Clay felt confident in his skills, he knew he could learn even more by working with Vern. On this trip, they would focus most of their collecting activities on larger mammals.

Clay arrived in Lamy shortly after noon. He had over an hour before the train would leave for Albuquerque, so he decided to have a nice meal. At the suggestion of the station master he went to the El Ortiz Hotel, one of the string of restaurants operated by Fred Harvey. It turned out that it more than exceeded the expectations set by the station master. Clay left the hotel full and ready for a nap when he boarded the train for the final leg to Albuquerque.

It wasn't long before the satisfaction of his meal, the warm weather, and the sound of the train wheels clacking upon the tracks put him to sleep. He slept soundly, just as he had for the past week since arriving at St. Anthony's.

He was awakened by the conductor's voice calling out that they were arriving in Albuquerque. It was a larger station than the one at Lamy. Climbing out of the passenger car, Clay looked up and down the platform. At the end of the platform on his left, men were unloading bags and crates from the boxcars. Looking to his right, he could see that this was the location where passengers would meet those coming to pick them up. Clay went in that direction carrying his pack and bags. At the end of the platform, he looked behind the station and saw a number of wagons waiting. It only took him a few moments to recognize Vern. He hopped off the platform and headed in that direction.

Vern saw Clay coming toward his wagon and called out, "Hey, Clay, over here!"

Clay waved at Vern and picked up his pace. As Clay approached the wagon, Vern jumped down and greeted Clay with a firm handshake. Dropping his bags, Clay grabbed Vern's arm with his left hand as he beamed, "It sure is good to see you, Vern!"

"Throw your bags in the wagon, and we'll head over to the hotel. I want you to meet the rest of the team." He briefly looked Clay over. "You look healthy, my friend. You must have been eating well."

Since they had last met, Clay had grown taller and stronger. He felt good that Vern had noticed a difference. "It's all that good mountain living. And, I've been working hard." Clay was eager to know how Vern felt about the specimens he had been sending to Dr. Merriam. "I hope you've noticed an improvement in my specimens as well. I've really been trying to follow all the details that Dr. Merriam has prescribed for the collections. I want to be sure that my work is meeting Dr. Merriam's expectations. Well, and, of course, your expectations, too." Clay realized he was talking very fast as he showed his excitement about his work.

Vern laughed, a polite laugh. "Clay, your work is just fine. Dr. Merriam was pleased to see how quickly you picked up on the details required. He's mentioned in particular the completeness of the written records that you provided with your specimens. As far as I can tell, it's better than most . . . with the exception of yours truly, of course." Now they laughed together.

The next few days were quite busy completing the setup of the wagons and the teams, organizing the collecting equipment and chemicals, and ensuring everyone on the team had their specific assignments. It was up to Clay to check and double check the chemicals, papers and supplies they would need for specimen preparation. Everything they had was organized for ease of access according to whatever the task would be. They had a chuckwagon and a cook to ensure they were filled with good food. Clay was especially glad for this as he had grown less fond of his own simple camp cooking.

Clay was able to select his own horse at the stable. He found a nice golden buckskin mare that was a good fit for Clay. He was glad the mare was not too large. It would be easier to navigate through trees and small gullies on her. When Vern saw Clay's selection, he made mention that Clay had made a good choice.

The wagons, horses, pack mules, and all the supplies were loaded onto the train a few days later. It would take a full day to get to the trailhead at Magdalena. Vern told Clay that they had put everything together in Albuquerque for two reasons. First, there were simply more, and better, equipment and supplies available in Albuquerque. Secondly, and perhaps most importantly, since Magdalena was the trailhead for the Magdalena Trail, the supply of good horses was quite limited. The few good horses were taken quickly, while the trail horses were too worn to be of any use to an expedition like they would be undertaking. Newer strings of horses might be available, but they were typically not trail ready.

On their first water stop for the steam engine, Clay decided to go back to the boxcar where his horse was stalled. He felt he had not had enough time to get to know his horse well, and he wanted to spend the rest of the day with his mare. She was a little jumpy being on the train, especially when they again got underway. Clay did his best to calm her, and offered her an apple he had in his pocket. She did not seem to want the apple at first, but then she nudged Clay's hand and took the apple eagerly. He rubbed her muzzle and forehead with his hand, and she accepted him as well.

Being as busy as he had been, Clay had yet to name his horse. She was a light golden color, with the exception of her black mane, tail and legs. He thought momentarily about her light gold color. He felt good around her; she was comforting to him. She was a new light in Clay's life; she was the light of gold. The light of gold. Clay thought about this as a name in Spanish. The light of gold in Spanish could be trans-lated as *luz de oro*. As Clay pronounced the Spanish several times, he heard the first part sound a little bit like Lucy. So, then and there, he decided that was her name – Lucy.

He spent the next several hours talking to Lucy. He told her about his life in Indiana, his move to the West, his convalescence from con-sumption, his friendship with the Azuela family, and his loss of Carlos and Analena. He told her about their upcoming expedition into the Mogollon Mountains and praised her for the good horse that she would be for him. He would treat her well and expect the same in re-turn. Clay felt as if she actually understood what he was saying.

1895

Chapter 21

THE MOGOLLON EXPEDITION

It was late in the afternoon when the train pulled into the station at Magdalena. Since it was past the peak season for the cattle drives, the town was quiet. That was fine for the group as they unloaded the horses and pack mules, the wagon, and supplies. They took the horses and pack mules to a nearby stable and bedded them for the night. They then proceeded to the one local hotel for rooms that Vern had secured ahead of time for them. After a good meal together, they agreed to meet early for breakfast at the hotel before heading out.

The first day was met with flat, dry desert well worn by the cattle drives from as far away as Springerville, Arizona. At Datil, the trail split with the northern branch going on to Arizona and the southern branch heading down through the valley that would take them to the Mogollon Mountains.

The next day was more of the same dry and dusty desert. Clay could not imagine how the cowmen could follow the cattle through this type of land. A typical drive took about twelve days, according to Vern. Most of the cowboys rode in the dust of the cattle herd for the entire length of the drive. Clay found it not to be the type of work that he would enjoy. He was glad they would soon be getting into the mountains.

After three more days, they passed Milligan's Plaza and arrived at Saliz Pass. It was here that they would make a camp and begin working the mountains to both the east and the west. This was the first of three general targets of their survey. This area, still north of the Mogollon Mountains, had been little studied compared to the areas further to the north. It was expected that the team would spend about six weeks in this first area.

The second target was the region around Alma. There were large ranches in that area, and they would be looking at the effects, if any, that cattle ranging on the land had on the plant and animal life. They expected that they would get a mixed welcome here, but they would be in and around Alma through winter and into spring.

Their final, and most extensive target, would be the Mogollon Mountains themselves. They would leave the wagon behind in Alma and proceed into the Mogollons. They would be collecting as they eventually worked their way down to Silver City by mid-summer. In all, Clay expected that the amount of time with this team would provide good company, new adventures, and a great opportunity for learning his trade.

Clay was putting his time on the trail to good use. Not only were he and Lucy getting to know each other well, but he was also getting to know the other men on the expedition. Vern had brought one experienced assistant and three newer Merriam's Men in training with him in addition to Clay. Art Howell was Vern's assistant who had been with Vern on a previous expedition to the northwestern United States.

James Gaut was a new collector originally from Tennessee on his first assignment with the Biological Survey. He had spent some time in Washington, D.C., before becoming a field naturalist on Vern's team. Bob Howler, Ben Holt and Clay rounded out the team of collectors. Bob, from Illinois, and Ben, from Pennsylvania, had backgrounds similar to Clay's. Like Clay, they had worked independently sending their specimens to Vern for the Survey. Bob was a little younger than Clay, and Ben was a little older. Unlike Clay and Bob, Ben had spent two years studying at a college back East.

Finally, there was Heinrich Alden, the cook, someone they were all hoping knew his job well. He was known as Henry and spoke with a strong German accent. Henry had been on three previous expeditions with Vern. Vern assured them all that no one would go hungry with Henry cooking for them.

Vern made it clear at the start of the trip that their work was important and that they would all receive specific training to bring them along as true professional naturalists and field collectors. The work would be hard, and their personal efforts would be closely scrutinized. Vern related his own experience to all of them. He had been self-taught, just as they had, but it was under the tutelage of Dr. Merriam that he was trained in the real skills of field work. He trusted they would all be willing to devote the time necessary to become the type of men expected by Dr. Merriam.

They had all learned the basic skills of trapping and specimen preparation. And, most were doing an adequate job of preparing the written records of their collections. It was in this last area that Dr. Merriam had the greatest expectations for the men. Yes, proper preparation of the specimens was important, but without the proper records and notations of the species and its domain, the specimen was worthless to the Department of Agriculture, and specifically to the division that was now being referred to by Dr. Merriam as the Biological Survey.

On previous expeditions, Vern had often felt out of place with some of the other field agents who had academic training and college degrees. He had learned a great deal working side-by-side with these professional naturalists. He had seen in these men what it would be like to be a career naturalist. In them, and especially in Dr. Merriam, he had seen the qualities that he admired most and desired for himself. He worked hard under the direct supervision of Dr. Merriam, beginning in 1887. He spent nearly four years in the field between 1887 and 1892. His knowledge of the American West and mastery of its flora and fauna was greatly admired by Dr. Merriam as well as many others. In 1890, Vern had been appointed as the Chief Field Naturalist for the Survey directly under Dr. Merriam, and he had published extensively of his collections.

Clay was greatly inspired after Vern spoke with the team about his own background and his expectations of the men he had gathered together. Clay was feeling good about his own future as a field collector. He was excited about the prospects of this particular expedition. He felt that this would be a turning point in his life.

They worked the first area for about six weeks, just as they had planned. Winter was setting in, but the party was gathering a good set of specimens. They had already identified an apparently new species of shrew. Vern was an expert when it came to shrews, and he was glad to have a new species to provide for Dr. Merriam. Mule deer were plentiful and easily obtained. Many smaller mammals preparing for winter were also easily acquired.

Gathering the specimens had not been a problem as the team moved about. They typically went out in two teams of three under the supervision of Vern and Art. Both Vern and Art were good leaders and teachers. While the days were long and grueling at times, Clay was learning a few new tricks of this collecting and surveying business. He was feeling good about his efforts until it came time to prepare the specimens.

They had set up a nice large preparation tent. All of the men were performing well preparing their skins. Then came the time to document their findings with field notes, catalogs, and specimen tags. Clay thought he had been doing a good job, until Vern began to teach them first-hand the recording standards required by Dr. Merriam.

Vern was hard on all of them. Measure and re-measure seemed to be ground into their minds. Observe, record, observe again, make corrections, observe again . . . there was a seemingly endless process in uncovering even the tiniest differences, or similarities, in specimens.

Dr. Merriam's expectations were meticulous. Vern shared with them how strongly he had been admonished by Dr. Merriam many times. Hart, as Vern always referred to Dr. Merriam, was quick to scold mistakes and slow to offer praise. Vern shared Dr. Merriam's never ceasing correction over his species identifications and his continuous chiding of Vern for leaving an area too quickly without getting a good series of specimens. As Vern progressed in his own skills and observations, Dr. Merriam eventually came around to voicing his satisfaction with Vern's progress.

Vern pursued the young naturalists' development in a meticulous manner that rivaled Dr. Merriam's, but he did so with a thoughtful and understanding demeanor, truly teaching rather than chastising. Every bit of the specimen required a measurement. Specimen weights were also key. As a series was collected for a particular mammal, even the most minor differences in males and females, young and old, were given the most strict scrutiny. If Vern questioned your results, you started over. Clay found that Vern's concerns were most always correct.

Clay and the other three newer members of Merriam's Men spent many late nights in the preparation tent revising much of their work. After a long day in the field checking traps, collecting specimens and preparing them, late nights were hard on the men. Still, they managed to enjoy a good cigar or pipe at the end of the day.

The four men found themselves offering much support to one another. Bob needed a push and encouragement from the others once in a while, while James eagerly moved ahead encouraging the others to speed up as well. While Ben was intelligent and eager, he sometimes got ahead of himself and, unfortunately, spent considerable time reworking his catalogs. Had he slowed down in the beginning of the process, he would have been way ahead of the others. Bob was more laid back and had a very caring nature about him. He was a good trail man, and Clay found himself learning a good deal about tracking from Bob.

While Vern drove the men on their identification and catalogs, Art assisted the men in preparation of the specimens. They had all learned refined skills from Art who shared very willingly and taught in the same manner as Vern. Most nights, Vern watched over their preparations while continuing his supper into the night. He was a big eater who was certainly able to put away the tasty biscuits made by Henry. In the preparation tent, Vern seemed to always have a biscuit in hand as some men might have a cigar.

Chapter 22

ALMA

There were many cattle ranches within the survey area. The region was large and rough, but they saw most of it, for they kept going through the late winter and into the early spring from place to place. The ranchers showed them every possible courtesy hoping to assure a favorable report to Washington.

The winter had been mild compared to the winters Clay had experienced back in Indiana. Throughout the winter, it appeared that more of the snow was being dropped far to their southeast, apparently more directly in the Mogollon Mountains.

Even in this early spring, small blooms and green shrubs could be seen scattered across the land. With a fine set of specimens from the surrounding area, the party returned to the Saliz Pass and headed south toward Alma. They followed the pine-forested, rocky valley until it opened wide. The valley unfolded into low hills, and eventually plains, that provided plenty of open grazing for the cattle ranchers of the region.

Two days after leaving the Saliz Pass, the team topped a slight rise, and a beautiful vista opened before their eyes. To the west were large fields of young, bright green alfalfa as far as the eye could see. From a distance, the crops appeared as level and as smooth as any city lawn that Clay had seen. To the east, surrounded by plenty of recently greened shade trees, stood a large beautiful house constructed of native rock. Behind this home, partly hidden by a row of trees, stood a group of fresh-looking barns and other ranch buildings. It was as if the buildings and fields and crops were designed by some great architect to be specifically placed in this location. This was a ranch unlike any that Clay had ever seen.

They neared the main house which was surrounded by a well-manicured lawn and fine oak trees planted in a neat pattern to accent the stone house. They stopped at a nearby corral where they were met by a welcoming ranch hand. He directed them to a table beneath a tree near the house where the owner was sitting. He was a distinguished looking man of about fifty years of age dressed in a fine tailor-made suit of clothes, a rare sight in this remote cattle country, Clay thought.

A bit self-conscious after so much time on the trail, Clay removed his hat and did what he could to remove the mud and trail dust from his clothing. Clay, Bob, James, and Ben stopped short of approaching the table as Vern and Art strode to the table to introduce themselves to the man who was now standing. The man moved from the table and walked toward Vern and Art confidently with his hand outstretched and a smile on his round face.

Clay studied the man as Vern and Art explained their business in the area. He appeared to be a proud man of wealth. His voice matched the pride and large presence of the man. Clay marveled at the man's correct English which had a strong, yet pleasant, Irish brogue. He almost seemed out of place on this remote ranch.

Since it was getting to be late in the afternoon, their host insisted that the party spend the night at the ranch. While a ranch hand led away their team to unharness and feed them, they continued to talk on the shady lawn where there was a cool, spring breeze. They were all invited to join the man at the table where lemonade was served to them. Vern explained the reason for their presence in the area to survey and evaluate the effect of the grazing cattle on the land and on the other animal life in the area of the ranch.

The group learned that Mr. French, William French, born in Dublin, Ireland, had been a captain in the British Army up to 1882. In 1883, he came to the United States where he met Harold C. Wilson and took up residence on the W S Ranch in Alma. The ranch had been founded by Wilson and Montague Stevens, hence the W S. Mr. French learned the cattle business working on the ranch over the next several years and became the ranch manager before becoming a U.S. citizen and, ultimately, a partner in the ranch. He continued to manage the large operation to this day.

Mr. French appeared to be well-educated in plant and animal biology. Since Vern had written many papers and described many new species of plants found in this territory, the two men had a lot in common to discuss. Mr. French showed them with pride a number of trees on the grounds that he had brought from his beloved homeland on the other side of the Atlantic Ocean. Some of these trees were forty feet tall and thriving on irrigation from the nearby San Francisco River.

Instead of being sent to the bunk house, the survey team was shown rooms in the large stone home. At dinner, they met his pleasant wife and nearly-grown children. Clay was in the most expensive home he had ever seen, with paintings, furniture, and furnishings far beyond his humble ability to appreciate.

Clay felt that a small piece of elegant Ireland had been planted in these desert mountains. His only other experience with Irishmen was far from the cultured character of Mr. French. Clay found himself gawking at the paintings on the wall, ignoring the dinner conversation. Bob poked an elbow in Clay's side to get his attention refocused. Clay quickly turned to Bob who quietly laughed at Clay's awe of the surroundings.

For several hours, Vern, Art, and Mr. French discussed forestry and cattle grazing. For many years, the owner had lived here and made expensive improvements. He grew alfalfa by irrigation to winter his better cattle, but he had always had free use of the open range near him for year-round pasture. Mr. French was curious to know why the government was so interested in the plants, trees, and mammals of this area. Cattle had been grazing this land for many years, and he could not see why there should be any question about the impact of the herds. Cattle, he said, were grass feeders and simply had no impact on the local mammal population. Nor were they having any impact, as far as he was concerned, on the plant life growing in the area. If anything, he felt that he had contributed to the development of the area with his improvement of the land, with the alfalfa planting, and with the movement of his herds in order to maintain the grasslands. The ranch man was managing the land quite well, and Clay was impressed by all that he heard.

Vern explained that the very reason his team was here was to confirm everything that Mr. French was telling him. If all was as he had said, then his report to Washington would say just that. Neither man was argumentative, but rather they were very understanding and listened to the other with rapt attention. As much as Clay was impressed by Mr. French, he also saw a side of Vern that he had not previously noticed. Vern gave all of his attention to the speaker and kept asking questions to get to the details that he wanted to know. It was as if he were gathering detailed specimen information of this very land from Mr. French.

As the evening came to an end, Mr. French let it be known in no uncertain terms that he wanted a favorable report made by Vern to Washington. He was not threatening in his tone, but rather he expressed a willingness to assist in the survey in any way that he could. Even with all of his pride and his strong personality, Mr. French remained very kind and cooperative to all of the men.

Early the next morning, Mr. French had their horses ready for the men and went with them to examine some small timbered areas nearby. Since the survey team had seen some timber a few days before where browsing cattle, probably half-starved, had killed large areas of young trees, they were rather surprised to find no damage at all on Mr. French's ranch. He explained, of course, that he managed the land and crops to provide proper nourishment for the cattle.

After several days of riding the surrounding countryside, they bid their host and hostess goodbye with a few regrets. The stop here had indeed been a pleasant interlude for all of the men. It made Clay feel good to see a man whose living was made off the land taking such good care of his holdings. It was obvious that Mr. French had a well-thought-out, long-term view of this ranching business.

Late that same afternoon, they approached the more typical ranch headquarters of the region. A group of weather-beaten one-story adobe buildings scattered over a bare hillside brought Clay's thoughts back to the real cattle ranch life. They were shown where to unhitch, then taken to their beds in the bunk house. A large group of cowhands was washing up at a horse trough to be ready for the supper call.

"Hoooo!!" sang the cook as he gave a triangle of steel hung on a wire a few blows with a hammer. "Come and get it, you sorry bunch of cowpunchers!"

Clay, the three other field collectors, and Henry joined the throng, while Vern and Art met with the ranch owner at the main house. The five men entered the low dining room where they were seated on a long bench alongside a table literally loaded with food. Bob looked at Clay with wide eyes. Clay noticed a wariness in Henry's face; obviously, he would be comparing the cooking to his own.

Whatever might be lacking in the quality of the food was certainly made up by the quantity. Clay found the beef, the soda biscuits, and the brown gravy just to his liking, so filled up to his capacity. There was little talk at the table, as all the men were hungry and ready to eat.

The cook's experience showed in the meal. Everything was seasoned to bring out the best in the flavors. Even Henry seemed pleased with the cook's repast. None of the survey men had any complaints about Henry's meals on the trail, and they were appreciative that Henry was every bit the cook as this local man.

After supper, Clay and the others watched a card game while enjoying a smoke. The local cowmen were more than happy to share their tobacco with the visitors. They invited the group to join in with the card game, but none of the team had any real experience in cards, and this did not appear to be the time to learn.

Clay was astonished at the size of these cattlemen. Many were six feet and over, and few were under that height. Clay thought that long days of hard work in the clean open air and eternal sunshine of the outdoors must be responsible for the size and health of these men. He stepped outside for a moment to knock the ashes out of his pipe. Gazing up at the stars, Clay felt the reality of how blessed he was.

At the break of day, the horse wrangler rushed into the bunk house shouting, "All out! All out! A grizzly has killed a cow in the upper pasture."

The ranch boss, a giant of a man in range garb, approached Clay and the four others. "Are you men ready for a bear hunt? We've got some good dogs we wanna try on this damned cattle-killing grizzly." The man was matter of fact but very firm in his manner.

They all, except Henry, grabbed a hasty breakfast as their horses were lead to the bunk house. They each had a rifle in a scabbard put on their saddles for protection. Clay noticed the eagerness of all the men as he put on his hat and mounted his horse.

Clay found his thoughts quickly turning to Carlos. He was suddenly hit with that feeling of revenge that he thought he had gotten over. He tried to get the notion out of his head, but it would not go away. *Will this be my opportunity to avenge for Carlos' death?* He was both excited and frightened by his own thoughts.

Word had been sent out to some of the other smaller neighboring ranches. Horsemen and dogs were arriving every minute. When all the men were ready, there were fifteen riders and at least a dozen dogs. Most of the dogs were familiar hunting hounds, but Clay also recognized a Spanish Shepherd and an Airedale in the pack.

Clay was able to learn that the bears lived in a very rough mountain range a few miles away. Every few weeks, one of them came down onto the flat at night, killed a cow, ate its fill, and returned to the jagged rocks. The men were anxious to eliminate this problem.

After twenty minutes at a steady gallop, they were at the place of the kill. A two-year-old heifer had been knocked down, and the amount of meat consumed by that bear was surprising to Clay. After circling the carcass, the dogs found the trail leading away, and the riders were off on the run.

The range in this area was open grassland without brush or trees or rocks, so their pace was brisk. They kept in a large open bunch with the dogs in plain sight at all times. As they rode along at a swift gallop, Clay asked the nearest rider, a young cowboy, which one of the gang of riders usually got to the bear first when the dogs ran it down. Clay wanted to be there for the kill.

"See that small man with only one leg on your left there?" he shouted at Clay. "Well, that 'puncher always gets there in time to shoot the bear. He's a small man, a horse-killer, and a ridin' fool, but he gets there every time."

Clay found that following a noisy pack of dogs in full cry to be an exciting business. Every man, and all the horses, felt its impact, for no horse intended to be left behind, to say nothing of the riders. As they went along, Clay studied Lucy. This was their first such run together, and Clay was not sure how she would react. The leaps she made over ditches and gullies showed that she was full of vigor and power. Nothing, it seemed, could keep the mare from staying with the bunch. Clay was now lost in the hunt, his mind now clearly focused.

Their trail began to show a gentle, but steady, grade upward. Their pace slackened as gravity began to exert its force on their mounts.

Soon, they were in the timber, but Clay was still urging Lucy on to keep that one-legged rider in sight. The heavier men and the more conservative riders who knew about the climb ahead were now stringing out behind. Clay tried to guide his horse around some low tree limbs, but she did not respond to the reins like a well-trained cow pony. Lucy now wanted to be out in front, and she took all the shortcuts, selecting the route that was best suited to it. Clay grabbed the saddle horn, then dodged from one side to the other of the mare's neck to miss getting killed. As he grazed his head on a big limb, Clay thought for a moment that he was gone.

The trail was now getting much steeper, and the pace slowed down even more. As Lucy slowed to a walk on the steep climb, Clay looked ahead for the one-legged rider, but he was out of sight. There were one or two others in front of him as they topped the first rise. Now, the dogs' howls had a new eager note for they had found the grizzly. However, they were far ahead of Clay and nearly out of hearing. On a level stretch, Clay urged Lucy once more into a rapid gallop and came upon a horseman who had stopped to listen. Away in the distance, they heard a dog's yelping in a voice that convinced them it had the bear stopped. Clay spurred his mount on alongside the nearest rider.

Finally, they met the one-legged cowpuncher with most of the dogs. He had sighted the fighting bear, but before he could pull his rifle from its scabbard under his knee, the brute had charged straight at his horse. As his mount whirled and got up to speed, the grizzly missed a swipe at its rump with a great paw. When the wrangler finally got his frightened mount turned, the bear was out of sight in a rocky, brushy canyon too rough for his horse to follow. This pack of dogs would hold the bear for a few minutes, but he always broke away and ran off. He was gone.

The dogs, after their seven mile run, were done for the day. They wanted water, and they needed it badly. After a few minutes' rest with all the riders and dogs accounted for, the group dropped into a deep, steep-sided canyon nearby where there was a good stream of water. The tired, hot dogs crawled into the water to cool off and then drink their fill. The horses were watered sparingly.

As they rode slowly back to the ranch, Clay talked with the one man who had seen the bear. It was, he maintained, a very large grizzly. He thought they needed to secure more fighting dogs to hold the bear once it was stopped. The hounds were very necessary to trail the brutes, but it took dogs with much more courage and fighting ability to hold these big fellows.

What a race they had undertaken – seven miles of run and now the return with tired out, sweaty horses. Clay was willing to recommend grizzly bear chasing on horseback as the best and most exciting American sport. But in the back of his mind, he still wanted revenge against that bear, or any bear, for what had happened to Carlos. He tucked that thought far away as he stabled Lucy.

Chapter 23

THE OLD PROSPECTOR

They left their wagon behind and took their supplies on the pack mules as they entered the Mogollon Mountains directly east of Alma. They worked the area around Willow Mountain, its peak at 10,780 feet. They continued south to the Black Mountain area, with a peak of 10,627 feet, and then pushed northeast to Turkeyfeather Mountain at 9,754 feet. They were covering a lot of new territory and collecting a very good set of specimens. They were hampered some by spring rains, but again, most of the stormy weather seemed to be ahead of them to the east and south.

The guidance from Vern and Art had paid off as their specimens, identifications, and catalogs greatly improved. Clay truly felt he was in the right place doing the right thing. He looked forward to every day that he spent in the mountains. They had all grown in their ability to work together as a team. Now, Vern was often deploying them in teams of two rather than three. Clay had grown close with Bob and appreciated their time riding and collecting together. Bob was one of the best readers of trails that Clay had ever seen, and he was sharpening this skill with Bob, who was always eager to share his knowledge.

Bob was from Illinois, just to the west of Clay's home state. The two of them had much in common when they talked about their homes, families, and childhoods. When their conversations turned to the topic of animal species, which was most often, they had yet to find a difference in the areas from which each of them had come. There was little geographic difference in the locales, so the similarities were to be expected. They both noted their awe of the discoveries they were making in the West.

Later in the spring, they made their way into the box canyon of the West Fork of the Gila River about forty-five miles above the Gila Hot Springs. The five hundred-feet deep canyon was steep-sided in the manner of a typical box canyon. In most parts of the canyon, the sides were so precipitous that there was no trail for miles where a man, horse, or burro could climb up or down. They were, however, able to find a good site for a camp in a wide area on the canyon bottom with good grass for the animals and plenty of water and wood for camp use. The water was plentiful from the spring rains and the snow melt from the higher elevations in the mountains.

One early evening, just about supper time, a traveler entered their camp, seemingly out of nowhere. Bob and Clay were cleaning up after preparing specimens when Bob nudged Clay in the side. "Hey, it looks like we're getting a visitor."

Clay lifted his head in the direction that Bob was looking. From the far end of their camp, down river, appeared a shadow of a man with two burros. All Clay could make out from the distance was the silhou-

ette of a stooped-over man leading the two pack animals. The silhou-
ette was small, wore a floppy hat, and had a very long beard.

Vern walked out to greet the stranger. They spoke momentarily,
then the two of them continued back to the main camp. Clay nearly
dropped his pipe at the sight before him. He was now able to more
clearly see the man. He was thin, yet appeared to be in good shape in
spite of his permanent stoop. He was an older man with gray hair and
beard. His clothes were quite tattered, indicating that he had been out
in the wilderness for some time. The load on his burros seemed to indicate that he was a prospector.

The man was warmly welcomed into the camp by Vern and Art.
After the old prospector took care of his animals, Vern brought the
man into camp and offered him something to eat. He eagerly accepted
the offer as he warily eyed the rest of the men sitting around the camp.
By all appearances, the man was what one might consider normal for
an old mountain prospector when observed from the waist down; otherwise, the old man hardly looked human.

His arms were crooked, and one side of his face was a terrible sight.
Try as he did, Clay could not keep his eyes off him. Clay felt his heart
pounding in his chest; momentarily, he was sure he was seeing the
ghost of Carlos. He could only imagine what Carlos might have looked
like had he survived and lived to become an old man. He recalled
Carlos' face as it was torn away by the bear, and could see that face replaced in this old prospector's face. Clay felt himself growing warm as
his eyes saw the old man turn into Carlos, and then back again. Clay
looked over at Bob to see if he too had witnessed the old man change.
Neither Bob nor anyone else seemed to have been startled by any such
phenomenon. Clay quickly realized it was his imagination running
away with him. After momentarily turning away from the old man, he
looked back at him.

The man's lower jaw had been broken in at least two places and
then healed in a crooked manner. Where his cheek bones should have
been, there were two huge, dark sunken scars. His nose was bent out of
shape, and there was a long scar and a sunken place across his temple

where it seemed part of his skull was missing. There were also some scars on his chin and throat. In spite of all this, he appeared fit and comfortable. Clay felt that he just had to know more about this man. He felt compelled to talk with him, almost to assure himself that this man was not Carlos.

When they had finished supper, Clay decided to begin a conversation and asked the old man if there were many bears in the Mogollons. The prospector replied, "There's still a good many here-abouts, though I hunt 'em all the time 'cause I got a grudge against all bears." The man's gruff tone matched the look in his sunken eyes. Any hint of contentment in the man quickly disappeared.

Clay felt that perhaps he should not have asked the old prospector any questions as he seemed to have stirred some unpleasant memories in the man. Deep down, however, Clay understood the man's feelings. He could not stop himself and kept right on putting questions at what he thought were the right places until he, at last, got the old man's story.

"Well, young man, it weren't far from this here very spot . . . up in the mountains . . . about twenty years ago." He had to work to get the words out of his mouth due to his injuries, and he spoke in a somewhat broken manner.

His eyes went to some far way place as he continued his story. "Ya see, I'd got tired of eatin' bacon and venison . . . so I fetched my double-barreled shotgun loaded with bird shot . . . and climbed up the mountain ridge fer some dusky grouse. I was sore lookin' forward to some fine tender breast meat." He paused and sipped some coffee from his tin cup. It was obviously a story he had told many times, but he told it as if it were his first telling of the tale.

He paused as he took a moment to enjoy a second sip of the hot coffee. "Say, this is mighty fine coffee you fellas have." He looked over his rapt audience, then he continued, "I bagged me a couple fine birds as it was nearin' sundown . . . like about now. I figured I needed to git myself back to camp afore dark set in full. I was nearly runnin' down a steep, narrow trail . . . lined on both sides with a thicket of tall oak brush.

"Well, I rounded a turn and entered an open space in the trail . . . there, ten feet away, comin' up the trail, was a mammoth male grizzly bear . . . That beast sure most thought I was attackin' . . . so it charged right fer me, rearin' onto its massive hind legs." The old man seemed to unknowingly do his best to stand straight to imitate the rising bear.

He slowly set down his coffee cup. His demeanor changed to display a seriousness and vengeance that also showed in the tone of his voice. "As that creature reared over me, I had me just enough time to unload both barrels of that shotgun into the brute's throat . . . That bear was takin' a swipe at me with his paw as I fired . . . I couldn't dodge that blow." He paused as if he were reliving that bear's attack; his face grimaced ever so slightly.

"The full mass of that bear was behind his strike . . . That one slap broke both my arms and caved in my ribs." He lifted his crooked arms and then motioned toward his lower chest, but he kept his eyes on the men.

"That bear followed with his jaws . . . I could plainly hear the snappin' and crunchin' of my own bones as that beast's jaws covered my face . . . I felt a second hit to my head . . . and then I was out." His entire body seemed to relax as he paused long enough that Clay wanted to pull the words from the old man's mouth.

"I come to my senses, but had no idea of how long I'd been out . . . I was covered with blood. The body of that dead bear had me pinned flat down to the ground . . . I could barely move. After what seemed to be hours of struggle, I wriggled my way free of the gigantic carcass.

"That bear was killt, but he'd nearly done me in . . . I somehow walked, crawled, and rolled downhill back to my camp . . . I managed to crawl into my bedroll, more nearer dead than alive . . . I passed out agin.

"Lucky for me, two cowpokes come by the next mornin' . . . They tied me on a horse, and after two days of agony, we reached the railroad and a doctor . . . That doc dressed my wounds and set my broken bones as best he could . . . I stayed there with the doc fer a few days until he placed me on a train bound for Kansas City." He seemed to be growing tired. Clay wasn't sure if he was physically tired, or tired of telling his tale. While he had been standing, he now very slowly sat down.

The old man picked up his coffee cup and took a long drink. Clay was not sure if he was done with his story, or just taking a break. There was nothing in his eyes or face to indicate what, if anything, was next. Clay felt himself wanting revenge for this man and for Carlos. He wanted those bears dead.

They all waited, and Clay was ready to ask a question about that revenge when the old man picked up his story. "I had family back in Kansas City, and they had the money to get a surgeon to take a look at me . . . The best surgeons did all they could . . . I was lucky to be a young man of robust constitution and in good physical condition . . . I was able to survive what would have killt many a man." He seemed proud to have survived what Clay thought surely would have killed many others, just as Carlos had been killed.

"After my final recovery back home in Kansas City, I took a look in a mirror. Yes, you all are seein' what I saw ... but inside that grotesque mask was me, James Moore . . . I was in there but no longer visible." There was now a sadness about him, and Clay felt the need for revenge more than ever.

He lifted his head, and the sadness disappeared. There was actually a hint of a smile in his misshapen face. "I knew then and there that I couldn't live among friends and relatives in civilization . . . so back I went to prospectin' in these mountains . . . prospectin' and bear killin'."

Now, twenty years later, he was still hunting bear. He continued to work out his revenge.

His story made a profound impression on Clay. He thought of Carlos the entire time that the old prospector was telling his story. The tale had sent chills down Clay's spine, and he had felt that need for revenge. He had to reach deep down inside to bring himself back to reality and to recall the talk with Sister Anne about letting go of the past, forgetting about revenge, and moving along with his own life and dreams.

It was a restless sleep for Clay that night. He thought deeply about James Moore living a life filled with revenge. He thought about the man's hurt and anger and reclusive life. It was not the life Clay wanted. He resolved to be done with the idea of revenge for Carlos' death. He woke in the morning with a renewed sense of the goodness of life. He wanted to say a few words to the old man, but he was gone.

Chapter 24

RIVER RESCUE

The winter had been long and steady, but not really overwhelming to the team in their continued survey through the cold. The spring felt refreshing to all of the men, and spirits seemed to rise as they continued along the West Fork of the Gila River studying all of the surrounding area.

It was now late spring as they entered the final deep canyon area about twenty-five miles above Gila Hot Springs. Melting snow and spring rains made the travel a little more difficult as the level of the river seemed to rise on a daily basis. Vern made sure that the men were always aware of the nearest exit out of the canyon should the water make a sudden rise. Rains to the northeast that might not even be seen from their location could result in a flash flood with little notice.

They spent a good number of days gathering specimens in the easier areas of access to the south of the river as well as trekking up some of the side canyons to the higher elevations to the north. Their mammal collection grew quickly as the spring brought forth life in all forms. The group was now performing at peak levels partly because of their work together over the past months, and partly because of the refreshing spring weather.

It was a clear day when Clay and Bob were told to make an advance search into the deepest part of the canyon as it meandered easterly. Not expecting to be gone more than a few days, they gathered minimal supplies taking only the horses they rode.

The canyon walls remained steep, but they were not as tall as they had been near camp. The ride was slow through the cold spring water that covered the rocky bottom. The river made a winding course through the canyon before reaching a long open stretch. As they came to the end of the open stretch, the canyon walls once again grew taller. Clay estimated the cliffs to be about eight hundred feet in height.

The river once again began to wind its way through the canyon. The pair rounded a nearly vertical canyon wall to the north and came upon a beach to the south that made a slow rise into the hills before taking a steeper rise. It looked like a good place to stop for some lunch before proceeding further into the steep-walled canyon.

They made their way up to a small rise before stopping and setting the animals free to help themselves to the small green shoots of new grass. While eating, they studied the next stretch of the canyon that headed toward a tight bend. There seemed to be a broad side canyon that they both agreed would make a good area to study.

As it was still early in the day, the two decided to take some time and head up into that side canyon on foot. They also decided to make their present location their camp for the night. So, before continuing down the river, they set up their tent and hobbled the horses. From this site, the head of the side canyon was less than a mile away. It would be an easy hike for the two, and they planned to carry minimal equipment with them, mostly some small traps.

As they neared the bend in the river, they noticed a cave opening about thirty feet above the river. They were aware that early Indian tribes had used the caves in these mountains in the past, and so the two men decided to explore the cave.

The way to the cave was steep, but there were footholds along a route up to the opening that seemed to have been man-made rather than any type of natural formation. They easily climbed the canyon side up to the cave entrance.

Standing at the cave opening, Clay noted the strategic nature of this location, "This is an incredible location for anyone seeking an advantage over an approaching enemy." His eyes scanned the area before them from the southwest to the southeast.

To their southeast, they could easily see around the bend in the river. To their southwest, they had a clear view of the area they had just traveled. Bob pointed to the location of their camp. "If they had any crops where our camp is located, they could have easily watched over that area. This is a really nice secure location."

Bob was already busily making notes about the area and drawing a rough map. Clay looked at the area of the immediate entrance of the cave. The ceiling was blackened from the obvious fires made in the cave dwelling. The walls seemed bare of any drawings or carvings which Clay had hoped to observe. The floor of the cave was also bare and covered with a layer of fine sand.

Bob completed making his notes and turned to Clay, "Well, let's see what's in here!"

Both men were eager to explore the cave. It was obvious that no one had used this cave in any recent time. There were no traces of activity near the entrance. Further in, however, they found evidence of a fire pit, now mostly filled with the same fine sand that was found near the cave entrance. Under several inches of sand, they found evidence that fires had been built here at one time.

The cave was not more than about fifty feet deep with the ceiling quickly lowering from about thirty feet in toward the rear of the cave. There was enough light from the entrance of the cave that their eyes easily adjusted to the dim light. They explored the walls of the cave and found some faded pictographs on the walls, mostly in one small area. Bob opened his notebook and began making drawings of the pictographs along with some notes.

Clay, in the meantime, visited every corner of the cave searching for any other access points. Near the back of the cave, Clay crawled on his stomach to the farthest reaches of the cave, but he did not find any other openings.

It was while on his stomach at the back of the cave that Clay heard a low rumbling sound. He was puzzled by the sound as it seemed to emanate from the very back of the cave. He listened carefully trying to determine the source of the rumble. He looked back at Bob who was still sketching in his notebook and did not seem to hear the rumble.

Clay backed himself out of the lowest, deepest part of the cave, and as he did so, the sound seemed to disappear. He made his way out to where he could stand fully and listened carefully. "Hey, Bob, do you hear a sort of rumbling sound?"

Bob stopped sketching and turned his head slightly. He stared far deep into the cave as if he might see the source of the sound. After a brief time, he looked back at Clay. "Not sure. I might." He then went back to sketching, and Clay continued studying the cave walls.

Moments later, Bob perked up, "Yeah, I do hear something."

The two men strode to the cave opening. Outside, there was a definite rumbling in the canyon.

"Clay, we've got to get back to our camp . . . and quick! That's the roar of the river! I think a flash flood is headed our way!"

They quickly exited the cave and made their way down the footholds to the river's edge.

"How much time do you figure we have?" Clay was concerned, but he was not panicked. *If we can get to the camp, surely we'll be above any flood waters.* Clay was hopeful, but his concern was growing.

"It's hard to tell, but I think we should have enough time to get back to camp." He cocked his head again to listen. "These darn canyon walls make it difficult to follow the sound. Let's not waste any time."

They scrambled along the north side of the river where the footing was easy. But, they realized that the tracks they had left on their way to the cave were already covered, and the water was rising at an incredibly fast rate. They neared the area where they had previously crossed the river. It was now flowing quickly and the water was waist deep and rising.

"Clay, we have to cross now! There's no looking for any place better!"

The two men plunged into the cold water which was becoming a muddy cauldron. Suddenly, from around the bend to the west came a wall of muddy water that was well over ten feet high. The two braced themselves as best as they could as they were pounded into the river by the powerful wall of murky water.

Thrown under the water, Clay was not sure which way was up. He swirled in a mass of confusion trying to right himself. He finally felt his feet strike the rocky bottom. As he did so, he manged to push himself away from what he hoped was the bottom of the river.

The water pressed against his chest, but he felt sure he was rising. *Where's the surface?!* How far under was he? He could not see anything and had no reference. Then, his head burst above the water, and he saw the sun above. He sucked in all the air that he could as he was pulled along down the river. He tried to get his bearings, but he could not find anything familiar.

Bob! Where's Bob?! He scanned the surface as fast as he could looking for any sign of Bob. Then he felt himself being sucked under the water. He fought against the current and again made his way to the surface. Unfortunately, he did not see that he was heading toward an outcropping of rock. He hit a boulder with his right shoulder, was thrown to his left, and again he was pulled beneath the surface.

He had not had time to grab a breath and felt like he was drowning. Now, he was panicked. He kicked his feet with all his might and popped up for the third time. Grabbing a quick breath he scanned about searching again for Bob, but also for the nearest shoreline. Farther ahead was another curve in the river, and he could see a small side canyon where there appeared to be a shore. He made every effort to fight the current and pull himself in that direction. The pain in his shoulder was enormous, but he knew he had to overcome it if he was to survive.

It was then that he saw Bob's head in the water not too far ahead. Bob was not headed to the shore, and he did not appear to be taking any action. Clay used every bit of power in an attempt to get to Bob. The pain in his shoulder was excruciating.

"Bob!" he called out. But the roar of the water was deafening, and he knew he was wasting his effort by calling out. He had to reach Bob before they passed the shoreline.

An experience from his early youth flashed into Clay's mind. He had been swimming in a pond with a childhood friend, Ed Taylor, when his friend went under the surface and did not come up. At first, Clay thought Ed was playing. When Ed's head bobbed to the surface, Clay laughed and called out. Ed raised an arm but disappeared a second time. Clay waited momentarily to see what Ed would do next, but he did not reappear. Clay puzzled another moment before swimming with all of his strength to the location in the pond where Ed had gone under.

Arriving at the location, Clay dove beneath the surface to look for Ed. He looked in every direction, but he did not see Ed. Running out of air, Clay surfaced, took a quick deep breath and dove again. This time he went deeper. Looking to his left he saw his friend in the weeds at the bottom of the pond. Clay grabbed Ed by his arm and pulled him to the surface.

Clay quickly dragged Ed onto the shore of the pond and rolled him over on his stomach. Clay's father knew that Clay and his friend spent a lot of time at the pond near their home as well as in the river at his grandfather's house. He taught Clay how to force the water out of someone's lungs in the event of a drowning.

Clay pressed with all his weight on Ed's back until he saw water come gushing from his mouth. Ed sputtered, coughed, and finally began breathing. He raised his head and began to cry. Clay cried with him.

Clay only hoped he would have the opportunity to provide life-saving help for Bob. *Bob, be strong! I'm coming!* He reached Bob as they continued down river. He grabbed Bob as best as he could with his injured right arm. He would need his left arm to pull the two of them to shore.

They bounced up and down in the rapids of the water while being pummeled by branches and shrubs carried along by the current. Clay fought the pain to retain his hold on Bob. He pulled with his left arm and kicked with his feet toward the shore that was quickly approaching. Clay spotted a downed tree and hoped he could reach it before passing the shoreline.

He thought they were moving down the river far too fast. *I've got to get to that tree!* He put his head down and gathered every last bit of strength he had left and pulled to the tree. They reached the top of the tree where there were just enough branches to stop their downstream race.

Clay struggled, working his way to the trunk of the tree, and finally to the shore. He pulled Bob to dry ground with his left arm, rolled him onto his stomach and dropped his entire body weight onto Bob's back. Nothing. Clay lifted himself and again dropped onto Bob's back. This time there was an expulsion of dark water from Bob's mouth and nose. *Good!*

"Come on, Bob, breathe!" Clay pushed and pounded on Bob's back several more times with his left hand to be sure all the water was out of his lungs. Nothing. He tried twice again, and Bob coughed, followed by a deep gasp of air. He breathed deeply and coughed several more times before regaining some awareness of his surroundings. Bob panicked for a moment, "What's going on?! Clay!"

Clay was quick to reassure him, "It's okay, Bob. You're fine. You're out of the water and safe. You need to take some deep breaths and cough up any more water from your lungs." He gave Bob a comforting and encouraging look. "You'll be fine. We're fine."

The water continued to roar past them having reached its crest. Clay looked out to the river and wondered just how far they had come. Realizing what he had just been through, Clay rolled over on his back and looked up at the clear blue sky. He laughed; then he cried. *Thank you, God.*

Chapter 25

THE QUESTION

Their expedition ended by mid-summer as they reached Silver City. Clay's dislocated shoulder had been put back into place by Vern and healed quickly allowing Clay to continue working. With specimens packed and shipped, they went to the hotel for a well-deserved rest and for much-welcomed hot baths.

The next morning, Vern told Clay that he needed to speak with him alone. Clay was unsure what Vern wanted to discuss, but he assumed it might be about his next assignment, something Clay was eagerly anticipating. After meeting in the hotel lobby, they walked together down to the stable to check on the horses.

"Clay, your skills as a field collector were good going in to our expedition. But, good is not what Hart is interested in." Vern, as usual, referred to Dr. Merriam in his familiar name of Hart. Clay, however, had a high regard for the man, and he had difficulty calling him anything other than Dr. Merriam. Vern continued as he noticed Clay's shoulders slump ever so slightly. "Art and me spent a lot of time with the three of you boys. We pushed you hard to make you better field collectors. We pushed, but it was up to you boys to put in the time and effort to make yourselves the type of men that Hart would be proud to call his own."

Clay was feeling a bit uncomfortable by now. He thought he had done everything required and more. Was Vern about to let him go, to tell him that he didn't measure up to expectations? Clay got a lump in his throat. He wanted to speak, but he waited for Vern to continue.

"Clay, I've had my eye on you. You've got a keen sense for this work, you work well with the team, and you certainly hold your own as an individual. Your work met – no, exceeded – the expectations that Hart and I were hoping it would."

Clay's slumping shoulders now lifted. His eyes moved up to Vern with a hint of a smile in them. "Are you saying that I can continue working for the Survey?"

Vern was now smiling. "Clay, you're the type of individual that Hart is looking for. However, there is one area that Hart feels you're lacking. While your records, notes, and catalog entries are as good as any at this point, Hart – and I must agree with him – feels you need additional formal education. We want you to have a better understanding of species identification and placement, of anatomy and geography, of geology, and of languages. While your catalogs are fine, you need to be able to write so that you can publish." He paused to let this sink in a bit, as well as to observe Clay's reaction at this point.

"Well, I don't even know where to begin with what you're talking about. I never quite finished high school. I read whatever I can, for example, Dr. Merriam's Life Zones paper. I try to soak in as much knowledge as I can from you and Art." Clay was confused as to where this was all going. He felt himself struggling to explain himself.

Vern noted the puzzled look on Clay's face. In as positive a manner as he could, Vern responded, "Clay, Hart wants you to get a college education. It'll round you out as a naturalist and place you in a position to lead your own team one day. Hart has a lot of confidence in you, and so do I."

"What does this mean as far as collecting? How do I go to school and . . . where do I go to school? How do I get in? I don't even know where to start." The questions came rapidly from Clay. He had mixed emotions at this point. He felt good about the assessment of his skills, but he was unsure about college.

Vern did his best to place Clay at ease. "That's where we'll help you out, Clay." Vern could see the concern on Clay's face, and wanted to quickly layout the plan. "There's a school not far from here in Las Cruces. It's the New Mexico College of Agriculture and Mechanic Arts. There's a Professor Cockerell there, Theodore Cockerell, who is willing to work with you and get you into the school. They offer college preparatory classes that'll transition you from your current education level into the college level. It's a perfect plan for someone like you!" Vern smiled brightly at Clay.

Clay was sure of his abilities as a field collector and naturalist. He felt he had proven himself on this trip. On the other hand, he was not sure of his ability to go to college. He saw college students as gentlemen in every sense of the word, but he looked at himself as a simple man without the mannerly ways to be a college man. "Vern, I don't know that I have what it takes to go to college. I like being in the field working as a collector. It's what I believe I have the skills and ability to do. How would a person like me fit in at college?" Clay showed a lack of self-confidence in both his words and his tone.

"Clay, trust me, you have what it takes. You're a smart kid who can adapt well to any situation. You've proven that. Clay, you can do this. It's what Hart is expecting of you." He paused, pondering what to say next. His face grew serious as he stopped and looked Clay squarely in the eyes. "You need to decide on this, Clay. It's an opportunity that'll not come 'round again. If you don't do this now, you never will. And, if you don't do this now, you'll likely not continue as a field collector for Hart."

Clay felt his face turn pale and his demeanor turned to a serious concern. "I understand, Vern."

"Clay, I need an answer by tomorrow. We can't wait. You know I have your best interests at heart. I wouldn't steer you wrong. This is the best thing for you, and if you see this through, it'll open up new vistas for you. Trust me."

Clay had a restless night. He had not written many letters to his family, but he wished he could talk to his father right now. He thought about what his father might say, and then he thought about his grandfather. Both men had such a tremendous influence on him. His grandfather had been his introduction into his interest in nature. His father had encouraged his work from a scientific perspective. That balance had helped place him in his current position. He was thankful for both of them. So, he listened to their voices in his mind. He eventually drifted off to sleep, deep in his thoughts, without arriving at an answer for Vern.

Clay fell into a dream. He had walked to his grandfather's farm south of town where the two of them were fishing on the bank of a pond fed by the Kankakee River. They were catching plenty of fish, more than enough for the two of them and a couple of Clay's cousins who lived nearby. Clay would throw in his line and immediately pull a fish out of the water.

In the dream, his grandfather spoke to him, "Clay, I still remember the first time you tried to fish with me. It was all you could do to lift your pole. The few nibbles you did have merely stole your worms."

Clay remembered the branch his grandfather had cut for him to use as a fishing pole. His grandfather had set up everything for him, and Clay baited the hook. He was excited about catching his first fish. Clay was now that little boy sitting on the pond shore with his grandfather.

After an hour of not catching anything, Clay was discouraged and asked his grandfather to catch a fish for him. He wanted a fish out of that pond. He looked seriously and longingly toward the man who meant so much to him. "Grampa, can you catch a fish for me? I can't do it." He moved the branch that held his line toward his grandfather.

"Sure, I could, Clay. But, what if I'm not around? What if you're on your own? Who's gonna catch a fish for you then?" He smiled and let Clay think about this for a moment.

Clay again looked longingly at his grandfather, but also a bit puzzled. "Well, I just want a fish now. You know how to do it. I can't."

"Clay, do you like sitting here with me fishing?"

He looked up at his grandfather with great respect. "Yes."

"But, you think you'd like it more if you could catch a fish? Would that make you happy?"

"Sure, but I can't do it." There was a bit of frustration in his voice.

His grandfather continued, "Well, if I catch a fish for you, then you won't have the joy of catching the fish yourself." He paused. "And, if I continue to catch the fish for you, then you'll never know how to catch a fish, will you?"

"No. Well, I mean, I just want one today. Then you can teach me next time." Clay felt he had made his point, and his grandfather would now comply with his request.

"Clay, I could catch a fish for you, and you'd smile at me and say 'thank you,' I'm sure. You'd be happy." He smiled brightly at Clay. "But, as I said a moment ago, what about next time? Or, what if I'm not around. You will again be unhappy at not being able to catch a fish." He saw that he had Clay's attention but that Clay was still hoping for a fish from his grandfather. "How would you feel if you caught your own fish . . . right now?"

"I'd be excited!" Clay's face brightened at the thought.

"And, would you say that you would be more than happy?"

"What do you mean?" Clay was puzzled. He'd be happy; he'd be very happy.

"Clay, there's something beyond happiness that is called joy. Both give us wonderful feelings." He searched deeply for the right words to say to the young boy. "You see, happiness is dependent upon things we do or places we go. It's based on those things that are happening around us. Here we are sitting at the pond, and it would make you happy to have a fish." He saw that Clay was listening intently, so he continued. "That would be a happy event. Joy, however, is something that is within our hearts." His grandfather placed his hand on Clay's chest. "Joy remains with us; whereas, a happy experience can be gone as soon as we forget about it. So, you may be happy now if I catch a fish for you, but tomorrow it won't mean much to you."

Clay was still listening intently to his grandfather. He had great respect for the man, and he knew he was being taught a valuable lesson. He wanted so much to fully understand what his grandfather was telling him.

"Now, think for a moment. What if I taught you how to fish so that you could come to this pond whenever you wanted and catch fish? You have learned to do something that remains with you. You have accomplished something. You have grown. You have a skill that cannot be unlearned. That would give you joy!"

Clay had a puzzled look, but it was a different sort of puzzlement. He wanted that good feeling within him that he could have by learning and accomplishing. He placed his hand over his heart. He was pretty sure he understood what his grandfather was telling him. Yes, he could have a happy moment if his grandfather caught a fish for him, but he wanted to learn to do it himself. He wanted to learn. He needed to learn!

"Come over here. Now, let's get a fresh worm on your hook." As he watched Clay place a worm on the hook, he continued, "Clay, see the shaded area under the tree near the shore . . ."

Clay awoke with a start, feeling like he had slept too late and missed giving Vern an answer. He located his pocket watch and realized it was not too late. He sat up in bed, rubbed his face, and decided then and there what he would do. Not only his parents and grandparents, but also several of his teachers had been good influences on Clay. Look-ing back, he recalled his teachers discussing his future and the possibili-ties he had before him. Education was key, both formal and informal. Clay decided he would go to college.

1896

Chapter 26

THE COLLEGE YEARS

Having written a letter of thanks to Dr. Merriam, and having given his thanks to Vern, and having said his goodbyes, Clay packed his belongings on Lucy and headed southwest. He planned to travel through Deming and then east to the college at Las Cruces.

He had considered taking the train, but he did not want to give up Lucy, and he could not afford to transport her on the train. And, he decided, it would only take another day or so compared to the train after considering the train schedules along the route to get to Las Cruces.

Further, he had talked with Vern about his ability to continue to do some field work while at school. Apparently, Professor Cockerell placed great importance on field work, and Lucy would provide him the freedom to explore at his own pace and inclination.

Vern had made all the arrangements for Clay to meet with Professor Cockerell. He had actually done this before Clay had given him his final answer. Vern told Clay afterward that he would have hog-tied Clay and delivered him personally to Professor Cockerell if that's what it took. They enjoyed a good laugh together about this.

Vern shared some background about Professor Cockerell with Clay. Born in England, Professor Cockerell was an experienced biologist, entomologist, and paleontologist who had already written countless papers on the subjects. As with many naturalists, Professor Cockerell had become interested in the studies of natural science at a young age and had actually written his first paper at the age of twelve. He was likely greatly influenced by his father, who was also a naturalist.

Vern further shared that, like Clay, Professor Cockerell had also had a bout with consumption. After a short time in Jamaica, Professor Cockerell moved to Las Cruces where he became a teacher in his areas of expertise. Vern explained to Clay that Professor Cockerell held the personal position that while formal classroom teaching was important, actual field work was critical to the learning process. He assured Clay that he would likely have plenty of time field collecting while at the college.

Vern's review of Professor Cockerell's background provided Clay with a good state of mind about attending college. The fact that Vern had personally made the arrangements for Clay to meet directly with Professor Cockerell when he arrived in Las Cruces lifted Clay's confidence. He was now truly looking forward to school.

At their first meeting, Clay found Professor Cockerell to be a warm and engaging gentleman. He showed a true interest in Clay's background and noted that, based upon Vern's comments and Clay's experience, Clay should do very well at the college. He encouraged Clay to become engaged in the many facets of college life, as every experience would add to his development as a well-rounded gentleman and professional. He explained his thoughts about immersing oneself deeply into every aspect of life. He felt there was more to be learned through experience than in classroom study. Clay was pleased to hear that sentiment.

Professor Cockerell also told Clay that to be the professional naturalist that he was going to be, he would need to be published. In order to achieve this, Clay would need to be focused in his studies, especially with languages and writing. The professor noted that he had helped several students publish papers, and he looked forward to doing the same with Clay. The recommendations from Vern and Dr. Merriam had set high expectations for Clay.

Clay settled into a small, two-room adobe dwelling in the old Mexican village of Mesilla just two miles from the college. Each of the dirt-floored rooms had a small fireplace in the corner, ideal for heating and cooking. There was a bed in one room and a small table with two chairs in the other. Small recesses in the walls accommodated the few dishes and utensils for cooking and eating.

Clay fell into a routine for his daily meals. After soaking beans overnight, Clay kept them cooking in a clay pot while he attended to his day. Returning to his rooms at the end of the day, his beans were ready to eat. He had a modest diet of oatmeal and brown beans, a diet that, while becoming monotonous, was nutritious. Of course as time allowed, he supplemented this meager diet with fresh meat from an occasional hunt.

Clay made good use of his trek to the college and back each day as he placed traps and captured specimens that he would prepare back in his small room. Clay was able to sell his specimens and used this as a means to supplement his college expenses.

Professor Cockerell was already helping Clay find current literature on his specimens, and Clay was soaking up every bit of knowledge presented to him. On one occasion, he prepared a weasel skin and presented it to Professor Cockerell who told Clay it appeared to be a new species. The professor suggested that Clay prepare a paper and name the new species. When Clay confessed his ignorance of this process, Professor Cockerell immediately proposed that they work on the project together. Clay was delighted.

The professor helped Clay find all the current literature on weasels and prepare a proper description according to current scientific methods. The paper was nearly complete when Professor Cockerell told Clay that since his own field of expertise was entomology, Clay's name should appear first in the paper they were completing. The following year, the finding was published in the *Proceedings of the Academy of Natural Sciences of Philadelphia*.

Professor Cockerell's interest in mentoring Clay continued, and the two of them went on many collecting trips together. Clay was learning something new nearly every day. His interests in natural history were broadening. He was witnessing the value of his school work as it applied directly to his field collecting trips with the professor. While Professor Cockerell's area of expertise was entomology, he seemed to be able to teach on nearly every facet of nature. Clay was finding himself especially drawn to the field of paleontology.

At the encouragement of Professor Cockerell, Clay started a local science club open to anyone, college student or not, in the local community. Using the science club, Clay published articles in the school newspaper that were of interest to local farmers as well as students. His study of hawks showed his growth as a natural scientist expressing a concern about the balance of nature and man's role in preserving that balance. He enjoyed his time in these various ventures, but he still spent most of his time focused on his field collecting projects.

Clay took the professor's advice and deliberately exposed himself to many facets of the college lifestyle. He had played football in high school and so joined the college team. He seemed more knowledgeable of the game than most of the other players, and so he also became coach of the team for the remainder of his time at school. In the first year, the team, under Clay's direction as coach, went undefeated. It was a feat that Clay would repeat the following years as the team went on to become the territorial champions.

As he continued to bloom as a college student, Clay joined the college's Columbian Literary Society. Here he participated in debates, most typically on subjects related to the understanding, or misunderstanding, of certain animal species. He never lost a debate during this time. Additionally, the society afforded him the opportunity to improve his social skills, a real need for Clay after spending as much time as he had in the mountains. Others in the society found Clay comfortable to be around and a valued friend with a quick wit.

The few female students at the college were quite taken with the young football hero with wavy black hair and his ability to speak with clarity on a growing number of subjects.

Clay was finding himself blooming in his romantic life as a result. While Clay maintained a camaraderie among the male students, he remained somewhat aloof around the opposite sex. To some of the women, this just made Clay all the more interesting and attractive. He did manage to develop a few good female relationships, including one with the daughter of a local judge that was becoming serious as Clay neared completion of his third year at the college.

Her name was Katherine. She was a pleasant looking girl, not beautiful, but charming in her demeanor. She was more refined than Clay, a quality that was not lost on Clay. He always felt a bit of awkwardness around her due to his own lack of refinement.

While she enjoyed listening to Clay talk of his collecting activities, she did not express any particular interest in his field work. She showed more interest in his school exploits, especially his talents on the football team. She had also encouraged Clay to become a member of the Columbian Literary Society, and even convinced him to take part in a college theater production.

Clay enjoyed their talks together and found spending time at the judge's home a nice change from his two-room adobe hut. To Clay, it seemed that the judge neither liked nor disliked him. He was a difficult man to read, but he seemed very supportive of any of his daughter's interests and activities.

Clay enjoyed evening walks with Katherine, and he eventually worked up the courage to kiss her. It was his first real emotional attachment with a female since his relationship with Analena. He found himself comparing the two girls, an action that made him feel guilty. What he was not admitting to himself was that he preferred the companionship of Analena, and her kisses had felt warmer to Clay.

In his field work, Clay developed a friendship with the individual in charge of the Agricultural Experiment Station at Las Cruces, Charles Townsend. The Agricultural Experiment Station was affiliated with the college but funded by the United States Department of Agriculture. Its purpose was to work with local farmers and ranchers and look for ways to improve their production by studying the influence of plants, mammals, and insects on the environment.

Townsend was known for his own study of insects. He had made a name for himself in the field and was working for the Bureau of Entomology in Washington before accepting a teaching position at the New Mexico College of Agriculture and Mechanic Arts. He had spent a short time in Jamaica and published extensively before returning to Las Cruces where he first worked at the Agricultural Experiment Station. Townsend had also made a number of collecting expeditions in the West, including one to the Grand Canyon.

Townsend and Clay became good friends and went on many collecting trips together. Clay's time in the field greatly increased over the next couple of years. Some of their collecting trips extended into the school year, but Clay managed to keep up with his studies. Many of Clay's early expeditions were in areas not far from Las Cruces and Mesilla – the Organ Mountains to the east, the Sierra De Las Uvas Mountains to the northwest, and El Paso, Texas, to the south.

More time was afforded for extended expeditions during those periods when school was not in session. Clay and Townsend were ranging farther from Las Cruces and managed expeditions to Bernalillo (just north of Albuquerque), Domingo Baca Canyon (east of Albuquerque), the Guadalupe Mountains on the Texas border, and the Sacramento Mountains to the northeast. With more experience and developing skills and interests, they ranged into the northern part of Chihuahua, Mexico, the Sierra Madre Mountains in Chihuahua, and to the Mormon settlement of Colonia Garcia.

The two worked together well, seeming to understand what the other was thinking as they made their way into some little-traveled areas. The pair was also publishing their findings in such publications as the *Botanical Gazette, Proceedings of the American Academy of Arts and Sciences*, and *Proceedings of the Biological Society of Washington*.

Despite the assistance from both Cockerell and Townsend, the process of publishing was not Clay's favorite activity. In fact, several times he told Townsend, "Why don't you just go ahead and write this up under your name?"

Townsend's position required him to publish. There was no such expectation of Clay since he was a student. Both Cockerell and Townsend let Clay know, however, that he needed the experience for his development as a professional. So, for the most part, Clay begrudgingly obliged.

Clay was finding Townsend to be a good friend, one he could talk to about his romantic endeavors with the judge's daughter. Being thirteen years older than Clay and married, Townsend was able to provide some very realistic advice for Clay regarding relationships with the finer sex. Clay felt he was getting the type of advice that he might have gotten from his father. He shared this thought with Townsend who, while pleased, jokingly admonished Clay for thinking of him as a man as old as his father.

Indeed, all seemed to be going quite well for Clay, until he became increasingly ill with typhoid fever and an acute infection, which the doctor called erysipelas, which caused a severe rash to cover Clay's body. He maintained a fever and was fatigued to the point where he could hardly get out of bed. His health problems put him down for a number of weeks. Fortunately, his fear that he had once again contracted consumption was eventually laid to rest. After a long and slow recovery, he thought of nothing better than a collecting trip into the mountains to bring him back to good health.

He and some friends prepared for a trip into the Sacramento Mountains with a plan to trap beaver. They camped in the mountains and valleys where the local Mexican farmers were appreciative of their work, as the beaver population was destroying their corn crops in the valley. The streams in the mountains were clear and cold, and the water had a good flavor that made Clay feel better.

The beaver trapping was every bit as good as anticipated, and Clay had a number of large skins to get ready. The size of his collection required a heavy base of arsenic and alum to prepare and preserve his specimens. As a result of his exposure to such large quantities of arsenic, Clay was hit with a bad case of arsenic poisoning. The poisoning caused a mass of red blotches and white-capped pustules to appear on his face. This was not the first time Clay had been a victim of arsenic poisoning, and he knew that when he quit using the powder for a few days, he would recover.

Clay returned to school for the fall semester feeling fully recovered from his illnesses. He felt his time in the Sacramento Mountains had been wonderful for him. When he returned to his studies; however, he found that he was having trouble with his eyes. He was unable to read as this caused his eyes to become irritated to the point of tears running down his face. He simply could not study.

Assuming he needed glasses, Clay consulted a local doctor. Unfortunately, Clay was told that glasses would not give him any relief. His eyes had been weakened by his bout with typhoid fever, and Clay would need to drop his studies and rest his eyes. The doctor advised Clay that, with time, his eyes should improve.

Realizing there was no quick fix for his ailment, Clay reluctantly left school. In the final months of his fourth year of college, Clay was just short of achieving a college degree, still an amateur in the world of the natural sciences.

1900

Chapter 27

SOLITUDE IN THE MOUNTAINS

Feeling a bit sorry for himself, Clay decided to head back to the Sierra Blanca Mountains above Ruidoso. He had been in that area on one of his expeditions, and he recalled the Sierra Blanca Peak as an area that was comforting. Something about it felt familiar and welcoming, and he had spent some time thinking of his family while spending a night under the stars at the 11,000-foot peak. It seemed to be a good place to ponder and wonder.

The route to the mountains took Clay through the Mescalero Apache Indian Reservation. His brief stop there once again made him aware of the pride of these people. But, at the same time, the elders were losing their way of life to the growing number of younger members of the tribe who were less interested in the old traditions and ways. Maybe Clay felt as many of these people did – conflicted about the tradition of the old ways and the development of the more modern ways. For example, the work he was doing in studying the beaver population was helpful to the tribe in increasing the bounty of the corn crop. The younger men were very interested in this work, but the elders were always suspicious of outsiders telling them to change their long-held methods of agriculture.

Clay did his best to convince the elders of the advantages of what he was showing them. Past experience with white men, however, had left them wary and unwilling to change. He hoped that, over time, the younger men would be able to prove to the elders the benefits of change. However, Clay was also aware that more of the younger generation were attempting to leave the life on the reservation. Clay was saddened by the perceived loss of tradition of the native peoples.

Leaving the reservation, Clay made his way north until he came to the south fork of Rio Ruidoso. He was not concerned with taking the shortest or easiest route to his destination. He simply wanted to be away and alone with his thoughts. He had Lucy with him and one pack burro for his trek. He was not even sure how long he would be in the mountains. He knew his eyes needed to heal, but he felt he needed healing in other ways as well.

He needed to understand who he was at his core. Sister Anne had helped Clay look into his relationship with God. But, he was unsure of how that relationship was progressing, or more specifically, how it was not progressing. Sister Anne had instilled in him a concern for his soul, and he wondered how much he needed healing in this regard. How could he develop a closer relationship with God? He was not even sure that he understood what that meant.

While he had done well at school, he felt like he was failing those who had placed a confidence in his abilities to excel as a student of the natural sciences. Clay looked up to Dr. Merriam, Vern, Cockerell, and

Townsend; he did not want to let them down. He realized that in let-ting them down, he would also be letting himself down.

At the same time, Clay felt good about the knowledge he had gained in his studies at college. He knew that, in spite of the fact that he did not get a college degree, he had developed and matured as an in-dividual through his class studies and his school activities. He saw the value of his education in pursuing his work in the natural sciences.

Further, Clay was encouraged by the development of his social skills. This had provided him with a renewed confidence in managing his future path in the natural sciences. Unfortunately, he had also made the decision that, for now, his career interests would take precedence over his romantic interests. He broke off his relationship with Kather-ine before leaving school. He found it not to be as difficult as he had expected. They enjoyed each other's company and good talks together, but neither ever really expressed a long-term romantic ambition. They parted ways on good terms with best wishes to one another for their fu-ture endeavors.

Clay couldn't help but wonder if he would ever stop thinking of Analena, however. Would he compare every woman to her for the rest of his life? Was there even someone out there for him, or would he be-come some reclusive mountain man like James Moore?

Clay's thoughts moved to his more immediate interests as a natural-ist. His study and application of Dr. Merriam's Life Zones enabled Clay to understand that the very mountains in which he was now journey-ing encompassed four of the Life Zones. The large elevation change and the resulting changes in both temperature and precipitation from the base of the mountains to the Sierra Blanca Peak, made the area he was now entering an easy study of the Life Zones in such a small area.

Americans were moving West at a greater rate with the railroad boom providing an easy method of transportation. It was important to Dr. Merriam that an understanding of these western areas be meticu-lously undertaken. Growing populations meant that agriculture needed every possible advantage when it came to the land, and to the pests that would do all they could to limit production. It was through the understanding of such scientific applications as the Life Zones and the study of the natural science of the flora and fauna that this land would support the growing number of immigrants from the eastern United States.

At this time, museums were calling for specimens to display for those interested in the many new species being discovered. This was important as, in spite of the western movement, there was still a very large eastern population that would never be able to travel to the West. Many scientists were interested in these new discoveries from the western lands. To Clay, it seemed to be a two-fold undertaking for Dr. Merriam's Biological Survey. His studies at the college had been very beneficial to Clay's ability to understand Dr. Merriam's mission.

Now, having dropped out of college and unable to read for what could be months, Clay was unsure of his next move. So, he planned to spend some time in the mountains collecting specimens, waiting for his vision to improve, and trying to make a plan for his life.

As usual, with some solitude, Clay's thoughts turned to Carlos. After all these years, he still felt blame and shame for not having saved Carlos. His experience with James Moore in the Mogollons convinced him that revenge was futile and pointless. He saw that James Moore had spent his life seeking revenge to no end. Clay wanted to ensure that he did not live his life that way. He was bothered by the way he had reacted to the bear hunt at the W S Ranch in Alma. *Wasn't revenge supposed to make you feel better?* He had talked with Sister Anne and the priest in Las Vegas. He felt better for awhile, but, just as today, he had too often let his mind run to these same distressing thoughts.

Camping this night, Clay called to mind his father and his grandfather. They had provided a good solid foundation for him. He knew right from wrong, he knew how to provide for his needs from the land, he knew the importance of learning – both learning from the book and learning by experience. He knew about dreams of a life befitting his very nature. Both men had told him about the "Golden Rule." He knew the importance of living a life that was thoughtful of others. He felt he was well-grounded because of the good people in his life. As the priest had told Clay, he truly did feel that his life was blessed.

Clay knew he had to talk with Carlos. He had done this before, and it usually made him feel better. By the glowing embers of his fire, Clay laid back on his bedroll and looked up at the stars as he and Carlos had done on so many nights.

"Carlos, you know I'm sorry for letting you down. The priest told me I was forgiven by God; I hope I'm also forgiven by you. I'm sorry for arguing with you at the time of the bear attack. I should've been paying more attention to our surroundings. This was my responsibility for the both of us."

Clay paused as if waiting for a reply from Carlos.

Hearing none, he continued. "Carlos, the priest told me that there is a reason for everything that happens. I'm still stuck on that one. I don't see any good reason for what happened. Your death was not good for anyone."

Clay paused again, and this time he thought about his parents. Clay was still confused on the idea of revenge. He knew it was not right to be vengeful toward another person. It was in the Bible, and had been taught to him by his parents and grandfather. It had also been discussed by the priest. *Vengeance belongs to God alone.*

"But this was a bear, not another human being. I want that bear dead!" But, Clay realized that he would never see that bear, so how could he take revenge on it? He had killed other bears, but there was no feeling of revenge in doing so. There was no satisfaction. No, his killings were to protect others or to obtain a specimen for study. Clay had not been vengeful to an animal, or to another man.

Clay sat up. "How do I atone for your loss, Carlos? The priest said that I've been forgiven of my sins. He told me there was no sin involved in your death. Still, I feel like I have to do something – anything! How do I get over these feelings of helplessness and hopelessness?" Tears were now flowing from Clay's tired eyes and running down his cheeks. His head slumped into his hands as he sobbed.

Clay, it was a terrible accident; it was not your fault. Please know that it was not your fault. Carlos' voice was soft, calm, and reassuring. *We were in that bear's territory, and he was only doing what was natural for him. Clay, you must know that I did not suffer; the attack was swift, and it was over instantly. Clay, I am not suffering now.* There was a momentary pause. *Be at peace with yourself. You will see.*

"Carlos?" Clay looked up through eyes blurred with tears, but he was alone. "Where are you? Can you hear me?" There was only the silence of the mountains. It was a comforting silence as Clay heard the whisper of the wind in the branches of the pines.

"What will I see, Carlos? Answer me . . . please!" But, still, only the wind in the trees.

Clay sat quietly. All he heard was that wind and the whispers of the pine trees. He did not hear any other sounds. No flowing water. No bird songs. No small creatures scurrying about. No wolves. There were no other sounds in the mountains. It was simply quiet peace.

Clay was not sure how long he sat completely still before he heard the sound of the nearby water flowing, the birds nesting for the evening, and the other animals preparing for the night. In the distance, a wolf howled. A renewed comfort came over Clay. He laid out his bedroll and went to sleep.

Chapter 28

CLAY'S BEAR

Two days later, Clay made his way along a small mountain stream feeding the Rio Ruidoso until he came to a place to make an easy crossing that would take him higher into the mountains. After the effortless crossing, Clay proceeded in a northwesterly direction through a low brushy area before ascending a rocky path up to a ridge above. The rocky area and ridge were sparsely populated with junipers before yielding to the larger piñon pines. Clay made note of the junipers as they provided a good source of food for all forms of wildlife at this time of the year . . . including bears. He kept very alert as he trudged ahead.

The lower branches of the junipers had been well-picked by the resident small animal population, but the berries were still plentiful higher up on the trees where the bird population had not yet stripped the branches. They reminded Clay of the deeper-colored blueberries back in Indiana. Blueberries grew easily back home, and they were deliciously sweet. He knew, however, that the juniper berries were not something to be enjoyed. They were bitter, but they did have some medicinal uses when properly prepared. Carlos had told him how his mother prepared them for stomach problems.

Clay moved through the thickening piñon pines following what appeared to be a little-used trail. As he continued at a slight incline, there were increasing numbers of the larger ponderosa pine trees. After some bit of travel, he noticed a nervousness in his animals. He now proceeded with greater caution with heightened senses for watching, listening, and feeling for bears. He would not be surprised by any bear lurking in the area. His thoughts immediately went to the guilt that he felt for not paying more attention to his surroundings when the bear attacked Carlos. Clay shook his head to clear those thoughts and focus on his current situation.

Then he saw it up ahead on the right side of the trail just near the edge of the ridge where it overlooked the stream he had crossed earlier. The large black animal was lying on its side. Clay stopped and quietly watched and listened for several minutes. From a distance, Clay could see the occasional rise and fall of the bear's rib cage. He knew it was alive, but why would a bear be sleeping at this time of the day and in this place? It did not make any sense. He would have expected the bear to be up and about eating berries and tree nuts, or maybe down at the stream wallowing in the water. He needed to get closer to make a better assessment.

He tied Lucy and the burro to some branches on a piñon pine before proceeding. Every step was taken with extreme caution, his 30-30 Winchester at ready. Close enough now, he saw the situation. The bear was caught in a foot trap. It had obviously been there for quite some time. All of the grass, shrubs, and small trees within the radius of the trap's chain were torn up from the actions of the animal and from the chain being pulled over the ground. The dryness of the torn up area indicated to Clay that the bear had been here for more than just a few days.

Whoever had set the trap had not returned to check it as they should have. The only scenario that made any sense to Clay was that whoever had set the trap had forgotten about it, or perhaps lost its location. It was not something a good hunter would have let happen; it was gross carelessness in Clay's mind.

Prior to his encounter with James Moore in the Mogollon Mountains, Clay had been nagged by a desire for revenge for the killing of Carlos. However, after seeing the life of rage and darkness in the soul of the man, Clay felt as if he were touched by an unknown force that made him let go of his own rage and appetite for revenge. While he still did not understand where this feeling for revenge came from, his time with Sister Anne and the priest had more clearly exposed the fallacy of revenge. His guilt, of course, was a different matter.

He now saw before him a suffering animal that should not be in such a situation. Whether through carelessness or accident, this situation simply should not have happened. Clay did not need the skin or the bear meat, or the specimen itself. It was simply a local black bear of which plenty had been obtained and studied.

Approaching more closely, Clay judged the bear to be a five-to-six-year-old male. His first thought was to put the bear out of its misery, not out of spite or revenge, but out of a concern for the suffering bear itself. Clay continued a careful examination of the situation at a cautious distance. The bear made no move toward Clay; in fact, its eyes were closed. It breathed slow, shallow breaths as it remained otherwise still.

Clay moved to get a good look at the leg trap. It was low on the bear's leg with much of the skin and meat torn deeply. The fur on the bear's hind leg was well-matted with dried blood. It was then that Clay observed that a large limb was also caught in the trap. On closer examination, Clay noticed that the branch had kept the trap from breaking the bear's leg. The damage was mostly superficial, but the trap had enough of a hold on the bear to keep it from gaining its freedom. The chain had been buried around the base of the large tree fully securing the bear. It was obvious the bear had tried to escape in every direction from the tree. After many days of effort without food and water, the bear was worn and weakened.

Clay quickly glanced again at the bear's head. His eyes were now opened. His breathing was ever so slightly deeper as Clay looked at the still bear. Clay retreated to Lucy and retrieved his canteen. Returning to the bear, Clay poured some water from the canteen into the bear's mouth. The bear's long tongue worked to move the water into his mouth as he remained in the same position, again breathing a little deeper, yet still very slowly. As Clay stepped back, the bear's eyes followed him. He made a slight, deep *hmmph* sound, but he did not growl.

Clay was now unsure what to do. "Carlos, this is not the bear that killed you. I know that. I know, too, that there is no revenge in killing this bear. If I take his life, it's only to put it out of its misery. But, can I save it? Should I save it?"

Clay, I do not need revenge. You are a good man, and you will do the right thing. I know you love nature, and you do not kill for revenge. Remember, you and I are scientists. Do what you can do.

Of course, Clay could examine the bear's foot and determine the extent of the injuries. The bear did not appear to be in any condition to charge Clay. He examined the bear's foot and the trap. Because of the branch that was also in the trap, it should be easy enough to open. The foot, while bloodied and shredded, did not appear to have a deep injury, and as he had previously observed, there were no broken bones. Certainly, he could free the bear with no trouble.

Before proceeding, however, Clay knew the bear would need more water and some food. He felt it wise to provide this while the bear was still trapped. He went back down the trail to gather some of the juniper berries. He returned to the bear and gave it another drink. He then poured about half of the gathered berries near the bear's mouth. The long tongue easily gathered in the berries. Again, a deep *hmmph*, but not a growl. And, again, the bear's eyes turned to Clay while his head remained stationary. He poured some more water in the bear's mouth and then placed the remainder of the berries nearby. The bear's tongue again came to life as it gathered in the remaining berries. The bear shifted his eyes slightly at Clay but remained quiet.

Clay moved along the bear's side and bent down at the bear's foot in the trap. He opened the trap and removed the bear's injured foot. The bear slightly lifted its head with another *hmmph*. Clay was extremely cautious with his gun at hand. He poured some water on the bear's foot to clean it a bit, and then he backed away. The bear gave a big sigh with a louder *hmmph* as it snorted through its nose.

Clay slowly backed away from the bear with his Winchester ever ready. He moved to what he felt was a safe distance and kept his eye keenly on the bear. After several deep breaths, the bear lifted its head and then its entire body followed. He made it to his feet while favoring the rear foot. He looked around at the mangled foot momentarily, then looked down the trail toward Clay. He lifted his head and gave a meager growl with his nose in the air. He then ambled toward the edge of the ridge limping on his rear foot. He moved slowly. Just before disappearing over the ridge, the bear looked back at Clay and again sniffed the air. Clay was upwind of the bear, so it surely caught his scent. It then disappeared, heading down toward the creek.

Clay stood silently, still a bit wary and ready with his rifle.

Clay, you did good. That bear has chosen you as a friend. Clay, I am at peace, and you will be, too.

Clay looked about expecting to see Carlos standing next to him. He stood momentarily and smiled. Carlos had provided that bear to help Clay heal from his guilt. "Thanks, Carlos. Thank you for your peace." Clay paused, and then felt compelled to give one more thank-you. "Thank you, God, for this moment with Carlos. Take good care of him."

1901

Chapter 29

THE SOUTHWEST TAXIDERMY & ZOOLOGICAL CO.

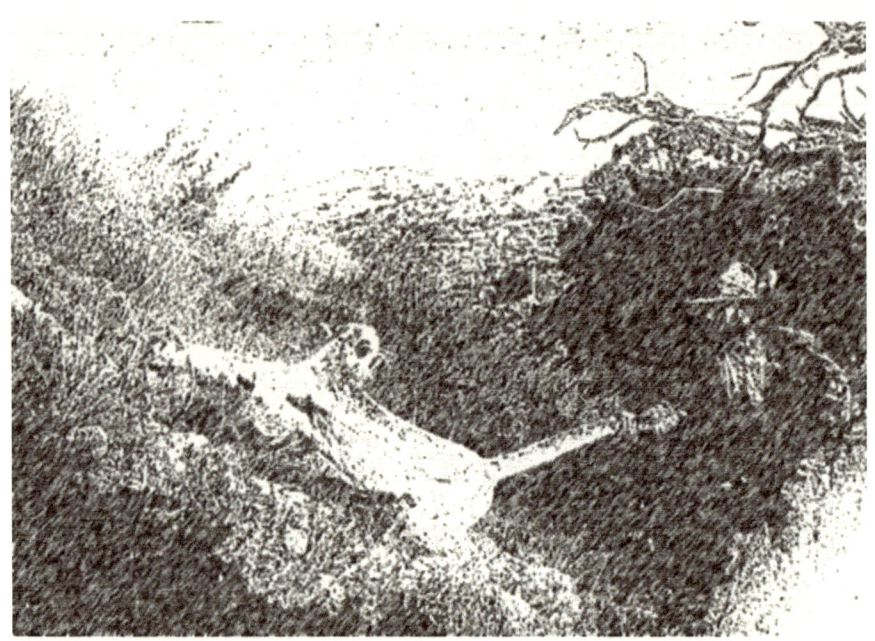

Clay spent just over six weeks in the Sierra Blanca Mountains. Because of his eye problem, he had not done any writing. The hunting and trapping he did was only to provide the necessary food during his stay. He could not see well enough to be able to prepare any specimens. He appreciated his time alone with his thoughts . . . and with Carlos. He had several more conversations with Carlos, and he now felt entirely free of his loss and hopelessness, and, most of all, his guilt.

He also thought a lot about what he would do next. He decided to open a taxidermy business in Albuquerque. On two field expeditions near there, he had the opportunity to visit the town. It was a large growing town, and he felt there would be a good market for taxidermy. This would provide him with an income while he decided on his next step. His eyes were much better, but he was not sure he was ready to return to school. He still enjoyed his time in the field, and perhaps he would pair field expeditions with his taxidermy business.

After coming down out of the mountains and making his way to Albuquerque, Clay opened a small taxidermy business which seemed to provide him more satisfaction than he had anticipated. He made the decision to divide his time between field collecting and preparing specimens using his taxidermy skills. He found over time, however, that his funds were continually coming up short.

It was on a day when he was pondering his next move that Clay received a letter from Townsend. Clay had shared with him his own concern in planning for his future. Townsend was suggesting they form a business together. They would provide hunting and field collecting expeditions into Chihuahua, Mexico, and Clay could additionally prepare taxidermy mounts for customers if he desired. Townsend suggested they set up a business in El Paso, Texas, where there was easy access to Chihuahua. Townsend had spent a great deal of time looking into the business, and El Paso was a prime location for hunters and collectors wanting to enter Mexico. And, there seemed to be a growing opportunity for this business, especially in the winter as the weather was much better in Mexico than in other farther north areas of the States.

So, it was not long before Clay was in El Paso, and he and Townsend opened a small shop north of town that would be their base of operations. Another one of their friends from college joined them as a business manager.

The Southwest Taxidermy & Zoological Company advertised in several journals reaching as far as Chicago and New York. They advertised field trips for entomologists, zoologists, botanists, and archaeologists in the Sierra Madre Mountains of northwestern Mexico. Their advertisements noted that in this tropical and temperate land would be found a variety of insects, reptiles, birds, animals, and plants, as well as wonderful cave and cliff dwellings rich in antiquities. The company would furnish saddle and pack horses, camp and cooking outfits, guides, and board in camp at reasonable prices. From a scientific perspective, they noted that each party would consist of only one specialist in a group, so that the members would not conflict with one another in their collecting. It was an appealing picture that proved to be effective in advertising for the business.

By late fall of the next year, the business of outfitting and guiding hunting parties had become quite profitable for the company. They kept all of their equipment and their pack and saddle animals in Casas Grandes, Mexico, to avoid problems with the Mexican Customs Office. In this manner, only the personal effects of those in the party had to be brought through Customs.

Most of the parties they led into Chihuahua were pleasant and good-natured. In general, most of the participants were men who wanted a bear or a mountain lion for their personal collection. Over time, Clay learned to easily determine the true interests of those in the hunting parties. While most were after a good specimen for their collection, there were others who merely wanted to brag about their kill. Many of the latter often looked to Clay to make the kill for them as they were not typically good hunters. Eventually, the business agreed to screen the members of the expeditions in order to refuse the men who were self-centered and self-possessed about the nature of their hunt.

There were some humorous incidents on many of the expeditions which were greatly enjoyed by all. While humorous in hindsight, Clay found himself on the wrong end of the gun on several occasions. There was a dentist in one of the parties that they took into the high Sierra Madres. The man had a particular excitability and unpredictability about him. This fellow looked forward to an annual excursion away from his business, as well as away from his wife and family.

While out with the dentist one day, Clay found himself pushing a deer toward the man for a shot. Clay was suddenly stunned by two quick shots near him on the ground that threw dirt and rocks all over him. Clay jumped for the nearest boulder for safe shelter. "Don't shoot me, you damn fool!"

The dentist apologized profusely to Clay for the accident. As the deer had obviously disappeared, the dentist pleaded to Clay for another chance the next day. Unfortunately for the dentist, Clay had vanished before breakfast the next morning. Townsend made up some excuse for Clay's absence that seemed to appease the dentist while leaving the man without a kill.

One incident was unknowingly precipitated by Clay himself. Clay and three greenhorns from the party were putting out traps for bears and mountain lions one morning. Clay was explaining to the group why the traps were placed as they were, how they were properly baited, and what the expectations for trapping an animal were. One of the men, an inexperienced city dude, said to Clay, "Say, Beckley, when you catch one of those lions in a trap, how do you kill him?"

The eyes of all three men turned to Clay, likely most of them also wondering about the same thing, but afraid to ask. Clay pondered for a moment as he wanted to have a little fun with the men. "Well, Jimmy, you just sneak up behind the cat, grab him by the tail, and pop him in the head with a club."

Clay made the statement in a very matter-of-fact way as though it was common knowledge among anyone with any hunting experience at all. All three men gazed at Clay in amazement. He could tell by their eyes that each one was hoping he wouldn't be the one asked to take the action.

Back at camp, Clay soon forgot about the conversation. That was not the case of Jimmy, a banker from Philadelphia, however. A few days later, they were making their morning rounds checking the traps. As they came over a rise, they saw a large mountain lion trapped by a front foot. Jimmy wasted no time at all and exclaimed, "Beckley, you grab him by the tail, but don't pop him! I want to take your picture."

The other men seemed pleased that Jimmy had immediately placed the foolhardy task upon Clay. Now, to Clay, mountain lions were not the feared creatures that most thought. He felt that the cats were cowards and fearful of man. Sure, he'd give this a try, but he first wanted to have some more fun with Jimmy.

"Now, Jimmy, you're paying me good money for this hunt. Wouldn't you rather be the one to have your picture taken with that cat?" He tried to remain as serious as he could, fighting back a smile. He left it there and stared intently at Jimmy.

Jimmy spoke quickly and nervously, "Beckley, this is all new to me, and I do not feel ready for this." He paused searching for what to say next. "Perhaps you could show us how this is done so we could learn." The other men were quick to agree with Jimmy's assessment.

Clay dismounted from Lucy and gave the reins to one of the men. That left Jimmy and one other man. Since Jimmy was going to take the picture, Clay enlisted the last man to distract the mountain lion while Clay made his way behind the animal.

With everyone ready for their assigned duties, Clay began circling his way around the cat. He gave a sign to the man to distract the lion. The man waved his kerchief, jumped up and down and whooped while ensuring he was at a safe distance. Clay cautiously approached the mountain lion from behind. When he was close enough, he reached out and grabbed the animal's heavy tail. Clay held on for dear life and yelled at Jimmy, "Take the damn picture!"

The mountain lion seemed quite distracted by both his foot in the trap and the jumping man before him. Jimmy had a huge grin on his face while he took Clay's picture. For his part, Clay kept a calm demeanor as he held the cat's tail and hoped for his life that the trap's jaw would hold the beast securely.

The party had an experience they would not forget. At that night's supper, the day's activity was the main topic of conversation. Townsend listened with interest and just shook his head and laughed. Clay never did share with the men that this was not really how to handle a trapped mountain lion.

As important as the hunting expeditions were to the business, the partners were finding an increasing interest from museums for the quality of the specimens that were being provided by Townsend and Beckley. An increasing number of their expeditions were guiding museum employees, or simply going out on their own to secure specimens for the museums. They were making some very good connections and earning a reputation for their excellently prepared specimens. Clay was certainly enjoying this type of work more than guiding the hunting parties. Fewer specimens were going to Dr. Merriam and more were being bought by museums who paid at a better rate.

A very successful hunt for a specimen of the Mexican grizzly bear yielded high praise from a team of collectors from the Field Museum in Chicago. Clay was establishing a good working relationship with the curator of mammals at the Field Museum. Their business with the museum was becoming a regular source of income for the company. Clay was truly enjoying his field work as well as his partnership with Townsend. They were working well together as a great team.

1904

Chapter 30

MEXICAN EXPEDITION

In 1903, Townsend's wife, Caroline, died suddenly and unexpectedly. The blow to Townsend was almost more than he could bear. He had two young children and left their upbringing mostly to his wife. Clay noticed that the life seemed to have drained from Townsend. They had some good long talks, but nothing seemed to help. He was becoming more distant on each expedition into Mexico. It seemed to Clay as if his heart was gone.

Finally, Townsend approached Clay one quiet evening and told him that he could no longer be a part of the business. He wanted to close the company and move away from the area. He told Clay that he needed to go abroad. He planned to take his children to a family member in New England, and he would then be going to the Philippines to study the insects of that country. Clay tried as he could to understand Townsend's need, but he also tried to talk him out of the plan. It was of no use. Clay could not argue against the manner in which Townsend needed to deal with his loss. The business closed in December of 1903. Clay had just celebrated his twenty-seventh birthday.

Fortunately for Clay, his endeavors with numerous museums presented an opportunity for him. Because of Clay's efforts for Chicago's Field Museum of Natural History on several collecting trips in Chihuahua, the museum was interested in having Clay come to work for them as a full-time field collector. Their planned expeditions for the next two years included Mexico, and they were aware of Clay's familiarity with the country. They felt he could easily deploy to their areas of interest and be very productive.

Clay was paired with Edmund Heller who would be head of this first expedition into southern Mexico. He and Clay hit it off well and seemed to have much in common. Clay learned that Heller was a graduate of Stanford University in California. He had spent some time in the Galapagos Islands and many months in Lower California honing his skills as a collector. Heller was pleased to know that Clay, while never having studied Spanish, had a good working vocabulary for the language. Heller himself was not at all comfortable with the Spanish language.

The pair of collectors spent the next year in the tropics of southern Mexico. In sweltering weather, they trapped and hunted in dense jungles. They had to sleep under mosquito netting at night. Their days were made miserable by ticks, chiggers, and more mosquitoes. Their bodies were covered with insect bites and itched continuously. These were all minor distractions to the two men, however, as they put their hearts into their work. Working directly for the Field Museum was a new and exciting opportunity for Clay, and he felt fortunate to be paired with a man of Heller's caliber.

The efforts of the two men were fruitful indeed. They were constantly discovering mammals that they had never seen. Their energy remained high with each new discovery. Busy hunting and checking traps during the day, their evenings were spent skinning and preparing specimens. Their days were long, hot, and miserable, but fulfilling to them in every way. The climate was just a minor expected annoyance of their research expedition.

One local man told them that in the tropical rain forest there was six months of steady rain followed by six months of just rainy weather. Because of these humid conditions, the larger skins had to be salted and dried at least three times over the course of a week. Smaller skins dried more easily. The dried skins were packed tightly into a hardwood barrel and saturated with a solution of salt brine. These barrels were shipped to the Field Museum where the skins were then tanned by experts at the museum.

Weeks in the tropics turned into months. Clay awoke one morning feeling ill. He soon became quite chilled, and then he developed a fever. A local doctor diagnosed Clay with a case of malaria and dosed him with quinine. After three days, Clay was too sick to move. He remained in bed, chilled to the bone and sweating profusely. Heller continued working alone for a week before he, too, came down with malaria. Heller responded well to the treatment and was up and active before Clay was even partially recovered. Clay forced himself to work at about half-pace for another week before he began to feel better. It was all just another inconvenience in the jungles of far southern Mexico.

Heller and Clay moved about to such places as Achotal, Oaxaca, San Geronimo, Niltepec, and Tehuantepec. Their collections included such exotic mammals as anteaters, kinkajous, peccaries, tapirs, agoutis, pacas, and coatis. There were also many new species of deer, raccoons, opossums, monkeys, bats, lizards, mountain lions, and jaguars. While focusing on mammals, the pair also collected many tropical birds including colorful parrots and toucans.

As Clay and Heller completed their survey in the south, they turned north toward Orizaba. There they planned to climb Volcan

Orizaba, known to the locals as Citlatepetl. At 18,491 feet, the peak was the highest in Mexico and the third highest in North America. Above the tree line, there were glaciers that existed year-round.

The two followed a well-worn trail from the base of the dormant volcano. Along the way, Clay was able to collect some large ground squirrels and brightly colored weasels, unlike any he had seen elsewhere. While the lower part of the mountain was rock-covered, the route was easy enough because of the frequent use of the trail over the years by potato farmers and sulfur miners. Clay and Heller both enjoyed the cool air that was already present in the place at even the lower altitudes. It provided them with a vigor that quickened their pace up the trail.

The trail followed an ascending ridge up the mountain. As they passed 9,000 feet, Clay noted the wheat fields that surrounded them. At 11,000 feet, they saw the last of the potato fields planted in the rich black soil. Clay wondered at the amount of difficulty that must be involved in harvesting these crops on the steep slopes. As they stopped to rest, Clay turned to enjoy the beauty of the checkerboard fields of corn, sugar cane, coffee, and bananas growing at the various altitudes below them. There was no such sight to behold in the flat cornfields of Indiana. He thought of how his grandfather would feel at seeing such a view.

It took them the full day to reach 14,000 feet where they made a permanent camp in an abandoned sulphur miner's cave. They had reached the timberline with 4,000 feet of grass- and snow-covered slopes up to the volcano's cone above. The glaciers near the lip of the crater shone brightly in the unfiltered sunlight.

Tired from the climb and slowed by the thinner air at this altitude, they limited their trapping and hunting to nearby level areas. Some large mushrooms caught Clay's eye as they began to think about supper. They looked so much like the morel mushrooms from back home that Clay gathered a large batch to prepare for supper.

After a few days spent at the camp, they made their way to the rim of the volcano where they cautiously peered into the crater. It was not a place Clay cared to venture. Here and there were plumes of smoke wafting from the dormant volcano. Clay wanted nothing to do with it. There were no animal tracks of any sort in the area. They had already added samples of the sparse grass to their collection, so they returned to their camp.

On their descent, they met two climbers on their way up to the crater. As the two teams closed on one another, Heller gave a hearty hello and a wave to the men. After a few more steps, Clay recognized the men, as well. It was Edward Goldman and Edward Nelson, collectors from Dr. Merriam's Biological Survey that Clay had worked with on his very first collecting trip in Arizona. After briefly sharing their recent ventures, the two teams went their separate ways but agreed to meet at Clay's and Heller's camp later in the day.

The four of them spent the next three weeks together on the mountain. Clay was amazed at the speed with which the other two men completed every activity. Even their specimens were some of the best Clay had ever seen in spite of how quickly they had been prepared. These men certainly knew what they were doing. Clay also noted that they were in great physical shape as they could ascend that last 4,000 feet to the summit quite rapidly compared to Heller and himself.

Chapter 31

PANCHO VILLA

After coming off the mountain and having a bath and a shave, Clay and Heller continued north by train. In Durango, they resupplied and made ready for a two-month trip into the high Sierras. They made camp in a virgin pine forest near an open valley. Nearby was a stream of cool, clear water and plenty of grass for the animals, all-in-all a great place for their permanent camp.

They found limited specimens of the large mammals they had hoped to find in the area; however, they did not see any bears. There were a few turkeys about, but most abundant were deer. They ate well while collecting a good series of white-tailed deer from the area.

While summer in the area had been pleasant, Clay did not feel they did as well with their collections in the place. They returned to Durango where they sold their worn-out animals and headed northeast to the plains of Jaral, a flat, dry land.

They hired a driver to take them out into the Mapimi Desert. In addition to their supplies, they carried six large barrels of water as there was no water to be found in the desert. The driver dropped them at their chosen location, then he took one of the fresh mules and rode toward home.

While there was some grass on the low rolling hills nearby, to the north and west there was the flat, dry floor of the Mapimi as far as the eye could see. Nothing more than a few dead weeds added to their surroundings.

Once again, they were looking for larger mammals. The following morning, they spotted a small herd of antelope about a mile away. Unfortunately, the dry flat land exposed their presence to the animals who were easily spooked. This meant that they had to drop from their mules at some distance from their prey and crawl on their bellies to get within range for a good shot. This proved successful for the hunt, but the hardened, shell-covered ground of the ancient seabed tore the skin of their elbows, knees, and bellies. Subsequent days proved less fruitful as the antelope seemed to have an even better sense of their presence.

Clay had an idea to improve their odds of securing the antelope specimens. He recalled his father telling him about hunting geese on the Kankakee Marsh in Indiana. He drove a horse with lines toward the geese while staying low behind the animal. The geese were not fearful of the horses, and when he was close enough, his father stepped from behind the horse and shot the geese. Clay convinced Heller that they could do the same with the antelope.

The next day, Clay drove a mule along in the fashion his father had told him about. Nearing a fine large buck, Clay shot from beneath the mule's chin. The mule was not happy about it, but Clay got a nice specimen. More days of hunting in this manner provided them a fine series without much trouble.

In the weeks that followed, they collected a nice series of pronghorn antelope, a unique animal with hollow horns. They also gathered a series of white-tailed deer from this area. Going up into the hills, they collected peccaries (medium-sized pig-like animals), and finally, a prized Mexican mountain sheep.

One quiet morning, Clay was in camp preparing specimens while Heller was out to the southwest checking trap lines that had been prepared the day before. He left early in the morning and would be gone for most of the day.

Clay was alerted to the sound of approaching riders from around one of the nearby low hills. The dust was stirred in the air as the men on horses approached. He was quickly able to count the seven riders as they neared. Clay remained seated at the table where he was working on some small skins. It was unusual to see other parties in this area, and it was particularly unusual to see a group such as this one. With caution, Clay made sure his Colt New Service 45 was at his side.

The group had only two small pack animals, and there appeared to be a minimal amount of supplies. As the riders neared, Clay stood with some concern. All of the men were carrying belts of ammunition across their torsos. They were certainly not a common hunting party, but they were well-armed. All were Mexicans wearing larger sombreros, and they appeared to have been traveling for some time. Both the men and their mounts looked worn.

The group slowed to a walk, and the apparent leader rode to the front. While the other men stopped outside of Clay's camp, the leader continued walking his horse right up to where Clay was standing beside his table.

"Buenos dias, Señor." The man spoke plainly and in a pleasant manner with just a hint of a smile on his sun-darkened face.

Clay replied in a similarly friendly manner, "Buenos dias."

The man smiled fully at Clay through a large mustache and shifted a bit in his saddle. His weapons were in obvious display, but his rifle was in its scabbard on the horse. Clay was relieved to see that all of the men had their rifles in their scabbards. However, they all appeared ready to move into action at a moment's notice. None appeared to be relaxed, other than the apparent leader.

"You are an American?" The man spoke English but with a strong Mexican accent. He had obviously recognized the inflections in Clay's words.

"Yes," Clay replied while remaining calm and confident. Clay estimated that he was about the same age as the man. Clay thought he was probably just a bit taller than the man in the saddle.

"I see." The man paused and looked around Clay's camp. "You are not alone. Where are the others?" He did not ask this in a threatening manner, rather he seemed to be asking with a curious interest.

"There are just two of us. My partner is out checking our traps." Clay pointed in the general direction to the southwest where Heller had gone to check the traps, and he immediately wished that he had not done so.

"You know there are silver mines in this area. You are perhaps miners?" He still continued to appear calm and matter-of-fact in his manner.

"Oh, no!" Clay replied, somewhat too quickly and earnestly. "We're collecting specimens for a large museum back in America." Clay recalled his encounter with Black Jack Ketchum – over ten years ago now – who had also inquired about silver mining, and he became a bit cautious. He felt an uncomfortable churning in his stomach.

"Specimens?" The man spoke the word slowly and appeared a bit puzzled.

"Yes. The museum has sent us here to study the types of animals in Mexico. We collect the skins to prepare samples that the museum will study back in Chicago, Illinois, . . . in America." Clay was trying to make his explanation as simple as possible hoping that the man would understand and believe him.

The man's eyes passed slowly over the camp with intensity. "You certainly do not appear to have any equipment that miners would use." The intensity left his face, and a slight faraway smile appeared as he continued, "I was a miner myself at one time." He paused and looked back toward his men. He then returned to Clay. "Perhaps you could show me what you are doing." It seemed to be more of a request than an order which put Clay somewhat at ease.

"Certainly, I can show you. Please, why don't you and your men get off your horses. We have a water supply here, and your men can water the horses while we talk." Clay was being as friendly as possible and hoping that Heller would return; although, he really did not expect him anytime soon. "There's a large barrel on the other side of the wagon that's filled with water. Tell your men to help themselves."

The leader turned to his men, said a few words, and they all dismounted. Three of the men took their horses to the barrel, and the other three remained where they had dismounted. The leader dismounted, removed his sombrero, slapped the trail dust from his hat and clothes, and approached Clay.

He placed his sombrero back on his head. "I am Pancho Villa," he said as he held out his hand to Clay. "My men and I are going into the mountains. As I said, I have mined in the past, and we are going to one of my mines." The man smiled at Clay. "You have not been to any mines?"

Clay shook the man's hand as he spoke, "I'm Clay Beckley. No, as I said, we're here working for a museum. We've seen some caves in other areas, but, no, we have not been to any mines." Clay was vaguely recalling a poster in El Paso with the man's name. He remembered seeing it, but he could not recall any of the details. He now wished he had paid more attention to the posters at the sheriff's office.

"Tell me of this museum. What do they do with these . . ." he struggled a bit for the word, "these specimens?"

"Well, as I said, the scientists at the museum study the animals. They also use the bones and skins to prepare exhibits of the animals that others can study. The museums are open so that anyone can come in and see the vast variety of animals from all around the world." Clay paused briefly to see if Pancho Villa might have a question, but he quickly continued. "One of the important studies that we do is observe the effect that animals have on the crops that the farmers are trying to grow in the areas we visit."

Pancho Villa lifted his eyes to Clay with interest. In the meantime, the first three men had returned from watering their animals, and the next three men moved over to the barrel. "Tell me, Señor Beckley, how are you helping the farmers when there are no farms in this area?" More than suspicious, he seemed to be genuinely interested.

"In this area, we're studying the animals as well as the plant life. No, we're not providing assistance for any farm opportunities here. However, we were farther south several months ago where we did do such work. We studied the smaller mammals in the area that were problems for the farmers' crops. For example, we made a detailed study of the rodent population. The scientists will use our studies to determine how to control the rodents and help the farmers have a larger crop yield."

Pancho Villa seemed quite pleased with Clay's response. "I know what a rodent is, but what are these mammals you speak of, Señor Beckley?"

Clay was now feeling more comfortable. "Señor Villa, mammal is simply a scientific word for a warm-blooded animal . . . like deer, coyote, mountain lions, beaver, and, yes, even rodents."

Pancho Villa shook his head in pleasure. "So, Señor Beckley, you and your partner are not farmers yourselves?"

"No, we are simply collectors for the museum. Our only possessions are the clothes on our backs and the equipment and supplies you see here." He wanted Pancho Villa to be aware that there was nothing of value in the camp. "We've been traveling from southern Mexico up to this area. We'll have been in your country for about a year by the time we return to the United States."

"I see. I will water my horse now." He smiled again and took his horse around the wagon to the barrel where the others had been. The rest of the men stood silently with their fatigued horses.

After returning to Clay, Pancho Villa had more questions. "So, Señor Beckley, what were you working on when we arrived at your camp?"

Clay proceeded to show Pancho Villa the skin he was preparing and how the chemicals were used for preservation. Clay explained how larger and smaller mammals were prepared. He showed the man several of the specimens that had already been completed. It all reminded Clay of the time he had spent teaching Carlos how to prepare specimens.

Pancho Villa took a real interest in Clay's activities while his men rested and talked among themselves. More time had passed than Clay realized when Pancho Villa indicated to his men to prepare to leave.

"Señor Beckley, I want you to know that Pancho Villa is a friend of the farmer and the poor. We do what we can to help those who are not being treated well by the rich or by our government. If your work helps the Mexican farmers, then I wish you and your partner well. You, too, are a friend of the farmer."

He mounted his horse, and his men did the same. "Remember Pancho Villa as your friend, also. Adios, Señor Beckley." He smiled broadly and tipped his sombrero to Clay.

Clay wished him safe travels in a friendly manner, "Adios, Señor Villa. Viajes seguro." The men turned their horses and headed northwest higher into the Sierra Madres. It seemed unlikely that they would run into Heller in the direction they were headed.

The remainder of the pair's time in the desert was quiet and productive. The trip had been good indeed. They packed up their camp and headed to Monterrey where they sold their animals and boarded a train for the good old U.S.A. They had been gone a full year and were looking forward to a good American meal.

1905

Chapter 32

GUATEMALA

After a very brief replenishment in the U.S., Heller and Clay were headed back into the field, this time to Guatemala. The areas they were to explore were more remote, more dense, and more hot and humid than Mexico. However, shortly before they were to leave, Heller was tapped to lead an expedition to Africa. Clay was sorry to see his partner for the past year take a new direction, but he certainly understood the opportunity ahead for Heller. And, for himself, Clay would now lead the expedition into Guatemala on his own.

He was to enter Guatemala from the Pacific Coast, so he headed for the port of San Francisco to board a Pacific mail boat bound for

Guatemala. Once again, he was taking a train west, and riding in the passenger cars rather than on them as he had so many times in his youth. The route would take him north of the New Mexico Territory, through Pueblo, Colorado Springs, and Grand Junction on his way to Salt Lake City, and across Nevada to Sacramento and San Francisco. Clay appreciated the time he would have to catch up on reading some of the latest scientific publications, some written by his contemporaries at the museum.

Clay knew the importance of publishing his findings from his work with Townsend. Townsend had made it very clear to Clay that getting his education and publishing his findings were very important in this type of work. Clay had written his first full report for publication in 1902 at Townsend's strong urging. While Clay had written for the science club he had initiated at college, this was his first real independent work for scientific publication. It was entitled "Notes on Little-Known Mexican Mammals and Species Apparently not Recorded from the Territory" and was published in the *Proceedings of the Biological Society of Washington* in October 1902. He had used his field journal from the years 1897 to 1902 to prepare the paper. He had been pleased with the details he had kept in his field journal, and he was proud of the finished report. It had been much less of a struggle than he had thought it would be. At the same time, however, he felt his work was not near the quality of the work of his colleagues.

Without Heller leading this expedition to Guatemala, Clay would have full responsibility for the final report of this collecting trip. Catching up on some of the most recent scientific publications was one way to prepare for his report. Clay had always been a quick study, and he was looking forward to the work ahead and the final report he would prepare for the museum.

From San Francisco, the ship passed around the tip of Baja California Sur and ported at Mazatlan in Mexico where they were allowed off the ship for several hours before departing and heading to the next port. They followed this same pattern for some number of days, porting briefly and then reboarding to proceed to the next port city. Clay noted that every day was hot and dry on the Pacific side of Mexico, very much unlike the rain forests he had worked in last year.

After fourteen days on the ship, days that Clay had truly enjoyed, they anchored offshore at the Port of San Jose in Guatemala. From the port, Clay transferred to a train which was headed for the capitol of Guatemala. After many hours of slow climbing, they passed Lake Amatitlan about twelve miles south of the city of Guatemala. The city of Guatemala had an ancient look to it with many large thick-walled one-story buildings. Clay learned that this was to resist earthquakes. Clay was anxious to get to work, but he found himself a little slow and lacking in energy.

Heller had provided Clay a letter to Don Guillermo Thorn who lived at Santa Elena, and Clay headed there on the back of an old mule. His baggage was ported on the shoulders of some large local Indian packers. They were paid a few cents a day, and they found their own food and lodging. His rented mule cost him three times what the baggage carriers cost per day.

Arriving at Don Guillermo's farm in Santa Elena two days later, Clay presented his letter from Heller. After introductions and some brief conversations, Don Guillermo told Clay that he had to go to the city on business. Don Guillermo gave the letter to his family, and then told Clay that he was entrusting his family's safety to him. Clay was taken aback, but he also felt good that the gentleman had such trust in Clay. It was obvious that Don Guillermo had complete confidence in the words of Heller.

The family gave Clay a spacious room in their large two-storied frame home. It was well-lit but not heated. Clay had noted a decided change in temperature as he climbed the mountain to this house. He was now around 9,000 feet above sea level, and, as night approached, there was a sharp drop in temperature. As he went down to supper, Clay found that none of the rooms had any heating apparatus. The hot supper warmed him up, but he soon went to bed to keep warm.

The sun was shining the next morning, but the air was quite cool as he started on a tour of exploration. A brisk walk soon warmed him up to normal.

All about him, the ridges were covered with virgin forests of gigantic mountain cypress trees. They were of large girth, tall, and the stand on the ground was thicker than one would expect. Clay recalled a similar tree of gigantic size growing alone at Chapultepec Castle near Mexico City. Here was a dense stand of these big trees, the most magnificent forest he had ever seen. He learned that this was a fog forest kept wet by regular morning fogs that rolled in from the Pacific.

Clay strung out a line of traps, then spent the rest of the day with his gun and collecting bag. The soil here was moist. Under rocks, he found a small salamander of which he collected a series. It appeared to him that it was likely a new species.

His trap line was fairly successful, so he had to sit and skin small mammals for hours every day. On foggy mornings, he got so cold on this work that his fingers would not function. He would then have to take a walk to warm up. He realized that the family went down to the kitchen stove to get warm at times, but he had not been invited there, although the family was very kind to him in every other way.

It was evident to Clay that most of his misery was due to his poor physical condition. Clay thought to himself that one who is not in the bloom of health should not go on a collecting trip to an unknown country. He kept working steadily, but the old speed and movement was not there, and the number of specimens that he was able to secure reflected this.

After a few months of working in the forests to the north and west, Clay made his way farther inland and east. His time in the jungles was hard going but fruitful. Travel was some of the most difficult Clay had experienced. He found himself easily fatigued over the next few months. He was fortunate to have a good group of locals to help with the collection activities.

Clay eventually moved back toward the Pacific to explore the areas around the two large lakes, Lake Atitlan and Lake Amatitlan, to the southwest. It was there that he met Seth Meek who had arrived from the museum specifically to study the fish in the two lakes. Clay was to assist Meek while still completing his mammal studies around the lakes.

The climate was even worse near the lakes. Clay began to become concerned about contracting malaria again with a population of mosquitoes like he had never seen. He knew his health was not the best, but he carried on using locals to assist him in his collecting work here as he had to the north.

Then one day, it hit him hard. He woke with chills and fever. For ten straight days, he had a chill every day in spite of all that a local doctor could do. This was no ordinary malaria but rather the terrible tropical strain with double infection. Forty grains of quinine taken daily did not seem to have any effect. Finally, the doctor injected quinine in his arms until they were sore. When the eleventh day passed without a chill, Clay felt a bit better.

The local doctor was a pleasant young man from the southern part of the U.S. He had a local Indian wife and two young children. The doctor informed Don Guillermo that Clay would need to get back to the States at once, or the next attack of malaria would be fatal. Clay was placed on the next fruit boat that docked at Puerto San Jose. He did not want to leave, but it was useless for him to continue working in Guatemala in his present condition.

Fortunately, after several days on the boat, Clay was beginning to get some strength back. He noted, however, that all of his clothes hung on his body like rags. He had lost a large amount of weight. He did not yet have a good appetite, so he knew he would continue to be a shadow of himself until he could regain his appetite.

At each port along the Mexican coast, Clay seemed to gain strength. By the time they neared Baja California, Clay was once again eating normally, but he still had little strength. Most days were either spent sitting in a chair on deck or sleeping in his small room.

Clay now learned that about the time they were leaving Guatemala, word had been received that there had been a terrible earthquake in

San Francisco. The reports received said that half of the city had simply slid into the ocean. And, apparently, the disaster was made worse by a fire that followed the quake and ravaged the city.

The captain, the ship's officers, the crew, and every passenger on board were going home to San Francisco where they and their families lived. They had received no word from their loved ones since the disaster. They did not know whether their homes were destroyed or if their relatives were alive or dead. No personal cables were allowed, hence their worry of the unknown.

Day after day as they traveled north, the catastrophe was the sole subject of conversation. Clay was the only person on board who was not vitally interested in conditions at San Francisco. He had never met a sadder group of people, all confused, hoping, and hopeless; all torn by fear of what might have happened to their homes and loved ones. He soon gave up any attempts to try to cheer the others up; it was a futile effort.

As they finally approached the Golden Gate, they saw a lot of half-burned timber floating in the sea. As the ship entered the Golden Gate, a cliff house seemed in good shape up on the bluff above. As the ship moved up the bay, the passengers crowded the deck for a first view of the stricken city. Finally, the rolling hills that were once covered with buildings began to come into view, but there were no buildings to be seen. A checkerboard of paved streets marked off those hills in squares. In some blocks, a few chimneys or the broken corner of a brick building were to be seen. Other solid blocks were completely bare now where once frame buildings had stood. On some more distant hills, there could be seen here and there a few large buildings standing, apparently uninjured like isolated sentinels.

What the quake had started, the fire had completely finished. Clay had been gone a year and was glad to see the U.S., but not this wreck of a once beautiful city. The poor passengers and crew who were so tense for news were now awed to silence by the devastated ruins of their city. Some were crying, but very few had any words to express their grief. It was much worse havoc than they had expected. The ship tied up at one dock that had not burned down to the waterline. The fire had been put out for nearly a month. Yet, Clay saw a few smoking ruins here and there.

On the deck, Clay heard that the post office building was still standing, so he started there hoping to receive expected funds from the Field Museum. Since there was no transportation of any kind, he walked down the middle of the streets to get there, dodging piles of debris that had fallen onto the pavement. Most of the inhabitants had been sent out of the city, so he saw very few people about except for the police.

The post office building had escaped serious damage because of its reinforced concrete and steel construction, but Clay saw a long crack in the pavement in front of it that seemed bottomless and was wide enough to hide a fence rail. Without transportation, Clay was unsure what to do next. He asked a policeman where he could spend the night. The policeman let Clay know in no uncertain terms that he did not belong in the area and that he must leave immediately.

Bluntly and directly, the policeman asked, "Where did you sleep last night?"

"On the ship I just came in on."

"Go right back to the ship to sleep," he ordered.

Clay explained to him why he was there and that he wanted to get away. He also explained that the ship had brought him there on a ticket, hence they would not allow him back aboard.

"Oh, yes they will," he answered. "Go right back to your ship."

While Clay doubted the policeman, he made his way back to the ship. There they gave him his room and fed him until the next morning. Again, Clay made the long walk to the post office with the same result – no letter from the museum.

Clay heard through conversation that Oakland, across the bay, was in better shape. So, he took a ferry boat across the bay, then a train to Stanford. At the gate to the campus of the university, he noted one big brick pillar that had collapsed. Up the drive was a new stone and steel library building that was partly finished. The stone and steel tower stood up intact, but some new stone walls along the building's side had been shaken down like a child's block house.

Clay called on a professor he knew at his home. His frame house looked normal on the outside, but, when Clay entered, he noted that the plaster had been shaken from the walls and ceiling. There were pictures hanging on bare lath walls. While the professor was polite, the entire situation was grim, and Clay again felt a helplessness in speaking with him.

Clay returned to the town of Stanford where he saw a cheap three-story frame building that had been shaken to pieces. Whole upper floors were tilted at all angles. It looked about like a crate full of empty berry boxes would look if a heavy man had stomped it to pieces.

There, a kind local policeman directed him to an old hotel building where he spent the night in a dirty, but comfortable, bed. The next morning, he crossed the bay and made the trip back to the post office where he finally received his long-expected letter from the museum.

With funds from the museum and help from his friend at Stanford, Clay was able to obtain a ticket for the train. As Clay hurried to the station, he passed down a street of ruin and desolation unlike anything he had ever seen. He saw a graceful lady dressed in a beautiful silk evening gown busily cooking lunch over an open-air fire. Just behind her fire was a rude patched-together shelter, roofed with crooked burned sheets of galvanized iron. Clay pictured in his mind the lady dressed in the gown attending a social affair where everyone was dressed in their finery when the earthquake hit. She was now apparently back home on her own property trying to begin a new life. As he boarded the train to Chicago, Clay was delighted to know he was leaving this nightmare of ruined hopes for so many people.

1906

Chapter 33

BACK HOME

B ack in Chicago, Clay had to see a doctor as he still had no energy. The doctor told Clay that he was still recovering from his recent bout with malaria and that he seemed to have a touch of pneumonia. Clay simply needed some rest.

Rest was something difficult for Clay to do. He needed to be in the field collecting, but he knew his health meant there would be no distant assignments from the museum. He spoke with Daniel Elliot, Curator of Zoology, and was able to convince the curator that he could do some localized collecting in Indiana and Illinois. This would allow him to spend some time at home and keep his travel light.

Clay first went home to La Porte where he could visit family and explore the lakes in the area. He had spent some time reading about local turtle species, and he was interested in seeing what he could find in the area. It would be easy work for him.

He spent about six weeks in the La Porte area staying at his boyhood home. His two youngest siblings were still living at home. Clay had not seen his youngest brother, Ira, who was named after their grandfather, since he was a toddler. Now thirteen, he was all boy and full of energy. He also seemed to delight in tormenting his sister, Minerva. She was sixteen and developing into a young lady. She was close to her mother and quiet in nature – a very different personality than her younger brother, Ira.

Clay's brother Mark was a twenty-two-year-old teacher having recently completed his education at Indiana University. The fact that Mark had graduated from college left Clay a little crestfallen about his own attempt at higher education. While the problem with his eyes that had caused Clay to leave college had eventually cleared, Clay had already moved beyond studies and was now actively immersed in his work. Mark also informed Clay that he would be getting married in the coming year.

Clay was closest to his brother Harry who, at twenty-seven, was two years younger than Clay. Clay had convinced Harry to join him on a couple of his expeditions into Mexico when he had first formed his business with Townsend in El Paso. While an able hunter, Harry had served as the expedition's cook on these two trips. Harry had enjoyed the time with Clay and appreciated the opportunity, but it turned out not to be the lifestyle that Harry was looking for in the long run. When he had returned to La Porte, he went to work at the La Porte Carriage Company where their father worked. He seemed to be following in his father's footsteps as a painter.

Harry was able to accompany Clay on his exploration of the lakes in the area. They had some good talks as Harry told him of what had been going on with the family. With his experience in the carriage business, Harry was excited to share his knowledge of the new horseless carriage trade that was developing. Henry Ford would be manufacturing his latest version of an automobile that was under development. He told Clay that by this time next year, automobiles would be seen in abundance on the streets of La Porte.

Clay was captivated not only by Harry's knowledge but also by the scientific progress in the world. His time spent in remote areas over the last several years had isolated him from such developments. Even back in Chicago, most of the talk with colleagues revolved around collecting and new species, as well as the developments in taxidermy being made by Carl Akeley. Little was even mentioned of items such as automobiles.

After about six weeks, Clay said his good-byes to the family. His parents had been especially glad to have him home, certainly for such a length of time. Clay and his father had actually had some good scientific discussions. His father had also been a good audience to Clay's stories of his travels. His mother, in a typically motherly fashion, was concerned about Clay's health. He was still very tired and had not put back on any of the weight he had lost. He assured her that he was fine as he gave her a gentle hug before leaving for the train.

Clay took his specimens back to the museum. He had collected a number of local turtles, his main point of interest, as well as frogs, toads, lizards, salamanders, and snakes. Immediately after delivering his specimens, Clay was on his way to southern Illinois. He was to collect in an area near Olive Branch in the far southwestern corner of the state.

It was after a few weeks in the area around Horseshoe Lake that Clay's cough seemed to be getting worse. He was still tired and lacking energy, and he attributed his cough to the slight case of pneumonia that the doctor had indicated was present. He hoped that he had not spread his pneumonia as there were two men at the boarding house where Clay was staying who had also been coughing.

He cut his trip short returning to the museum a few weeks earlier than planned. He had collected a very nice American Snapping Turtle which he knew would make a fine specimen for the museum.

Back at the museum, his spirits were lifted when he learned that Heller was back from Africa. The two men met, and Clay listened to Heller's stories with a fascination that made him all but forget about his health. Afterward, Heller let Clay know that Teddy Roosevelt was planning another trip to Africa and that he, Heller, would be accompanying him.

Clay perked up as he mentioned to Heller that his present situation made him available to be part of the expedition if it could be arranged. Heller provided what seemed to be somewhat of a feigned interest in the idea. He finally had to tell Clay that he did not seem fit for the trip.

"Clay, look at yourself. You're so thin and weak. And, do you even realize how bad your cough is?" Heller was sincere in his concern for Clay.

"It's simply a touch of pneumonia that will be cleared up in no time!" Clay forced himself to be as powerful as possible in his response to Heller. "The doctor even gave me the okay to make some small expeditions in Indiana and southern Illinois. I'll be fine in no time. I think being out in the field just a bit has been good for me." Clay had to fight back the urge to cough as he replied to Heller.

"Clay, I hear what you're saying, but you do not appear to have fully recovered from your last bout of malaria." He looked Clay squarely in the eyes. "Clay, you're not okay. You can't go into the jungles of Africa like this. The jungle diseases there are much worse than what you and I faced in Mexico."

"But, Heller . . ." Clay's voice broke as he began coughing with great force. His heart was broken at the thought of missing this opportunity, but he also knew that Heller was right.

Heller put his arm around Clay and helped him stand. Clay continued coughing and bent over as he did so. When he finally stopped, he stood straight, moving his eyes to contact Heller.

"Heller, you're just afraid I'll get lost in those jungles, like I did that time in Mexico, and embarrass you in front of Teddy Roosevelt." He grinned, and Heller returned a smile as he patted Clay on the back.

"Yes, you fool, can you imagine me having to convince the president of the United States that we had to hold our expedition while we searched for you?!"

They laughed together before Clay again started coughing.

"When did you last see the doctor?" Heller's laughter ceased.

"I don't know. Time flies by so quickly. I suppose it's been a couple of months." Clay knew it had been a long time.

"Don't you think you ought to see him again? Surely, you should be improving to some degree by now." He thought for a moment. "I'll tell you what, Clay. We'll go see the doc tomorrow. We'll see what he says about your health and go from there. Just don't get your hopes up until we do this." He paused again. "You look terrible you old fool. Let's get you home."

Clay had a restless night and his coughing grew worse. Near dawn, he sat up with a fit of coughing that produced blood. Clay looked at his handkerchief, and his heart nearly stopped. He remembered the last time he had coughed up blood. That time it had been consumption.

1907

Chapter 34

CONSUMPTION AGAIN

Heller picked up Clay in the morning to see the doctor. This doctor was a specialist in lung ailments who saw patients in his clinic. This was new to Clay as previously he had had the physician come to wherever he happened to be. It seemed unusual to be going to a physician's office. Perhaps this was how these "specialists" worked in a changing world.

The trip to the doctor was quiet except for Clay's occasional cough. Clay did not tell Heller about the blood he had been coughing up. He had also taken some of the medicine that was supposed to control his cough. It seemed to work for a short time.

The doctor that Heller had arranged for them to see was new to Clay. Initially, Clay had assumed that they would be going to the same doctor that Clay had seen previously. Heller told him that this new doctor was recommended by Dr. Elliot at the museum. Clay was surprised to hear that Dr. Elliot had taken a personal interest in his well-being.

After questioning and examining Clay, the doctor took him into a room to take an x-ray picture of Clay's chest. The doctor explained that the x-ray would allow the doctor to see the condition of his lungs. It should be able to provide a definitive answer to what was going on with Clay. The doctor told Clay that with his malaria, his loss of weight, his lack of energy, and his previous case of consumption, the prognosis might not be good. Clay would need to come back the next day to get the results.

This x-ray was something new to Clay, he had listened intently, and his curious nature gave him an interest in this whole process that was outside of his illness. How could this machine take a picture of the inside of his body? Clay wanted to ask the doctor more about the machine, but he was now tired and simply wanted to get back to his bed.

After another fitful night, Clay was picked up by Heller in the morning, and they went once again to the clinic. Heller went into the doctor's office with Clay to hear what the results of the x-ray showed. The doctor wasted no time in letting Clay know that he had consumption, or tuberculosis as the doctor now scientifically referenced it. The doctor informed Clay that the x-ray photograph could not distinguish between new formations of the tubercle bacillus and scarring from his former infection. The doctor said the good news was that he did not appear to have a severe case of the disease; in fact, the doctor referred to Clay's case as mild. It also seemed that he was still fighting his malaria, and the combination made his symptoms worse. Clearing up the malaria would provide Clay a quick improvement in his condition.

Somewhere in the back of his mind, Clay had a concern that he might once again have consumption, but he had suppressed this thought and was hoping it was merely another course of malaria. The diagnosis was a real blow to Clay. Hadn't he been cured of this once? Why was it showing up again? Was the doctor sure about this? Questions ran through Clay's mind, and he was unsure of which ones he had asked aloud. But in the end, despite the doctor's assurance of a mild case of tuberculosis, Clay was devastated by the outcome.

Clay was glad that Heller was with him. Heller was very supportive and positive about Clay's ability to once again beat the disease. The doctor had explained to both of them that there were some advances in treatment. He also recommended a newly-opened sanatorium in Booneville, Arkansas, where he felt Clay would get the best treatment. He prepared a personal letter to the Arkansas Tuberculosis Sanatorium which would assure Clay's acceptance into the facility.

Clay's spirit was down as Heller took him back to his apartment. "Well, I guess this for sure rules out the African expedition," Clay said with both a lack of energy and a crestfallen heart.

"Look, Clay, let's just get you to that sanatorium in Arkansas and get you healed up. Look how you've recovered from your bouts of malaria and your previous course of consumption. You've beaten these things before, and you'll do so again." Heller kept a positive and cheerful tone for Clay's sake. "There will be plenty of other expeditions once you've recovered."

"Heller, I appreciate your positive outlook, I really do, but I don't share it. I'm not sure what's going to happen to me." He was attempting to be realistic in his thoughts, but he continued to be despondent.

"Clay, let's take the first step and get you on the road to recovery in Arkansas."

"Why Arkansas? I did pretty well in New Mexico."

"Look, this doctor is an expert in this field of lung problems and consumption. Elliot called in some favors to get you in to see him. Elliot wants to ensure you get the best care."

Heller had received an update from Elliot on the Arkansas facility. It had only recently opened, and so afforded the latest in care and treatment. It was under the direction of Dr. John S. Shibley, the leading authority on tuberculosis in Arkansas and respected nationally. Elliot had an acquaintance with the doctor through a colleague. Elliot had met the doctor on one of his trips to visit the Mayo brothers' clinic in Rochester, Minnesota. Dr. Shibley had taken a keen interest in the work of the museum at the time.

Dr. Shibley had graduated with high honors from the medical college at Nashville, Tennessee. During the Civil War, Dr. Shibley had been a compassionate caretaker for the sick and wounded. After the war, he returned to Arkansas to practice in a community named Roseville located on the southern bank of the Arkansas River just below Fort Smith. He subsequently moved to Paris, Arkansas, and became one of the leading physicians of the state. He was known and loved by all for many miles around. He became known as the leading authority on tuberculosis in Arkansas, and, at the completion of the sanatorium in Booneville, which he worked hard to establish, he was appointed by the governor as its first superintendent.

Located on Pott's Ridge south of Booneville, the site for the Arkansas Tuberculosis Sanatorium embodied the locations chosen for sanatoriums in the eastern U.S., especially around Saranac Lake, New York. The site was in a mountainous area away from large cities where the air would be fresher, to bring better relief from the disease.

The creation of the Arkansas Tuberculosis Sanatorium was a reflection of the progressive stance that Arkansas had taken against some of the most prevalent diseases of the period, a stance that was often ahead of many other states. The site of the sanatorium near Booneville was seated among the pines, high enough for refreshing breezes in summer but not high enough for the cold fogs of winter. There was a bountiful supply of excellent water and perfect drainage. The climate the year round was unparalleled by any in the South or the West, according to Elliot, free from the winter's dampness of the Gulf Coast and from the sand storms and excessive heat of the southwestern arid regions.

Only in its initial phase, the sanatorium was small at this time, with a capacity to care for about 75-80 patients. The facility was also set up to focus on mild to moderate cases of tuberculosis. Everything about the sanatorium was a perfect fit for Clay. There would be highly personalized care under the direction of a leading physician in a near-perfect environment. And, while the rate of $10 per week was about the standard rate, the museum had committed to pay for half of that amount on Clay's behalf.

Heller had not shared this with Clay until today. Clay was even more impressed by the care his friends had shown to him. It helped to lift his heart just a bit.

Heller continued, "If Elliot says that this is the best place for you to be, then you can rely on his words, Clay."

"Hmmm," was all Clay could manage, but he felt extremely good by all that Heller had told him.

While Clay went back to bed at his apartment, Heller began making preparations to get Clay to Arkansas as soon as possible.

Clay awoke during another restless night. He had opened the windows in his apartment as he knew the fresh air was best for him. As dawn neared, Clay made a decision on his future. He would go to the sanatorium in Arkansas as the doctor had recommended. That was an easier decision to make than his second decision. He knew that he would not be able to be a field collector in the near future, if ever again. He could not see himself sitting in a museum office working on the specimens collected by others. Clay needed to be in the field, and he saw no future for this with the museum. So, he decided he would resign effective immediately. He wrote a short note to that effect, and he set out to the museum to deliver it to Dr. Elliot. He knew, however, that he must first inform Heller. It was the right thing to do for someone who had become such a close friend.

He found Heller in his office working on preparations for the African expedition with Roosevelt. After exchanging pleasantries, Heller told Clay of a meeting he had had with Dr. Elliot the previous day. He had informed Dr. Elliot of the outcome and thanked him for the support he had provided for Clay. The two had also discussed Clay's future with the museum. Elliot told Heller that Clay could retain his position while he recovered at the sanatorium. Heller was very pleased to hear of Elliot's position on Clay's absence.

"Clay, you'll have a position waiting for you when you return. Not only that, but you'll still be on the payroll while you are at the sanatorium. Now, tell me that doesn't make you feel just a bit better!" Heller was excited to share this good news with Clay.

"Heller, I can't begin to tell you how grateful I am for all that you, and Elliot, have done for me. Of course, this makes me feel good about the museum. It has been a home and a family to me."

Heller interrupted Clay, "I knew you would like this. Now, here are all of your arrangements for the trip to Arkansas. We have you on a train tomorrow morning."

Clay stopped Heller. "Heller, thank you. Again, I'm very grateful. And, I will be on that train in the morning. But, there is something I need to tell you." He suddenly found it difficult to talk. He strained to look Heller in the eyes. Heller looked back at Clay questioningly.

"Heller, I am quitting the museum. Here's my resignation that I'll give to Elliot today." Holding out the letter he had composed, Clay could not go on and stared blankly at Heller.

"Clay, I don't understand. Why would you do this? This is a very kind offer from the museum."

"You and I both know that I'll no longer be fit for field work, at least not anytime in the foreseeable future. And, you know very well, Heller, that I can't sit in an office and work on the specimens from some other collector. I'm not cut out for that type of work." He felt a sense of relief as he continued. "I think it's best for me to get to Arkansas and ponder my future while I recover. I know it will not include an expedition to Africa, and certainly not with a president." Clay managed a smile.

"Clay, I would sure like to talk you out of this, but I know you are a stubborn fool . . . probably from too much time spent with those mules of yours." But he would make one last attempt. "Are you really sure, Clay?"

"I'm afraid so, Heller. I feel so blessed by the friendships I've made at the museum, and especially our friendship. I could not have asked for more. But, it's time for me to find a new way."

"I understand. I will sorely miss your camp talks, especially the stories of your family in Indiana. Clay, I'm really sorry we won't be going to Africa together. But, I am so thankful for our work together in Mexico. I wish a speedy recovery for you."

They said their good-byes, and Clay dropped off his letter of resignation at Elliot's office. Elliot was out of the office for the entire day. Clay was sorry he did not have the opportunity to say thank-you to Elliot for all that he had done for him. He did leave a note of thanks with his resignation letter. Clay left the museum and went back to his apartment to pack his belongings.

Chapter 35

ARKANSAS

Early the next morning, Clay departed on the train headed to St. Louis. The doctor had given him some medicine to control his coughing for the trip. It made Clay drowsy, and he nodded off from time to time. Fortunately, he was alert enough to hear the conductor's directions for all of his arrivals and departures on his way to Fort Smith, Arkansas.

Three days later, he arrived in Fort Smith. There had been a spur line to Greenwood, but it was no longer in service. So, Clay boarded a horse-drawn coach for the remaining forty miles to Booneville. It was a quiet, dusty drive in some beautiful countryside. Having previously read about the geology of this general area of Arkansas because of his growing interest in prehistoric turtles, Clay found it as expected with ridges and plateaus. Millions of years ago, during the time of the dinosaurs, this area had been part of a vast ocean. Clay hoped to spend some of his recovery time studying the geology and paleontology of the area.

By mid-afternoon, the coach turned south out of Booneville, and ahead could be seen the hill in the distance where the sanatorium was located. The short ride from Booneville to the sanatorium was pleasant, but flat and plain. As they approached the property of the sanatorium, the area became more densely wooded with tall pines as the elevation increased in steps. The entrance was framed by two tall stone pillars and a curved sign reading "Arkansas Tuberculosis Sanatorium."

The main road rose to the top of the hill where there was a small cottage-like building. A sign outside the building read, "Arkansas Tuberculosis Sanatorium, Administration Building." The coach stopped near the entrance to this building. As Clay began to exit the coach, two men approached. One man opened the door for Clay, and the other man asked the coachman to identify Clay's belongings so that he could retrieve them. They escorted Clay into the Administration Building where he was asked to take a seat. Only moments later, a man approached and took a seat beside Clay. He introduced himself as Thomas Sparrow, an administration officer. He let Clay know that he would not take a lot of his time at this moment, but rather he would get him settled in a room. He took some basic information from Clay and showed some surprise that he had come from Chicago. Mr. Sparrow told Clay that the sanatorium had been established for residents of Arkansas. As he reviewed notes on Clay's case, he saw that special arrangements had been made with Dr. Shibley's approval.

He looked up at Clay. "Well, you must have friends in high places to get yourself a spot here. We've only been open a few months, and you are patient number 71. Right now we can handle about 80 patients, but we will be growing the facility quickly over the next year."

Clay paid attention and felt a twinge of guilt being here. "Yes, I'm very fortunate to be here as I've heard many great things about Dr. Shibley."

"I'll tell you what, Mr. Beckley, let's get you settled into your place. You can unpack and rest until supper. You have an appointment with Dr. Shibley at nine o'clock tomorrow morning."

With that, Clay was escorted to a frame ward building where he was placed in a small, sparse room. The attendant told Clay that he would return to take him to supper at six o'clock. The attendant suggested Clay rest in bed after unpacking his belongings.

His sleep was better than usual that night. In the morning, he was shown to breakfast precisely at 8:00 a.m. Breakfast ended precisely at 8:30 a.m., and he was escorted to the superintendent's office for his 9:00 a.m. appointment.

On his way to the superintendent's office, Clay noted three other small frame buildings, a couple of cabins, four stone cottages, and some type of tent-cabin structures. The superintendent's building was a stone cottage. Out in front of the cottage was a sign that read, "Superintendent's Office." Below that was a smaller sign with the name, "John S. Shibley, MD."

He found Dr. Shibley to be very warm and welcoming. He talked with Clay about his life and activities prior to coming to Arkansas. He asked about Dr. Elliot back at the museum. He wanted to know how his travel had been. He was not just making small-talk, he displayed a real interest, and Clay felt that he must be like this with everyone. He had a most gracious demeanor about him.

The doctor eventually got around to Clay's health. Clay shared many of his experiences as a museum collector and of his bouts with malaria. As they talked, the doctor took notes and reviewed the x-ray photographs of Clay's lungs. He confirmed that Clay's case was mild. He felt that as Clay fully recovered from the malaria, his recovery from tuberculosis should follow closely. He certainly expected Clay to be released in well under a year, and, perhaps, in six months.

"Mr. Beckley, you have a generally healthy disposition. Your work in the open in the West and Mexico has been good for you. I believe we can get you on the road to recovery in a relatively short time."

That prognosis lifted Clay's spirits, and he displayed a pleasing smile. He felt good about this doctor. He could see that things would be similar to what they had been at St. Anthony's in New Mexico, but with even tighter control over every minute of the day.

Dr. Shibley confirmed this. He explained to Clay that in spite of a better understanding of the tuberculosis bacteria, the treatment remained much the same. "Here, there is a very strict regimen of diet and exercise. Our patients are given three meals every day, and a glass of milk every four hours. We will have you outside in the open air for as much time as possible."

The doctor shared with Clay the daily schedule for the sanatorium:

7:15 – Rising Bell
8:00 to 8:30 – Breakfast
8:30 to 11:00 – Rest, or Exercise as Ordered
11:00 to 12:45 – Rest on Bed
1:00 to 1:30 – Dinner
1:30 to 4:00 – Quiet Hour. Rest on Bed. Reading, but No Talking.
4:00 to 5:45 – Rest, or Exercise as Ordered
6:00 to 6:45 – Supper
7:00 to 8:00 – Rest on Bed
8:00 to 8:30 – Nourishment if Ordered
9:00 – All Patients in Residence
9:30 – Lights Out

Strict schedules for eating, sleeping, bathing, and using the bathroom were enforced. "Everything which is not expressly allowed is forbidden. Our complete focus is on getting you back to your normal duties as soon as possible."

Clay was to learn that the cornerstone of the sanatorium treatment was self-control. He was taught how to control his coughing and spitting. He was taught to be vigilant against depression and morbid thoughts. Long lists of rules controlled every aspect of his day. Rest meant rest. There was no activity of any sort, not even sitting up in bed or in a chair. This was far more regimented than St. Anthony's, but he was more than willing to comply in order to recover as quickly as his body would allow him.

A nurse by the name of Flora Mae Hastings was assigned to Clay. Flora was from Flint, Michigan, about 200 miles northeast of Clay's home in La Porte, Indiana. Clay had not been to Flint, but he had been north along the Lake Michigan coastline. He understood that Flora had made many trips to the lake.

Clay learned that Flora had attended nursing school at the University of Michigan in Ann Arbor. After working locally for a few years, she was offered the opportunity to work with Dr. Shibley at the Arkansas Tuberculosis Sanatorium. Although she was close to her family, she felt a real calling to work with the tuberculosis patients.

Flo could not say enough about Dr. Shibley. Of course, he was a very skilled physician, but he was one of the most caring people Flo had ever met. His heart overflowed with charity and kindness, and his demeanor around patients was always uplifting. Flo noted that he began every day in prayer and included it as a part of the healing process. He often sat and prayed with patients in their darkest moments. Flo felt that his life was devoted to the overall betterment of mankind.

Clay found himself touched by the doctor as he had been by Sister Anne at St. Anthony's. Over the coming weeks, he developed a close relationship with Dr. Shibley. And, while he may have developed such relationships with most of his patients, the doctor always made Clay feel special and gave him the sole focus of his attention.

Clay was glad to share with the doctor his stories of museum collecting. The doctor listened intently, and Clay discovered that he had been a bit of an amateur collector of bones in the area. This further encouraged Clay's interest in the world of paleontology, especially in Arkansas.

After several weeks, Clay's malaria had cleared up. This already made him feel a bit better, and he felt some strength returning. It was too soon, however, according to the doctor, to begin exercise therapy.

Clay needed rest, and a lot of it. So, most of his time was spent in bed, and the time he was allowed for reading was limited.

He had received a number of publications relative to his interest in paleontology and turtles and was anxious to devour the words. Clay wrote to the Field Museum and asked for recommendations on books he could study. Some days when he was not supposed to be reading, Flo would read to him. She struggled a bit at first with some of the terminology, but she was a quick study and was aided by her medical knowledge. Clay was impressed how easily she retained much of the material. It was good to have her work with him, and she seemed to enjoy their time together as well.

Lying in bed, even out on the open veranda, was very boring. Clay had memorized every species of plant he could see, and he was now working on the birds. Flo had expressed an interest in the birds, and Clay was more than happy to share his knowledge of bird species with her.

Clay improved at a good pace over the next couple of months, and he was able to increase the amount of exercise in his daily regimen. He especially looked forward to walking about the sanatorium grounds. It was a large area, over 800 acres he had learned. In the time he had been at the facility, there was regular on-going construction to expand the number of buildings. Most notable, however, was the foundation of a new large structure. Flo told him that this would be a new full-care hospital for the sanatorium.

As he improved over several more months, Clay found himself looking forward to daily walks which allowed him to study the local plants and birds. But most of all, he found himself eagerly anticipating the time with Flo. She was easy to talk to, and she had a real enthusiasm for Clay's interests as a naturalist and as a budding turtle expert. He began to wonder if she took this much personal interest in all of her patients, or if he might mean something more to her.

As well as he was progressing in his health, Clay could not imagine himself being at the sanatorium much longer. However, recent blood tests showed he was still infected with the tuberculosis bacteria, although the count was decreasing. A recent chest x-ray photograph also showed some improvement in his lungs. Dr. Shibley seemed to be able to distinguish between old scarring in his lungs and the more recent evidence of his current disease. Yes, he was definitely getting better.

Three days later, a nurse Clay did not know showed up in his room for his morning exercise. Clay tried to be very casual in asking her where Flo was. She informed him that Flo had a meeting with Dr. Shibley, but she would be back in the afternoon to work with him. She smiled at Clay in a manner that let him know that she knew it was more than a passing interest that he had in Flo.

At four o'clock that afternoon, Flo appeared right on time to walk with Clay. She smiled as they quietly readied to leave the building and go for their walk. She seemed, however, to be unusually quiet. Clay supposed that it had something to do with her meeting with Dr. Shibley, and he thought it was probably none of his business.

They took a path that went slightly uphill to a small meadow. It was one of their favorite spots near the growing campus. Reaching a wooden bench at the edge of the meadow, they sat together. The silence was too strong for Clay.

"Flo, is there anything wrong? You seem awfully quiet and distracted this afternoon." He did not mention anything about her meeting with Dr. Shibley, but he wondered if that was the reason for her demeanor.

She was looking at the ground near her feet. She slowly lifted her head and turned to face Clay. "I'm leaving the sanatorium, Clay." Her mouth smiled at Clay, but her eyes seemed sad.

Clay turned his head slightly to the side trying to think of what to say to Flo.

But Flo continued, "Dr. Shibley has given me an opportunity to be the head nurse at a thermal mineral spring that is opening for convalescents of tuberculosis and other lung diseases. He sees it as another opportunity for the care of tuberculosis patients, and he is so dedicated to helping them." She paused and straightened up. "He has hand-picked the doctor to head the facility, and he wants me to be in charge of all the nursing care." Again, she paused and took on an air of confidence. "Clay, it is a wonderful opportunity for me. I'm honored that Dr. Shibley has selected me." She finished and smiled at Clay.

Clay knew he had a dumbfounded look on his face. He blinked his eyes as if he had just awakened from a dream. "Uh, Flo, I'm real happy for you." He immediately regretted his hesitation and lackluster response. "I mean, what a good fortune for you." He hesitated briefly before continuing. "Based on the way you've helped me, the good doctor could not have made a better choice!" He forced a nice smile onto his face and looked directly into Flo's eyes. "I'll miss you sorely, for sure."

"Clay, you're doing so well. You'll be leaving the facility in no time and probably be heading to some remote area in search of your ancient sea turtles."

They both seemed a bit more relaxed now, but Clay was feeling something he had never felt before. He knew it was more than just saying good-bye to a dear friend. He felt a new kind of connection to Flo, and he did not like the idea of completing his time at the sanatorium without her. He suddenly found himself reaching out to touch her hand. Their eyes connected at the touch. Clay wondered if she had the same feeling as he did, but he could not bring himself to ask her.

She drew her hand away and said, "Well, Clay Beckley, we need to get on with your exercise and get you stronger so you can get on with your life."

Flo stood, Clay stood with her, and they continued their walk. "Flo, where is it you'll be going?"

"Oh, I'm heading to Hot Springs. It's less than a hundred miles southeast of here. There is a family there by the name of Fordyce that has about 1200 acres just outside of town. They have agreed to the development of one of the thermal springs on their property in the area. Dr. Shibley told me that the facility will be ready within the next six months. He wants me to go there right away to work with Dr. Deaderick – he's the doctor who will run the place – to ensure the needs of the nurses are included in the planning as the facility is completed and prepares to open. I believe I will be quite busy in the next few months."

Flo stopped as she realized she had blurted out everything she needed to say without pausing.

Clay could see that Flo was excited about the opportunity in Hot Springs. She was an intelligent, strong, and caring woman who would certainly do well. "Well, you do sound excited about it all! That's so great, Flo." He tried not to hesitate as he said, "When do you leave?" He looked to the right and into her eyes.

"I will be leaving at the end of the week."

"Oh, that is quick."

They walked for a bit without saying anything. Clay felt he should lighten things up. "So, who are you going to burden with listening to my collector stories and my longings for prehistoric sea turtles? I sure hope it's not that nurse who works with Al down the hall from me. She never seems to let Al get a word in edgewise."

"Clay, she might be exactly who you need!" She laughed, and Clay followed suit.

They continued the walk in their normal manner with Clay identifying plants and birds. Flo surprised him several times identifying a species before Clay. Clay longed to take her hand, but he could not bring himself to do so.

1908

Chapter 36

HOT SPRINGS

Clay spent more time reading and studying on his own after Flo left for Hot Springs. His walks with his newly assigned nurse were much quieter. His main focus now was on completing his cure and getting out of the sanatorium. The place just seemed like a big, and growing bigger, hospital. He was thankful for Dr. Shibley and all of the staff, and he knew the blessing it had been to be able to come to this place. But, he wanted out. He found himself exercising as if preparing to scale Mount Kilimanjaro in Africa.

The day came when Clay had his final examination by Dr. Shibley. The doctor pronounced Clay cured and wished him all the best for his bright future. Clay expressed his gratitude to Dr. Shibley for his care, for the staff, and for the organized methods which helped Clay recover in a manner that was more than Clay could have hoped for.

Clay took the carriage back to Fort Smith where he planned to take some additional time to determine his next move. He felt his interest in the prehistoric sea turtles gnawing at him. He knew he had to plan some field work to begin his collecting and research. However, he needed funds. While the museum had been more than generous in assisting with the cost of the sanatorium, there were still expenses that Clay had to cover, and his funds were now nearly depleted.

But there was another gnawing that was even deeper than his newfound paleontology interest – he longed to see Flo. He missed their walks. He missed their talks. He missed her interest in him. He missed her caring personality. He was having trouble putting his finger on it, but he knew he missed her in some other way that he could not quite express.

From his paleontological studies, Clay learned that Hot Springs and other areas to the south were ideal for searching for prehistoric fossil remains. The area was near the shore and the shallow waters of the sea that had existed there about 65 to 145 million years ago. He found himself growing in enthusiasm about relocating to Hot Springs. He could find a job there and use his free time for fossil hunting. And, he could reconnect with Flo.

He decided to write to Flo and tell her of his plans. Her response was joyful and enthusiastic. Clay's spirits were raised at her reply. She also made mention of the Fordyce family and their many developments in the area. There were certainly opportunities to be afforded for Clay in Hot Springs.

Clay left Fort Smith on the train to Little Rock. There, he picked up the train to Hot Springs. When he arrived, he went to the Arlington Hotel where Flo had arranged a room for him. It was an exquisite place, a bit too royal for Clay's taste. He knew right away that he would need to make other arrangements as soon as possible. Still, he was very thankful to Flo for all she had done to make him comfortable.

Over the next few weeks, Clay found out more about Flo's work. She was very happy with the progress being made on the hot springs facility. She introduced Clay to several individuals in the area, but he seemed to develop a simple and easy rapport with John Fordyce.

Fordyce was an amateur archaeologist, and showed a great interest in Clay's plan for fossil hunting in Arkansas. Clay eventually moved into a small cottage on the Fordyce property and was placed in charge of a small dairy goat farm that Fordyce wanted to expand. Clay liked the job as it kept him outdoors most days and provided him an opportunity to be around animals, an enjoyment for Clay.

As Clay developed the goat farm, he hired some help which allowed him to make week-end trips into the gullies of the surrounding area where he began his work as an amateur paleontologist.

At the same time, Clay and Flo were spending much of their free time together. Flo enjoyed being around the goat farm as it reminded her a bit of the farm where she had grown up. Clay now knew the cause of the gnawing he had been experiencing – he was in love with Flo. He found an ease in being with her that he had never known with anyone else. Clay realized that what he had with Flo was far beyond his relationship with Analena. He had grown close with Townsend, Cockerell, and Heller, developing friendships that he would treasure the rest of his life. He had shared a great deal with Katherine as he grew into a young man at college. But, none of those relationships, as close as they were, could compare with his feelings for Flo. He was even becoming confident that she had similar feelings for him.

She was settling into her new role, and Clay was beginning to have the goat farm functioning even better than expected. He even managed to save a little money. He made the decision to buy a ring and ask Flo to marry him.

It was a Saturday afternoon, and the two of them were walking in the woods of the Fordyce property not far from the goat farm. It was a beautiful day. Clay heard more birds singing than usual, and the sky seemed a more beautiful blue than it had ever been. Nearing a meadow, the flowers laid out a soft quilt of colors before them. They stopped upon entering the meadow. Clay reached out and took Flo's hand. She turned and looked at him with that most gentle of smiles.

Clay's heart was pounding as he tried to remain calm. He had to say something, but his mouth was not cooperating. The silence seemed long and unbearable, while Flo continued to stare into his eyes almost as if she knew what Clay was going to ask her. She turned her head slightly to the side and reached up and touched Clay's cheek with her other hand.

"Flo, you're so beautiful. And, you are as beautiful on the inside as you are on the outside." Momentarily, Clay felt that maybe he sounded too much like a field collector describing a specimen. "What I mean to say is . . . you mean so much to me. You're so easy to be around, and you're such a good, caring person. I so enjoy our time together, our walks. You listen and understand me, and we share so much with one another." He felt his courage building. "Flo, I want to spend the rest of my life with you. Will you marry me?" He slipped the ring out of his pocket and held it out to Flo.

Her face lit up with joy, and with some surprise. "Clay Beckley, I've been waiting for you to ask me that question for quite some time. I was hoping I wouldn't have to ask you! Yes, I'll marry you!" She threw her arms around Clay and kissed him.

Clay was both pleased and relieved. He had gotten the words out, and she said yes! He was thrilled beyond anything he could imagine. He could feel the entire meadow touching them with its beauty and goodness as they kissed. They stood and stared into each other's eyes. Clay felt blessed as he had never felt before.

"Flo, John has agreed to sell me the cottage and goat farm. It'll be ours. You can make the cottage our home in any way that you want. You've always seemed to enjoy it there. Would that be okay with you?"

"Clay, I'm okay with being with you wherever that is. But, yes, I love that little cottage, and it's the perfect place for us." She kissed him again.

"Well, put that ring on my finger!" Clay placed the ring on Flo's finger, and her face shown bright with joy as she looked at it.

1938

Chapter 37

THIRTY YEARS LATER

C lay and Flo spent the next 30 years living in the cottage and managing the goat farm. Flo continued working at the thermal springs convalescence facility nearby. Flo traveled from time to time, and Clay made fossil collecting trips in Arkansas, Texas, Georgia, and Florida. Flo would sometimes take extended trips with her sister, and Clay used the time for lengthy collecting trips, often with other collectors from the Field Museum.

Clay kept in close contact with the Field Museum, although he did not work for them directly. When possible, he sent his collections to them with rare consideration for any other museum. Occasionally,

Clay asked for money to support his expeditions. The museum nearly always supported Clay's efforts in the field, and he had made substantial contributions to the museum's specimens from the Late Cretaceous Period, the time of the dinosaurs. Only rarely did Clay need to sell his collections to other museums in order to provide funding for expeditions that he wanted to make.

Clay had a keen eye for fossilized remains, and especially for the sea turtles that he had studied so thoroughly. Clay would find bits and pieces of fossil shells in an area. He could tell by looking at them that they were part of the same shell. He would send these fragments back to the museum where workers would put them together like puzzle pieces.

One late fall, Clay was successfully working along a riverbank when the weather turned bad for the season, forcing him to abandon the location for the winter. When he returned the following spring, the weather had exposed new fossils. Clay recognized additional pieces of the same shell that he had collected many months earlier. Back at the museum, these were the final puzzle pieces to complete the shell.

It was in 1937 that such an expedition by Clay uncovered bits and pieces of a shell that he knew was different. Over the course of the next months, the pieces were collected and put together. Clay was convinced that he had uncovered a new species of prehistoric sea turtle.

It took the museum from 1938 through 1940 to put all the research together and publish a paper on Clay's find. It was, in fact, a new species, and an important one at that. Other paleontologists had predicted that such a species should have existed, but none was ever found. Clay had discovered a missing species, a missing link, in the line of prehistoric sea turtles. The Field Museum described it as the most notable turtle to be discovered in North America since 1900.

While Clay was proud of his find, he was, in his usual manner, more concerned about offering gratitude to the others for the work they had done on his find. Clay felt that since he was an amateur in the field of paleontology, the work of others should receive the recognition. His career as a collector had never been about himself, but rather it was about contributing to the good of the understanding of the natural world. Those professionals in the museums needed to have published works to maintain and advance in their positions. Clay was fine with helping them to do this.

On many of the expeditions that the Field Museum supported, museum collectors joined Clay. Clay welcomed the company of new and old friends on these trips. Oftentimes on these trips, talks around the campfire provided Clay with a renewed energy as much as the collecting itself did.

As the years went by, Clay began to feel his age, and ultimately realized that his field days had to come to an end. He wanted to quit while he still had a good reputation for the work, which indeed he did. He made his last expedition in 1949 into Alabama.

Clay and Flo subsequently moved to her home town of Flint, Michigan. Here Clay managed to work a few odd jobs until he found out about an opening for a curator at the local county museum, the Genesee County Historical Society Museum. He looked forward to an opportunity to see what he could make of a local small museum after his many years of working for a number of curators at the Field Museum.

He moved into the position with a great enthusiasm. It was, of course, nothing on the scale of the Chicago museum, but he put his best efforts into it. As word grew of his tales of the early collecting days, he was often called upon to make presentations to various local organizations. With time, he honed his presentations and became better known as a story teller along with whatever museum objects he was displaying.

Flo noticed a new energy in Clay, but at the same time his health was taking a turn for the worse.

1954

Chapter 38

THE STORYTELLER

It was near the end of the school year in 1954, and many local schools were making field trips as their last class activity. The county museum in Flint, Michigan, was one of the highlights for many of the sixth grade students this year as it had been for a number of years. The museum contained many artifacts from earlier days that allowed the kids to have some idea of earlier lifestyles and living conditions. But, also among these lifestyle artifacts were some interesting collections of dinosaur bones, as well as bones of other long-gone species, and some stuffed rare animals.

Clay managed the collections as the curator of the small museum in his wife's home town. He had to oversee the historic clothing and dolls and furniture pieces that were amply donated to the museum. But, he had also been able to include some of those items that were near and dear to his heart. Some of his own special collections from his work as an amateur paleontologist were on display. On several occasions, he was also able to borrow from some of the collections at the Field Museum in Chicago for special displays. The students seemed more interested in these items than the lifestyle pieces. Clay understood why.

Clay looked forward to the visits by the sixth graders. They displayed a real fascination with the collections. The old ways of working and living seemed to both amaze and puzzle the students. They could not imagine anyone living in such a manner. But most of all, they became focused on Clay when he showed them some of the paleontology displays. Then, Clay finished with his much anticipated stories of the old museum collectors of days long gone by.

He was nearing the end of the time with this group of students with one last activity remaining: the bear story. It was almost a right of passage to sit through one of Clay's bear stories.

Sitting on the floor of a small room that contained several animal specimens, including a black bear from northern Michigan, they gathered around Clay who sat in a comfortable wooden rocking chair with his old pipe in his hand. Many of the students glanced over at the bear as they sat down. While some viewed the bear cautiously, a few of the boys wanted to display their bravery by getting as close to the bear as possible.

The bear was positioned standing on its hind legs, and its shoulders were at a height of about five feet, surely large to all in the group. Clay explained that the black bear had weighed about 300 pounds. There were some gaping mouths at the size. Clay told them that the bear he was about to tell them about was a grizzly bear that was over twice the size and weight of the black bear on display. There were numerous gasps to imagine anything so large.

Clay set the scene in the Sangre de Cristo Mountains in the New Mexico Territory about 1901. Clay had been in the mountains collecting specimens. He found himself at a camp of several local cattlemen. After introductions and some coffee, the men informed him that they were trailing a large grizzly bear that had killed some of their cattle. They were now certain they had him surrounded in a box canyon. They asked Clay if he would like to join him as they could use the extra hand.

"Of course, I joined right in! I was ready to help those fellas out, and I relished a good bear hunt and the prospect of a nice specimen for the museum.

"So, come first light in the morning, we mounted our horses and headed into the box canyon. There was only one way out for that bear, and that was through the group of riders.

"Now, these huge bears leave an easy trail to follow, so we knew right where we were going. The canyon was thick with brush and small trees, making it difficult to see very far ahead, however. We rounded trees and rocks and hills not sure what to expect the next moment.

"I have to tell you that a good horse has a way of knowing when a bear is nearby. By late morning, we knew we were getting close by the nervousness of our mounts. My own horse, Lucy, was used to hunting, however, and she was very well-behaved on the hunt. I had every bit of confidence in her."

A hand shot up from one of the boys sitting near the black bear. "Did you have a gun?"

"Oh, yes. Every man was well-armed and ready for that bear. I was carrying a 30-caliber Winchester Model 1895 rifle, a powerful rifle in 1901, and a good one for bear hunting."

Clay slowly lifted his arm and pointed to the rear of the room with the stem of his pipe. All eyes turned in the direction of Clay's outstretched arm. "That rifle on the wall there is such a gun. It was a fine weapon for its time, and it's still used by hunters today."

Clay lowered his arm, and all the eyes returned to him. "Back to our story. As I said, some of the horses were getting nervous, and we knew we were getting closer to that bear. Moments later, we heard one of the men who was in the lead call out that he had seen the bear. We all made a mad scramble through the brush and over the small hills. The riders kicked their horses in the side and drove them forward. The lead man was on the bear's trail. But, as big as these bears are, they are quick and agile. That bear was running mighty fast and busting down the brush, and even small trees, as he tried to escape.

"Soon, we were in a large area of dense trees and brambles. The bear had gone in where the horses couldn't go. We listened for that bear hoping to hear him breaking through the trees . . . but it was silent. Some of the horses were very nervous, stamping the ground." Clay paused momentarily and looked ever so slightly away with a hint of a smile on his face.

"Roarrrr!" With all of the breath he could muster from his weak lungs, Clay had every child jumping and screaming. "Out of those trees shot that giant beast with his ferocious teeth ready to tear us apart! He was coming fast and hard. The lead rider turned his horse as there was no time for him to take a shot. The bear continued after him swiping his giant paws at the horse's flank in an attempt to bring him down. None of us could take a shot as the bear was too close to that cowboy.

"Then, the cowboy turned his mount sharply to the left. There was a brief moment to take a shot, a bit of a risky shot. I swung my Winchester around, took a quick aim, and made a shot. I missed that beast, but I did kick up some rock in front of him just enough to distract him from the fleeing horse and rider." All eyes were fixed on Clay. Many mouths were gaping open in anticipation of what would happen next.

"The rider continued on and disappeared over a small rise. The bear, a bit stunned and confused, stopped momentarily, looked at the small group of riders, and then it, too, disappeared over the hill. Immediately, we all took off in a beeline for that hilltop.

"We continued to kick up rocks and dirt as we scrambled to the aid of the cowboy. As we came to the top of the rise, we could see the bear once again gaining on the cowboy. And, again, we were not in a position to take a shot.

"The rider was approaching a large tree, and I could see what he had in mind. There was a branch just low enough that he should be able to grab it from his saddle. He was pushing his mount hard. He neared that branch and raised his arms. He swung up and out of his saddle. The bear stumbled to slow down as it took a swipe at the swinging man. Fortunately, that cowboy was able to pull himself up onto the branch just as the giant claws took a swipe at the man's rear end." Clay paused as the wide-eyed students seemed to have some sense of relief about the situation. But, he could tell they were still wondering what would happen next.

"The bear decided to leave that cowboy who was out of reach, and he turned toward the group of riders. Many guns were raised at the bear as he pounded the ground toward us.

"One, two, three, four, five shots rang out, but that bear kept charging! The nearest man now became the object of the bear's attack. As it neared him, the rest of us were not able to shoot without risk of hitting the cowboy. He pulled his horse to a stop, raised his rifle, and nothing happened. His gun had jammed! He only had one chance to swing his horse around and flee.

"Once again, the bear was in pursuit of a cowboy and his horse. This time, though, the bear seemed to be slowing down. As he did so, I could see that a safe shot could be taken. So, one more time, I raised my Winchester and fired. This time I hit the bear . . . but he continued on. I quickly took a second and a third shot hitting the bear with each. The bear finally stumbled and fell.

"As the dust settled, the bear stopped breathing. He was finished. The men all gave a big 'Hurrah!' at the site of the dead bear. One of the men rode over to the tree to help the cowboy down. After retrieving his horse, they met us at the carcass.

"'Beckley,' one of the cowboys said to me, 'that was some good shootin'. We were mighty lucky to have you with us. Your experience as a hunter sure saved the day.'

"I was glad that no one had been hurt. I told the men that if they would allow me to have the bearskin, I would cook them up a good bear steak with all the fixin's for supper. They were more than happy to oblige. After skinning that giant beast, I found he had eleven bullet holes in him. He did not go down easily."

The kids all looked a bit more relaxed by now. A hand was slowly raised by one of the girls. "You ate the bear?" she asked timidly.

"Why, yes. When you're out in the mountains for months at a time, you make good use of all your resources."

"What did it taste like?"

"Well, I have to tell you, it was not very good. It was an older bear, and old bear meat is just not very good. Steaks from younger bears, however, are quite tender and good. And, biscuits cooked in the grease from the bear meat are very tasty."

Another hand. "How many bears have you killed?"

Clay's mind went back to that place long ago when Carlos was at-tacked by the bear. He had killed many bears since that day, but that bear attack had never never left his thoughts. "Well, I never really kept count, but I only killed the bears that needed to be killed, and never more. You see, my job was to collect specimens – like that black bear – for museums so that others could have a chance to see them. So, I took only what we needed for museum specimens, or, like in the story I told you, those that were a danger to others, or to the cattle."

"Now, see this?" Clay held up a bear claw that was attached to a piece of leather lacing. All eyes were fixed on the object. "This claw, nearly five inches long, came from the front foot of that very grizzly bear." He offered it to one of the boys sitting nearby. "Pass it around."

The stunned boy took the bear claw in both hands and stared in awe. Several other boys quickly gathered around him all wanting to hold the claw.

As the students prepared to leave, the teacher asked them if they had forgotten something. In one voice, they all said, "Thank you, Mr. Beckley." Clay smiled with appreciation and waved at them.

Before leaving, the teacher took Clay by the hand and thanked him personally. She told him the story was well-presented. She had feared that it might contain too much "detail" for the students, but she saw that Clay had done a good job in leaving them with a memorable experience. Clay was glad to have her evaluation and told her how much he enjoyed telling the stories to the students. And, by the way, he did have many stories with much too much "detail" to ever share with most people, let alone school students. He was thinking in particular of Carlos. The teacher said good-bye without noticing that Clay's eyes were beginning to fill with tears.

While the session with the students had worn Clay out, he still very much enjoyed every opportunity to tell his stories. Clay sat and rested for a bit. His cancer was wearing him out more each day.

The once heavy man was now skin and bones. He picked up his old pipe and placed it in his pocket. He rarely smoked it anymore; he just enjoyed having it with him like an old friend.

Four weeks later, on June 23, 1954, Clay passed away at home, sitting in his favorite chair with his pipe on the table beside him.

FACT AND FICTION

The Backdrop of the Historical Novel

The fun part of writing a historical novel is weaving the fact and fiction together. The facts of history provide a springboard from which to launch the overall story as well as to develop specific scenes.

In the case of *Hill of the Bear*, there are two overarching historical backdrops to the story. The first is the time of the Gilded Age, or the Victorian Age, as it was known in England. This period of our history began around 1870 and lasted through the very early 1900s.

This time has often been equated to a time of excesses in society and substantial growth in our economy. It was during this time that the railroads made their way across America opening up the West. However, it was also a time when people were fascinated by order. It was a time when the natural world was being opened up with a desire to order and classify living specimens. Museums were built to bring the elements of the natural world to the masses.

With this backdrop, in 1885, Congress created an Office of Economic Ornithology in the Department of Agriculture. By 1886, the name was updated to the Division of Economic Ornithology and Mammalogy. By 1896, the department was renamed to the Division of Biological Survey. Its early work focused on the effect of birds in controlling agricultural pests and on mapping the geographical distribution of plants and animals in the United States.

The department gradually grew in responsibilities and became the U.S. Biological Survey in 1905. The organization was transferred to the Department of the Interior in 1939. The Bureau of Fisheries and the Biological Survey were transferred to the Department of the Interior in 1939. In 1940, they were combined and named the organization we know today as the United States Fish and Wildlife Service.

The first head of the original organization was Clinton Hart Merriam who headed the Bureau for twenty-five years and became a national figure for improving the scientific understanding of birds and mammals in the United States. Merriam is one of the key historical figures in this novel.

The second part of our backdrop is the life of one of the men who worked during this period of our history as a field collector. The field collectors, naturalists as they were known, were those individuals who spent months and years working in the remote western United States, areas of Mexico and Central America, and around the world. These men were rugged individuals with the rigor of natural scientists. They spent months and years studying and collecting the natural history in wild and remote areas. They often relied on none but themselves for survival.

Charles Melvin Barber, my great uncle, was one such man, and it is his story upon which is built the fictitious main character of *Hill of the Bear*, Clay Beckley. Charley, as he was known, actually wrote some stories based on his time as a field collector. Some of the stories in this novel are based upon, and in some cases include parts of, the writings of Charley.

Nearly all of the locations in the story are real places, and Charley Barber worked in most of them. You could actually follow all of Clay's adventures using Google Maps™ to plot his routes. Charley himself surveyed the Halls Peak area, but it is not likely he went further south along the eastern range of the mountains. He also did not spend time in Las Vegas, New Mexico, nor in the Booneville area of Arkansas, as Clay did in the story.

Chapter 1. Rails West (1890). Charley Barber, the real person on whom Clay Beckley is based, hitched west on trains. The only details relative to his travels are the towns he visited. He did actually spend twelve hours in the Dodge City jail for vagrancy. The young boy, Will, and all the surrounding events are fiction.

Chapter 2. The Beginnings. Charley Barber, Clay's real-life counterpart, lived in La Porte, Indiana, where he was born in 1876. The family had originally settled in Kingsbury, a small town six miles south of La Porte. Charley had a real interest in nature. The stories of time with his grandfather are all fictional. We are introduced to Clinton Hart Merriam in this chapter, as previously mentioned, a real historical character. Charley corresponded with him as a young man, and he did send him some specimens.

Chapter 3. Riding the Rails. As was previously mentioned Charley Barber, the model for Clay Beckley, rode the rails west as a young man. While his father worked at the La Porte Carriage Company, it is not known if Charley began his journey at the company. Again, the small boy is purely fictional.

Chapter 4. Before the Judge. Pure fiction.

Chapter 5. On to Arizona. The real person of Charley Barber did not join the Merriam expedition into the San Francisco Peaks, although this was an actual expedition undertaken by Merriam. Charley did, however, walk to Raton, New Mexico, from La Junta, Colorado, as Clay does in the story. Charley was also witness to the actual events of U.S. troops marching on the civilians in Raton during the nationwide railroad strike of 1893.

Chapter 6. Working the Expedition. This was a real expedition undertaken by Merriam. The Life Zones concept conceived by him is also fact. Vern Bailey is introduced in this chapter. He was a real field collector who was Merriam's right-hand man. Also real individuals are Ed Goldman and Ed Nelson, collectors Charley met later in life in Mexico (see Chapter 30).

Chapter 7. Consumption. The real person of Charley Barber originally went west because he had tuberculosis, or consumption as it was known at the time. He ended up in Raton, New Mexico, where he met a friend by the name of Ed Taylor.

Chapter 8. Recovery (1891). It is not known what type of treatment Charley Barber undertook for his consumption. There is no mention of him spending time at a sanatorium. The treatment described in this chapter was standard for consumption at this time in history. St. Anthony's was the location of a tuberculosis sanatorium run by the Sisters of Charity, but it opened a few years later than the time of this story.

Chapter 9. The Azuela Family (1892). The Azuela family is purely fictional. Charley worked in the railyards at Raton where it is known that he was an engine watchman. The *El Camino Real de Tierra Adentro*, the Royal Road, is true history.

Chapter 10. Analena. Again, the Azuela family is fictitious.

Chapter 11. The Halls Peak Expedition (1893). Charley Barber undertook his first expedition to the Halls Peak area at the age of 17, about 1893. He was proceeding at the direction of Merriam. Charley's friend from Raton, Ed Taylor, accompanied Charley on the first part of the expedition, but he eventually returned to his home in Raton.

Chapter 12. On the Trail. According to Charley Barber's account of the Halls Peak Expedition, they passed through Horse Thief Gap and then turned into the mountains.

Chapter 13. Black Jack Ketchum. Black Jack Ketchum and his gang were real outlaws in New Mexico, and they were still around at the time of this story. Charley Barber did not have an actual encounter with the gang.

Chapter 14. Return to the Trail. Since there was no actual encounter with Black Jack Ketchum, this chapter is fiction.

Chapter 15. Halls Peak. Some of the details of the expedition were taken from Charley Barber's stories.

Chapter 16. Working the Expedition (1894). Again, some of the details of the expedition were taken from Charley Barber's accounts. The story of the snowstorm, the cabin, and Charley's snow blindness are true.

Chapter 17. Cerro del Oso. It is not believed that Charley traveled farther south to this location. The account of the bear attack is fiction; Charley never experienced such an encounter. Field agents who were trained according to Merriam's strict standards were known as Merriam's Men. The Wheeler Survey mentioned in this chapter was a real expedition.

Chapter 18. Loss. Continued fiction from Chapter 17.

Chapter 19. Unburdened. This is fiction, other than the fact that St. Anthony's was a real place.

Chapter 20. Luz de Oro. This account is fiction.

Chapter 21. The Mogollon Expedition (1895). This expedition is fiction; however, the places noted in the story are real. In 1900, Charley Barber participated in a survey of the Gila Forest Reserve for the federal government. This survey was to assess the area that was to become a national forest preserve. Charley and Professor E. O. Wooten also spent time on the W S Ranch and met with the manager, William French. Real characters in this chapter include Vern Bailey, Art Howell, and James Gaut, all who worked for the Biological Survey. Clay's friends Bob Howler and Ben Holt are fictitious, as well as is Heinrich Alden, the cook. Charley took part in a bear hunt as in the story.

Chapter 22. Alma. As with the other locations, Alma is a real town. William French and the W S Ranch are also real. The incidents in this chapter, including the bear hunt, are based upon Charley Barber's actual accounts at the W S Ranch.

Chapter 23. The Old Prospector. While Charley Barber was surveying in the area of the Gila River National Forest Preserve, he ran into the real-life character of James "Bear" Moore. The description of the man and his story are taken from Charley's true account of the encounter. Charley's actual words were used to create the dialogue.

Chapter 24. River Rescue. This is a fictitious adventure. Caves like the one noted in the story are found in this area of the West Fork of the Gila River.

Chapter 25. The Question. This is fiction. Charley Barber was actually convinced to attend college by some of his high school teachers.

Chapter 26. The College Years (1896). Most of the accounts in this chapter summarize Charley Barber's time at the New Mexico College of Agriculture and Mechanic Arts. Katherine is a fictitious character based upon Charley's mention that he had dated a judge's daughter while at school. Charley became close with the real-life persons of Theodore Dru Alison Cockerell and Charles Henry Tyler Townsend. Charley actually dropped out of college because of problems with his eyes.

Chapter 27. Solitude in the Mountains (1900). While Charley Barber spent time in the area around Sierra Blanca Peak and the Mescalero Apache Indian Reservation, the account in this story is fiction.

Chapter 28. Clay's Bear. There is no evidence of such an event as having taken place.

Chapter 29. The Southwest Taxidermy & Zoological Co. (1901). After a brief stint as a taxidermist in Albuquerque, Charley Barber formed a business with C. H. T. Townsend at this time. The business was the Townsend-Barber Taxidermy and Zoological Company located in El Paso, Texas, as described in the story. Many of Charley's personal stories cover this time of his life. One of the expeditions has been documented with photographs. The story of grabbing the mountain lion by the tail is true, and the illustration at the beginning of this chapter is taken from one of the actual photographs from the expedition.

Chapter 30. Mexican Expedition (1904). The business that Charley and Townsend started was, in fact, dissolved when Townsend's wife died. Charley went to work for the Field Museum of Natural History in Chicago where he was employed as a field collector from 1904 through 1908. Charley was paired with Edmund Heller, a real-life individual, for a year-long expedition into Mexico. The events summarize some of the actual stories of the expedition. They spent time on Mount Orizaba where they met Ed Nelson and Ed Goldman (from Chapter 6).

Chapter 31. Pancho Villa. Pancho Villa was a real leader in the Mexican Revolution. Charley, however, never had an encounter with him. Until 1910, Pancho Villa alternated episodes of thievery with more legitimate pursuits. It was in 1910 that he became involved in the Mexican Revolution.

Chapter 32. Guatemala (1905). This is a bit of a summary of Charley's expedition into Guatemala. Don Guillermo Thorn was a real individual, and Charley did lodge at his family's farm in the mountains. Charley actually made two separate expeditions into Guatemala, the first through the Atlantic side of the country, and the second through the Pacific side. The account of porting in San Francisco after the 1906 earthquake is real. Most of the words in the story are from Charley's actual account.

Chapter 33. Back Home (1906). Charley returned to his home town of La Porte, Indiana, after his last expedition to Guatemala. While the story here is fiction, the names of Charley's real siblings are used in the story.

Chapter 34. Consumption Again (1907). Charley did not have a second tuberculosis infection. The account is fiction.

Chapter 35. Arkansas. This chapter continues the fictitious account of a second round of tuberculosis. The location of the Arkansas Tuberculosis Sanatorium is real. Dr. Shibley was the real doctor who pursued the sanatorium and was able to get it operational. The character of Clay's love interest, Florence Mae Hastings, is fictitious.

Chapter 36. Hot Springs (1908). Charley and his real wife moved to Hot Springs, Arkansas, where he ran a dairy goat farm. John Fordyce, who owned a large amount of the land that is today's Hot Springs National Park, was a real individual whom Charley did know. The hot springs facility where Flo worked in the story is fictitious. The goat farm was Charley's home base for his paleontological expeditions. Charley, in fact, made a significant discovery with a prehistoric turtle, *Podocnemis barberi*.

Chapter 37. Thirty Years Later (1938). Charley Barber and his real wife moved to Flint, Michigan, in 1943. Eventually, Charley became the curator of the Genesee County Historical Society Museum, today known as the Sloan Museum.

Chapter 38. The Storyteller (1954). The scene of Clay telling bear stories is fictional. June 23, 1954, is the actual date of Charles Melvin Barber's death.

Looking for More?

Charley Barber's real life is as good a story as any about the place in history that brought out the need for such men. This novel dramatizes some events, but it also takes some scenes directly from Charley's life as he described it in his own words. His life and the lives of his contemporaries were a true adventure.

The Collector, the Guide and the Bone Digger, 2nd edition, (The Other Road Publishing, 2016) is a biography of Charles Melvin Barber. It also contains many photos from one of his expeditions into Mexico in the early 1900s. It can be found on Amazon at https://www.amazon.com/Collector-Guide-Bone-Digger/dp/0692641734/.

Charley's own writings of his time as a field collector are contained in the book *Recollections of a Museum Collector* (The Other Road Publishing, 2017). This book can be found on Amazon at https://www.amazon.com/Recollections-Museum-Collector-James-Barber/dp/0692930949/ref=asap_bc?ie=UTF8.

www.ingramcontent.com/pod-product-compliance
Lightning Source LLC
Chambersburg PA
CBHW050013180626
46810CB00002B/404